D1066305

INTO
the
HEARTLESS
WOOD

JOANNA RUTH MEYER

PAGE STREET
PUBLISHING CO.

PAGE STREET
PUBLISHING CO.

Distributed by Macmillan, sales in Canada by The Canadian Manda Group.

25   24   23   22   21   1   2   3   4   5

ISBN-13: 978-1-64567-170-1
ISBN-10: 1-64567-170-4

Library of Congress Control Number: 2020936366

Cover and book design by Laura Benton for Page Street Publishing Co.
Cover images: Illustration of trees © Shutterstock / Nikiparonak; illustration of violet © Shutterstock / Aluna1; vector of woman © Shutterstock / logozilla; illustration of heart © Shutterstock / Bernardo Ramonfaur
Author image by Gary D. Smith

Printed and bound in the United States

FOR ARTHUR—

Love you so much, love you so cool.
Love you always, Bear.

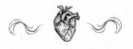

Prologue

MONSTER

I WAS BORN A TREE. IT WAS EASIER, THEN. ALL I NEEDED WAS THE earth and the wind and the rain. All I needed was the sunlight warm in my dappled leaves.

There was no fear, just growth. No wanting, just sky. No thirst, thirst, thirst.

Only starlight.

But my mother wanted daughters, and she chose the birch ring.

I remember the day of my birth: the stretch of wood becoming sinew, of leaves becoming hair. I felt the dirt under my toes and I opened my eyes for the first time and saw what I had never seen before: the deep green wood and the wide blue sky, the gray and white forms of my seven sisters.

And my mother, who is neither tree nor woman nor anything that there are words for. She is power and beauty and binding. She does what she wants, and woe to anyone who stands in her way. I understood that, in my first moment of life, and I bowed before her, my green and yellow hair spilling around my shoulders like a shining stream.

What I did not understand was that I was born to be a soldier. What I did not understand was that I would no longer be free.

At first, I thought I loved my mother. She opened my eyes and loosed my tongue. She taught me the names of all the things in the wood; she taught me to sing. And the music, music, music, that welled up inside of me and spooled out from my lips was a thing of such wonder, such beauty, that I thought it was good, because how could it not be? So I sang and I grew, and I allowed her to shape me into her monster without realizing she did so.

When I was old enough to lure a man with my song, to trap him in the heart of the wood and break him like so many dead branches, I did it without question, without thought.

And when I had done it two times and ten and twenty, when I had lured a hundred men to their deaths in my mother's forest, I forgot that I had ever been a tree.

I forgot I had ever been anything but my mother's youngest monster.

Part One

LEAVES

Never go into the deep parts of the forest, for there are many dangers there, both dark and bright, and they will ensnare your soul.

— Robert Beatty, *Serafina and the Black Cloak*

Chapter One

OWEN

THE GWYDDEN'S WOOD IS QUIET TODAY. THERE IS NO HIGH, eerie melody woven into the air, pulling at my mind and my body, tempting me to come among the trees, though I know very well what would happen if I did. I'm more able to resist the music than most. But it's easier when it's quiet.

The wood smells as it always does: of loam and earth and the sour hint of decay. Branches hang over the chest-high boundary wall my father built too late. Leaves scrape against the stone; they're a luminescent green, new-furled. But they can't trick me into admiring them—I know what they conceal.

What they've taken from us.

Awela tumbles like a new puppy in the grass, nearly in the shadow of the wall. She doesn't understand the danger that lurks so close. How could she? She's only two. She doesn't remember our mother. She doesn't hear our father's gut-wrenching cries in the dark of night when he thinks I'm sleeping. Father would be angry that we're out here at all, but Awela is part wild thing. She can't be kept indoors all day. Besides, there's no music coiling out of the forest at present, and Father is away working at Brennan's Farm. He doesn't need to know. And it's not like I take my eyes off her, even for a second.

I don't think Father's wall can keep the trees out if they really want to come in.

Awela races about in circles, squealing with joy until she's so dizzy she falls down. There's dirt on every inch of her, and she's managed to rip her dress. Her skin is freckled and tanned from the sun, her dark curls—the same ones I have, inherited from Father—springing out in every direction. She never sits still long enough for me to properly comb her hair, which right now is tangled with grass and twigs. She has Father's brown eyes and Mother's broad smile and more mischief than any person so small should be able to contain. She exhausts me, and I adore her to bits.

"Awela!" I cry, as she trots up to the wall and stretches up her tiny hand, reaching for a low-hanging branch.

Panic jolts through me, and I leap up from where I've been sprawling in the grass. In another heartbeat I'm at her side, grabbing her wrist and tugging her back to the safety of the open sky.

She screams at me and wriggles loose, but I catch her again and twirl her around and around until she laughs, forgetting her desire to run back to the wall and that devilish branch. I don't dare fetch the axe from the shed and hack the branch off. Not even Father would dare. I try to forget my own uneasiness, try not to hear the faint thread of a song coiling out from the depth of the wood.

"Time for a bath, little one," I tell my sister.

"No bath!" Awela shrieks.

But she trots along after me as I fetch the wash basin and fill it from the pump in front of the house. When it's full, I put the basin by the garden—the flowers and vegetable seedlings will appreciate the water Awela is absolutely going to splash out.

I strip her of her grimy dress and plunk her in, grabbing a bar of soap and scrubbing vigorously. She shouts and laughs and splashes, thoroughly enjoying herself. I finish scrubbing and let her play in the water, my eyes wandering sometimes to the wood beyond the garden and my father's wall, and sometimes to the house I've lived in for as long as I can remember.

It's a small stone house, ordinary except for the tower that serves as my father's observatory, the silver dome closed until evening, the telescope safe inside. Flowers wilt in the bright blue window boxes, like they never did when my mother tended them instead of me. I've tried to keep all the pieces of her alive. I've tried not to surrender the whole of her memory to the Gwydden's Wood.

Everyone says we're fools to live on the border of the wood itself. Maybe we are.

But there was nowhere else far enough away from the village for my father to observe the stars in solitude. Few people know he's an astronomer. No one knows he charts the stars for King Elynion himself, on the king's coin no less. Father works as a day laborer at Brennan's Farm to keep people from asking questions about how he earns his money and adhere to the king's condition of secrecy. Brennan is our closest neighbor, a three-mile walk northeast of our house. The village is another five miles north, and even that's considered perilously close to the wood.

It grows chilly as the wind picks up. Clouds knot dark over the sun, and it smells suddenly of rain. The music is stronger now, loud enough to hear clearly over the rising wind. It pulls at me. I shudder, clench my jaw, steel myself against it.

"Time to go inside, little one," I tell Awela. I pour a pitcher of clean water over her head and she screams like I'm murdering her. I just tickle her chin and scoop her out of the basin, wrapping her in a large towel and carrying her toward the house.

The music follows, sinking into me with invisible barbs.

The same music that lured my mother into the wood, where she was lost forever. I wonder if anyone heard her scream when the Gwydden's eight monstrous daughters fell on her and rent her to pieces. I wonder if any part of her remains, or if she is nothing more than dust now, strewn about the forest floor amongst the molded leaves.

I carry Awela up the two steps to our front door in a hurry, reaching for the handle.

"Is Calon Merrick at home?"

I jump at the overloud voice, turning to see what is obviously one of the king's men striding up, his long cobalt coat fixed with gold-plated buttons, his smart blue cap trimmed with gold to match. A tall oilcloth satchel hangs over one shoulder, and he's somewhere between my father's age and my own seventeen years. He has dark brown skin, which speaks of Saeth descent.

"I'm Owen Merrick," I reply. "My father isn't here right now. You've come for the star charts?"

The king's man's eyes flick between me and my baby sister with obvious distaste. He taps his ears, and I realize he must have put wax in them, to protect against the tree sirens' song—he can't hear me.

I open the door and wave him inside. He steps through, but only takes the wax out when the door is shut firmly behind him. His eyes flick uneasily to the wood outside the kitchen window. "I'm here for the charts."

"I'll fetch them," I promise. "Just a moment." I set the kettle on the stove while I find Awela a cloth diaper and a clean nightgown. She scampers about, shrieking. The king's man frowns, pressing his back against the wall by the fireplace because he physically can't get any farther away from her.

I scowl at him when he's not looking—does he suppose he sprang from his mother's womb as fully grown and thoroughly dull as he is now?

I leave him with a cup of tea at the kitchen table and carry

Awela up to the observatory with me to collect the month's star charts. Ordinarily I wouldn't take her, but there's no chance in hell I'm leaving her downstairs with that dullard.

"Don't touch anything, little one," I instruct with great futility as I set her down in the middle of the observatory. For a few moments she stares around her with huge, fascinated eyes, and then the next instant she's racing round the room in circles, shrieking with mad delight.

The charts are in bundles on the bookcase beside the telescope. I gather them under my arms and manage to herd Awela out of the room in front of me.

She half tumbles down the stairs—it's past time for her nap.

"Here they are," I tell the king's man, piling the charts on the table for him to examine.

I give Awela some milk and sit with her at the table; she nestles into me.

The king's man takes each chart from its casing and gives it a cursory glance before putting it back. He's clearly new to this job—King Elynion normally sends the same few servants to collect the charts and bring my father's payment, and I've never seen this man before. I can also tell by the way his eyes dart around the star charts that he doesn't actually know how to read them.

"Everything appears to be in order," he says when he's perused the last one.

I don't call his bluff. I'm annoyed that he hasn't even touched his tea, leaving it to go cold at his elbow. I shouldn't have wasted it on him.

Outside, the clouds break, and rain slants hard past the window. Awela is half asleep in my arms.

"Your father's payment, as agreed upon." The king's man takes a blue velvet pouch from an inner pocket, and sets it on the table with a faint clink of metal. "You can count it, if you wish, but be quick about it. I want to be back in the village by nightfall."

Nightfall isn't for hours, but I see how his gaze travels once more to the window, to the shadow of the wood that lies just beyond his view. I wonder if he's ever laid eyes on it before today.

"I don't know how you stand it," he says in an undertone. "I don't know how you sleep at night, so near her wood. So near *her*."

The Gwydden. Few say her name aloud, but everyone thinks it: the witch who rules the wood, powerful enough to bend the things of God to her own will, just as she bends her daughters, the tree sirens. She wields them like weapons, commanding them to sing, to lure men and women into the wood and devour them.

"We don't bother her." I shrug, attempting nonchalance. "She doesn't bother us. But I don't need to count the money. I trust His Majesty."

Awela rubs her eyes and I stand, hefting her up against my shoulder. The king's man stands too, awkwardly bundling the star charts and stuffing them into his oilcloth satchel. The satchel is deep, but a good third of the charts still poke out the top. He studies me for a moment, as if debating whether or not to say something. "Do you know why he does it? His Majesty, I mean. Why he pays your father for these charts every month?"

I shrug. This man really must be new. None of the other servants the king has sent to us ever questioned him in such a way. "If my father knows, he's never told me. But I'm sure *you* know the importance of—"

"Secrecy." The man scowls at me. "I'm not a simpleton. Just wondered if you knew. That's all."

Personally, I like to imagine King Elynion as a bit of a scientist, that he keeps his hobby to himself to avoid appearing superstitious. If the people of Tarian knew their king consulted the stars on a monthly basis—whatever his real reason—they would distrust him. He's their hero, their champion against the Gwydden and her wood. If they thought he was seeking his future in the stars, they might whisper of magic; they might begin to think he was no different than the witch and her monstrous daughters. There is a thin line, after all, between magic and science.

The king's man hesitates at the door, pulling two lumps of wax from his pocket but not putting them back in his ears yet. He clearly doesn't relish the thought of going outside, even if the alternative means staying in here with me and Awela.

"Just seems like a waste of coin," he says. "It could be going to the railroad."

Awela lays her head against my neck, yawning. The tree sirens' song is slipping through the cracks in the stones and into the house now. I might be stuck with the king's man for a while—I don't know that he can resist the pull, even through the wax. "What's wrong with the railroad? It's been running smoothly for a year now."

The king's man grimaces. "It was until the wood grew up around the tracks."

"It did *what?*" I stare, shocked.

"Just west of your village, the train to Saeth runs almost entirely through the wood. Been that way since the winter."

"Since the *winter?*" I'm repeating things stupidly, but I don't care. Horror grips me. Along with the telegraph lines, the railroad is one of King Elynion's crowning achievements, making travel swift and safe across Tarian, strengthening ties with our neighboring country and trade partner, Saeth. When he built it, the wood was *miles* away, the tracks running over long stretches of grassy plain. And now . . . "How is that possible?"

"The wood witch grows stronger, year by year. I'm surprised she hasn't tumbled down that wall of yours." He glances out the window. "But it's worse than you know. The tracks in the forest are being torn up. The metal is twisted, the railroad ties ripped from the ground and set to stand upright like the trees they once were and hung with garlands of flowers. No matter they were never *her* trees;

we brought all the lumber in from Saeth—His Majesty plays by the rules. It happens at random, delaying whole shipments. We have to repair sections of track nearly every week now. There will be trouble with Saeth if we can't sort it out."

He's right. Tarian imports wood and coal from Saeth. We would be in bad trouble without it. Besides the slow, perilous sea routes, there's no other way to *get* to Saeth, unless one was foolish enough to go through the wood on foot—horses won't go near her trees.

Awela shifts on my shoulder, her small hands fisting my shirt. Outside, the rain drives on and on, and the tree sirens' song fades into nothing. "You've been in the wood, then," I say, not missing his use of "we."

He shudders and nods. "I worked on the railroad six months, and I'm often sent out to guard the repair crew."

My pulse throbs in my neck. "Have you ever seen them? The— the witch's daughters?"

His hands twitch, the star chart casings in the oilcloth satchel rattling against each other. "Once. It was two months ago, the first time we were sent to repair a section of the track in the newly grown wood. We stuffed our ears with wax against their songs. We armed ourselves with knives and guns. But when they came, it wasn't enough. There were three of them, and their devilish music was loud even through the wax. They were fast as snakes, with glowing eyes and bony hands, and they bound our bodies with living branches that twisted and squeezed, winding into our flesh."

I stare at the king's man in utter horror.

"It was our captain who saved most of us, with a bundle of kerosene-soaked rags and a packet of gunpowder. Scared the devils off long enough for us to escape. But our captain died anyway. He'd lost too much blood."

I eye the king's man with new respect.

He shakes his head, as if to shake the memory away. He seems to realize the music has faded from the wood. "Good day, then." He stuffs the wax into his ears and steps outside, shutting the door behind him. I'm not sorry to see him go. I tuck Awela into her little bed on the first floor, then climb up to the second floor, passing my and my father's bedrooms before taking the narrow stair to the observatory. Assuming the storm passes, it won't be dark enough to use the telescope for some hours yet, but I like the quiet peace of this room. When the dome is open, the glass ceiling is a window to the sky; when it's shut, there's only a small window to the left of the cast-iron stove operated with a crank. I turn it and stare into the Gwydden's Wood, my eyes straining to see past the rain and into the heart of the forest. No one touches the Gwydden's trees—they are sacred to her. The stories say she thinks of them as her children, that she even *made* children from them: her eight daughters, the tree sirens, whose eerie song twists up again through the window.

There was a time when the wood was significantly smaller than it is now, but it grows year by year. More rapidly, according to the king's man's report, than I realized. I wonder if by the time Awela is as old as I am it will have swallowed all the world the way it swallowed my mother.

For a moment more I stare into the trees, listening to the song of the Gwydden's daughters. The music rakes through me with jagged claws, and I find myself leaning out of the observatory, stretching my hands to the trees. Awareness slams through me. I jerk my head back inside and crank the window shut again.

Chapter Two

OWEN

I T MAY BE SPRING, BUT THE CHILL OF WINTER LINGERS WHEN THE evenings come, so I shovel coal into the downstairs stove before I start cooking supper.

I'm a fair cook, which is not generally thought dignified for a boy, but I enjoy it: the rhythm of chopping vegetables, the satisfaction of stirring flour and butter and sugar together to make Awela's favorite little cakes. I'm proud I've kept all three of us alive since the day Mother was lost to the wood, even though it meant leaving school a year early.

Tonight I stir cawl in a pot bubbling on the kitchen stove, and mix tea-soaked dried currants into my bara brith dough. I shape the dough into loaves and leave them to rise overnight—they'll go straight into the oven in the morning. Awela wakes up from her nap and comes darting out into the kitchen, wrapping herself around my legs and giggling as I walk with her attached to me.

"Wen, Wen!" she cries, pleased.

Father steps through the door just as I am spooning cawl into three bowls, and Awela launches herself at him, searching his pockets for the chocolates she knows he's tucked away for her there. She finds half a dozen, which I confiscate from her, promising she can eat them after dinner. Father pulls off his boots, hangs his cap on its wall peg, and stretches, his skin weathered and tanned from his long days of work in full view of the sun. He perches his spectacles onto his nose—he never wears them in the fields, for fear of breaking them—then washes up and comes to sit at the table.

We eat, and afterward Awela plays on the floor by Father's feet while he reads his newspaper, glancing down at her affectionately every minute or so. I step outside for more coal, shoveling it into the coal scuttle from the bin outside the kitchen. The bin is running low—I'll have to walk into the village soon to buy more. Long ago, the people of Tarian burned wood in their fireplaces, just like Saeth and Gwaed across the mountains. Some people still do, if they can't afford coal, collecting loose twigs or branches the wind has broken off. Only the greatest of fools would dare cut down a whole tree.

King Elynion tried to burn the Gwydden's Wood, once, in the early days of his reign. He scorched miles of trees, and she retaliated by slaughtering an entire village of people. He thwarts her in different ways, now. With the train. With the telegraph wires running for miles under the ground to make communication with Saeth and Gwaed swift and cost effective. But if the king's man is to be believed, she is finding her own ways to fight back.

I return to the house, lugging the coal.

The mantel clock chimes eight, and I scoop up the protesting Awela for bed. She gives Father four slimy kisses and then I take her into her room, changing her back into her little nightgown, tucking the covers up to her chin.

"Story, Wen," she says in her high squeaky voice. "Story."

I tell her the story I do most nights, about the man who watches the stars, about his wife who goes away on a long journey and can't find her way back to him. She makes herself into a star so he can always see her, so that, in a way, she can always be with him.

Awela doesn't understand, but she likes the sound of my voice, the familiar rhythm of the story. I turn down her lamp and kiss her forehead and shut her door.

Out in the main part of the house, Father has already gone, his newspaper and spectacles absent from their place on the little end table by the stove. I don't know how late he stays up reading every night before falling asleep in the room that must feel empty without my mother. But I do know it's up to me to fulfill his contract with King Elynion, as it has been every night since my mother was lost.

I set our stewpot to soak in the sink, and climb up to the observatory.

I light the lamp on the worn wooden desk that waits beside the telescope, and absently spin the rings of the brass armillary sphere my father brought back from his university days. I put the kettle on the stove that hugs the back wall and make a pot of cinnamon tea; its potent sweet scent fills the whole room. Then there's the dome to open and the telescope to adjust, this evening's empty star charts to take from their drawer and lay out on the desk.

I settle into the chair in front of the telescope and peer into the eyepiece. Thankfully the storm has broken apart, so I have a clear view as the sky grows dark. The planet Cariad is the first to rise, bright near the horizon. I mark its position on the first of tonight's charts with a scratch of my pen. I wait for more planets to appear, watching for red Rhyfel and the paler Negesydd, and of course the first of the stars.

There are millions of stars in the sky, and scientists speculate there are millions more we can't see, even with the aid of telescopes. What I do every night—what my father used to do, before my mother was lost—is mark down the positions of all the stars we possibly can: the ones that make up the constellations, the ones between and around the constellations. The planets. The phases of the moon. I have an empty chart for each position of the telescope, with curved lines marking the path of the ecliptic. There's one whole chart to mark the Arch of the Wind, the spray of stars that look like handfuls of snow strewn across the sky.

The stars are predictable—that's what I like best about them. I've been charting them by myself for a whole year now, watching them move in their set patterns across the celestial sphere. I really *don't* know why the king hired my father to do this, why he demands secrecy. When I was younger, I used to pore over the charts, looking for patterns and predictions. There are stories about the constellations, about the movements of planets and their proximity to each other predicting the future, plotting out the events of your life. But I've only seen order. Wonder. Besides Awela and my parents, the stars are what I love best in the world.

Slowly, methodically, I begin the process of charting the stars, shifting the telescope to a new part of the sky when each chart is full.

I've marked only three charts when the observatory door creaks open, and I look back to find my father there, his spectacles perched on the end of his nose. His presence surprises me. He looks exhausted, as he has ever since my mother was lost, but there's a determination in his eyes that's been gone so long, I forgot it was ever there.

"May I join you?" he asks, hesitant, as though he fears I'll turn him away.

I grin. "Of course, Father. I've only been keeping up the work in your absence."

"I'm not chasing you away," he clarifies.

A knot I didn't know had formed in my chest loosens again. I pop up from the desk and drag a second chair over. Father pours himself some tea, and we settle in together, taking turns at the telescope, trading off marking the stars on the charts.

Contentment fills me. I've missed my father—he's been here and yet not here, gone in a different way than my mother. This is how it used to be: my father teaching me how to chart the stars, the two of us staying awake long into the night drinking cinnamon tea.

The work goes faster with him there, and when the charts have all been filled and bound safely in their folder to be given to the king's man at the end of the month, Father and I linger in the observatory. I get the feeling that he has missed this, perhaps even more than I have.

"Owen," he says, as the lamp burns low and we drain the dregs of our tea, "can you forgive me?"

"There's nothing to forgive, Father."

His brow furrows, and he puts his hand on my shoulder. "We would have been lost, if not for you. The king's coin. The house. Little Awela. Without you holding us all together, I don't know what would have become of us. I shouldn't have left you to fend for yourself."

My throat hurts; the subject is perilously close to Mother's absence, which I'm not sure either of us have the courage to discuss just now. "I've been all right. Really. God gave me strength enough."

Father smiles at me, setting down his tea mug to place his hands on my shoulders. "I am blessed to have such a son. But I have too long neglected you, Awela as well. It's time for you to start thinking about learning a trade, apprenticing with someone in the village. You're old enough now."

I stare at him, entirely blindsided. "I don't want to learn another trade—I'm going to be an astronomer like you. Besides, you need me to keep the house and watch Awela. Help chart the stars."

Father shakes his head. "Let me worry about Awela. I need to get both of you away from here before the wood—" The word chokes him. He takes a breath. "Before the wood winds itself into your souls. It's something I should have done long ago. I can't lose either of you. I won't."

I want to point out that we've been perfectly safe for the last year, but I think of the music, oozing more often than not from the trees, of Awela stretching up her tiny hand to reach the branch hanging over the wall, of myself hanging out the observatory window.

"If you would rather, you can attend Saeth University in the fall," Father continues. "I've put money aside for it." His forehead creases, and I know he's thinking of my mother—they met at the university. She was a cellist, and he an astronomer, and they used to tease each other that they would have to live on love, since their professions would take them nowhere.

My throat tightens. "Father, I'm not going to leave you."

He claps his hand on my shoulder as he rises. "You are young yet. There is plenty of time to think beyond the confines of this house and the sky. Just promise me you'll consider it—you don't have to make a decision immediately."

I get up too, dousing the lamp and following him from the observatory.

"I'll consider it," I tell him. I don't mean it. I may only be seventeen, but all I've ever wanted is the sky.

Chapter Three

OWEN

I

T'S ONLY WHEN I CRAWL INTO BED THAT I REALIZE I FORGOT TO tell Father about my errand—his unexpected plans for my future drove it right out of my mind. I wake early enough to catch him before he leaves for Brennan's Farm, trying not to see his red eyes, the grief that hangs on him like a physical thing. I didn't sleep more than a handful of hours after leaving the observatory; he looks like he might not have slept at all.

"I'm going to Saeth University today."

Surprise sparks in his face. "That time of year already?"

I nod. Every year, my father files an abbreviated record of his annual star charts in the university library. Astronomers all across the continent do the same, scientists pooling our knowledge, collecting it for future generations. I went by myself last year, by train, and the three years before that, my mother went with merchants traveling along the old road across the plains.

"I'm to take the nine o' clock train from the village." I think about what the king's man told me yesterday, and wonder if Father knows the wood has grown around the tracks. "It will be perfectly safe," I lie. "I'll spend the night in Saeth and be back tomorrow evening. I've arranged for Awela to stay with Efa till then. I'm taking her the moment she wakes up."

Father scratches at the stubble on his jaw. "Perhaps we don't need to file the charts this year."

"I'll only be gone a day, Father."

He frowns. "I've heard the wood has——"

"The train is perfectly safe," I repeat hastily. "And fast. I promise I'll be all right—I'll send you a telegram the moment I arrive, so you won't have to worry."

"Very well." He sighs. "But I'll worry anyway. Don't open the window on the train. And take my knife." He nods at the decorative box on the shelf above the stove in the living room, where his hunting knife has resided for as long as I can remember. I don't think he's ever used it.

Then he's out the door in a rush and I put my bara brith in the oven and brew tea, obediently adding the hunting knife to my pack. The star charts I'm taking to the library are ready, bundled together in a waterproof cylinder and fitted with a leather strap to make it easy to carry.

Awela toddles into the kitchen just as I'm about to go and wake her. She gobbles down a thick slice of bara brith, and gulps milk and porridge as if I never actually feed her. Then I'm bundling her into my arms and slinging my pack and the star chart case over my shoulder. We start on the path to Blodyn Village.

It would be vastly easier if we had a horse, or even a donkey—Awela grows enormously heavy after only a short walk. But animals don't like being so close to the Gwydden's Wood. We had a goat for a while, when Awela was a baby—her milk dried up, and she jumped the fence and was never seen again. Even chickens don't last at our house; they stop laying after a week or two, then molt all their feathers and die off one by one. We gave up keeping animals altogether, and get our milk and eggs and meat from Brennan's Farm now.

At least the garden grows, so we're never short on fruits and vegetables. Sometimes I swear plants grow *faster* in our garden than they really ought to, as though they pull some kind of invigorating magic from the soil that feeds the Gwydden's trees.

What I really want is a bicycle. I don't travel long distances often enough to really *need* one, and I couldn't ride one with Awela, but I want one all the same. The newfangled contraptions are all the rage in Breindal City, according to Father's newspapers, and there are a few in our village now, too.

It's faster to carry Awela than to let her walk, even if my arm muscles are screaming by the time Brennan's Farm comes into view. I leave her with Efa, Brennan's wife, and then trudge into the village alone, waving at my father, who's hard at work in the fields and probably doesn't even see me.

The air smells fresher and the sun burns hotter the farther I trudge away from the wood. Dust swirls beneath my feet, and I've grown quite hot by the time I arrive at the village train station. It really doesn't warrant the word *station*, being more of a small wooden platform sandwiched between the telegraph relay station and the inn, which is where you purchase your ticket.

I step inside the squat stone building. It's dim and cool, a welcome relief from the sun. I wait for my eyes to adjust before stepping up to the counter. A dark-eyed girl stands behind it, polishing glasses with a rag, her long hair tied back at the nape of her neck with a bright ribbon. Her cream blouse has puffy sleeves with cuffs tight at her wrists, and her high-waisted skirt has buttons running all down the front of it. The sight of her makes my face warm. There aren't many young women in Blodyn Village, but

Mairwen Griffith is by far the prettiest. Smartest, too. She's a poet, and has had several pieces published in the Breindal City newspaper. Someday I'm going to work up the nerve to talk to her. Properly. About astronomy or music or books. Maybe marry her—I haven't quite figured out all the details yet.

"Morning, Owen. What can I do for you?" She smiles at me, and for a moment I lose the power of speech.

"Uh . . . ticket," I remember. "For the nine o' clock train to Saeth."

"Barely made it," says Mairwen, glancing at the small clock on the wall behind her. She pulls out a paper ticket from the till and writes in my name.

I hand over the fare. For a moment I don't move, just stand there awkwardly, trying to think of something clever to say.

She smiles at me again, her eyes bright and laughing. "Better hurry, Owen Merrick. You'll miss your train."

I stammer something nonsensical in reply and step outside and onto the train platform, upbraiding myself for being such a coward.

But there wouldn't have been time to properly speak with her anyway, because she's right—the train rattles up that moment and I climb aboard, handing over my ticket to the dark-skinned steward in the blue and gray cap. I slide into a seat by the window.

The car is at the very end of the train right before the caboose, and it's mostly empty, the only other passenger a pale-skinned old man in a tailed coat reading a newspaper. The headline says something about King Elynion drafting soldiers into his army. The old man's top hat sits in the vacant seat beside him, and I realize I've forgotten my own in my hurry to make the train. I'm not in the habit of wearing it—it's still stuffed in the coat closet somewhere. At least I put on my one and only suit, although it's rather too small for me now—I'll have to ask Father about getting a new one. Mostly I just wear Father's castoff shirts and trousers—I haven't been to school in a year, and Awela doesn't care how I'm dressed.

I settle deeper into my seat and take a book out of my satchel. The train lurches into motion, the village and farms passing in a blur. It's not long before we plunge into the wood, the leafy green swallowing us whole; I push away my uneasiness, try to lose myself in the book.

The old man across from me momentarily lays down his newspaper to pull his window shut.

I wonder how many passengers are riding in the cars ahead of us. I wonder if the engineer has wax stuffed into his ears. I try to comfort myself with the thought that perhaps the noise of the train is loud enough to block out the song of the Gwydden's daughters.

Yet I can't help but feel we're hurtling into danger.

Hours pass. I eat my lunch: another piece of bara brith, with a fat slice of ham and hot tea from my thermos. The train clatters on, the motion of the wheels on the rails dragging my eyelids down.

A horrific *SCREEEEEECH* of metal jolts me awake. The train car wrenches sideways and I'm thrown hard into the seat across the aisle, inches from the old passenger who lies limp against the shut window. His neck is bent at an odd angle, and there's a smear of red on his temple. I stare at him, my thoughts dull and slow with shock. This is a nightmare, and in another moment I will wake up.

But I don't.

The train car shudders as it settles on its side, causing me to slide into the old passenger's body. He is stiff and cold, and a scream tears from my throat as I frantically, desperately, pull myself back into the aisle. I am shaky with horror, with the dawning awareness that gnaws at my mind.

The train windows are over my head now. Branches press against the glass. They scratch and they scrape, like they're trying to get in, and I know, I *know*, even before the music twists suddenly through glass and metal and puts its claws in me.

A tree siren derailed the train, and she's going to kill us all.

The music calls me, commands me. The barbs dig deep and *pull*. Something inside my head thrashes, screams, fights.

But my body obeys the siren's call.

I pull myself across the seats, toward the door that leads to the next car. It's sideways now, bent and jammed from the crash. The tree siren's song clamors in my head, yanking me like a beast on a chain. I don't want to leave the train. I want to hide from her. I want to tuck myself into a shadowy corner and pray she passes me by. The music doesn't let me. I put my shoulder into the door, throw myself against it again and again. I'm dimly aware of the pain in my arm, of the wound in my side from being thrown against the seat. The music writhes in every part of me. It's splitting me apart. I do not want to go to her. And yet—I *do*.

There is terror and desire. A distant horror, a further distant pain. I must get through the door. I must, I must.

The door gives. I push through, hissing as a piece of jagged metal slices into my leg. The music pulls me, pulls me. I haul myself from the train, and tumble out into the wood.

Chapter Four

OWEN

IRT GRINDS UNDER MY PALMS. THE CUT IN MY LEG DRIPS blood on the ground.

I gulp for air, my limbs strangely heavy. Screams echo in the wood ahead of me, a jarring counterpoint to the music that twists into my soul. The train has been torn off its tracks, the cars scattered on the ground like discarded toys. They stretch on into the wood, out of my sight line. Other passengers crawl from the cars ahead of me, some with broken arms or legs, many with wounds from the impact of the crash. All of them lie on the forest floor, limbs dragging across the tracks. All of them wait, as I do.

The music overwhelms me, pins me like a bug to the earth between the railroad cars. I can't move my arms, my legs. Her song commands me to stay, to wait. My mind is screaming for me to *run*. My body doesn't listen. I can't move, can't think. I can hardly breathe. She will come. She will devour me. And I will let her do it.

Horror is a yawning gulf inside of me.

I will never see Father or Awela again.

From the front sections of the train comes the same sound again and again, the pop and crack of something breaking. I realize that it's bodies, that it's bones.

Overhead, wind ripples through the trees. Branches groan and leaves whisper. Through it all her song swells and swells. It will swallow the world. It will swallow me.

I don't even have the will to clap my hands over my ears, to shut out the all-consuming sound of it.

I just lie here, and wait for her to come.

I shake, shake.

Father. Awela. Tears blur my vision.

I glimpse the siren through the trees, a flash of green and silver. The screams grow louder, swelling toward me like an ocean tide. But they do not block out her song. They don't even muffle it.

She comes nearer, to a car five down the line. She has the vague form of a woman but she's very, very tall, and unnaturally thin. Her skin is silver-white bark, and she's clothed in green and gold leaves round as coins. Branches burst from her hands and catch hold of the train carriage, ripping it open as easily as if it were an egg. She drags a passenger out by the throat, and with one vicious twist she snaps his neck and flings him to the ground.

A scream tears out of me. I try to fight against the music. I tell myself to get up, to run, but my body will not obey me.

So I just lie here. I lie here and watch her slaughter them all.

Bodies. So many bodies. She scatters them over the grass, flings them onto the wreck of the train. They're broken and bloody, some with twisted limbs, some with their final screams frozen in their vacant eyes. Vines spring out of the ground, and pull them into the earth.

She is two cars down from me. One. With every person she kills, she kneels beside them for a moment, and something hanging at her throat pulses with a silver light. She never stops singing.

I feel her music in every part of me, throbbing in my veins, heavy in my bones. It will be the last thing I ever hear.

An eerie red light slants through the trees, and some distant part of me realizes that beyond the wood, the sun is setting.

I won't live to see the stars. Won't have the chance to tell my father and Awela goodbye.

I weep.

There are no passengers in the train car ahead of me, or if there were, they were killed in the crash. A mercy for them. I think of the old man and his newspaper, dead on impact. He will not have to die as I will—in the grip of a nightmare, at the hands of a monster.

She comes toward me, her movement wavering and strange, like a tree bowing in the wind. She will put her claws in me. She will break me in half, and fling me to the ground for the earth to swallow, like it swallowed all the rest.

But she stops three paces away from me, and closes her mouth. Her song is cut off. She stares at me. The tree siren *stares at me.*

She is even more monstrous up close. Her hair is silver, tangled with yellow leaves. She wears a crown of violets. There is blood on her hands.

I shake, dimly aware that my will is flooding back to me. My body buzzes with needle-like pain, blood rushing back into limbs that have been asleep. My mind is a riot of terror. I still can't move, fixed by her gaze as I was fixed by her song. There is a pendant at her throat, hung on a twist of vine. It glows a faint silver, reflecting in her eyes.

She opens her mouth and I shrink back. I have lost my chance. I should have fled the instant she stopped singing.

"*Run,*" she snarls.

Chapter Five

MONSTER

THE ORB AT MY THROAT IS HEAVY WITH SOULS. THEY WEIGH ON ME.
There is a boy in the dark.
He stares, but does not cower.
There is a strangeness about him.
A difference in his soul.
A familiar spark.
I do not want to kill him, to feel his blood warm and wet on my hands.
I do not want his soul.
I do not need it.
The orb is heavy.
She will not know.
He runs
into
the
night.
I let him go.

Chapter Six

OWEN

I TEAR INTO THE DARK, MY FEET SLAPPING AGAINST THE RAILROAD ties, my breathing ragged, frantic. Pain stabs under my ribs. I stumble on one of the cross ties, but I haul myself up and keep running. I can't stop. The moment I do, I'm dead.

Oh God.

Bodies. So many bodies. The images crowd in my mind. I can't run fast enough to shake them loose.

Oh God.

A sob tears out of me. The trees murmur and scrape above my head, an eerie wind seething past my hot face. I run and run and run, following the train tracks, the only possible route of escape. But how far did the train take me into the wood? How many hours was I asleep? Maybe I was nearly to Saeth. Maybe I should have run the other direction.

But *Oh God, no.* That was the way *she* had gone. The tree siren. The monster.

Slap slap slap go my feet against the railroad ties. My pulse is so quick I can't count the beats. I gulp air like I'm drowning and maybe I am. Drowning in leaves and branches and the horror of her eyes.

Now I know the color of a demon's eyes. Yellow.

Slap slap slap.

I run and run. I can't feel my feet. My body seems separated from my mind, like I'm floating somewhere far above, watching my own futile dash to freedom.

She stopped singing. That is the only reason my will returned to me. I have no illusions that she really let me go. Why would she? She is a cat and I am a mouse, and any moment now she will catch me in her claws, bat me back and forth between them, leave my broken body on the forest floor like she left all the others.

Oh God. My body is screaming to stop running. My mind is screaming to keep going.

She was green and gold. Silver and violet. There was blood on her hands.

The trees watch me as I stagger on. I run until I collapse, and then I pull myself along the railroad tracks, tearing holes in my trousers and scraping my legs raw. I don't make a conscious decision to stop, but I grow aware that I have, huddled between the rails, shaking and shaking.

Oh God. I am going to die here. I'll never see my father or Awela again. Never have the chance to talk to Mairwen Griffith.

Silver and yellow, violet and green. Blood on her hands.

My head throbs and my body aches. Silver and yellow, violet and green. Red and red and red.

Suddenly it's not the train passengers I see—it's my mother, her body bloody and broken, her eyes staring into nothing, a last ragged bit of her hair gleaming gold as the vines wrap over her and pull her under the earth. No one should have ended that way, least of all my mother. Not her, not her.

I weep for her, understanding for the first time that she's wholly, entirely *gone*. My father understood it from the beginning. It broke him, body and soul.

Exhaustion crowds my mind. Creatures rustle somewhere in the underbrush. The wind rattles the leaves away overhead. .

I want to sleep. I don't want to see silver and yellow, violet and green. I don't want to see red. I let unconsciousness steal over me, piece by piece. I let the horror of the Gwydden's Wood lull me to sleep.

I wake to the blear of orange light and hands under my armpits, hauling me upward. I look into the gaunt face of my father, his mouth pressed into a grim line. "Are there any others?"

I don't understand the question. I'm bleary and bewildered. Every part of me aches, and for a moment I forget why I was lying on the train tracks in the middle of the wood. I don't understand why my father is here.

"Owen," he says gently. "Are there any other survivors?"

Remembrance slams through me and I stagger under the weight of it. My father keeps a steady hand under my elbow.

"She slaughtered them." The words choke out of me. "She slaughtered them all."

He nods, like he was expecting this. "Stay close. We have to move fast." He shoves wax in my ears and ties a scarf over my head, then does the same for himself.

The world is suddenly muffled.

Father grabs the torch lying on the ground—the source of the orange light—and brandishes it ahead of him like a sword. He takes my arm, and I stumble along with him down the railroad tracks. I feel as if I'm in a dream. Perhaps I am.

We walk quickly. The trees don't like my father's torch. They hiss and draw back, and I pray to God they're not calling for their mistress. She would laugh at the fire while she sank her claws into us, while she broke us like so many twigs.

Around us, the sky begins to lighten. I never expected to see another morning, and yet here are the ragged edges of dawn. The sight of it chokes me.

And then we're stepping from the forest, turning south toward our house. We don't take the scarves from our heads or dig the wax from our ears until the observatory tower comes into view, bright in the morning sun.

We stop at the garden gate, and Father turns toward me, clapping his hands on my arms.

My jaw works as I reach for adequate words to express my gratitude and sorrow and relief. I realize none exist.

"How . . . ?" I say instead.

"I went to the telegraph office last evening on my way home from Brennan's Farm. There was no telegram from you, so I sent one inquiring after your train. It had never arrived."

I'm shaking. I can't stop. It's only my father's presence that grounds me. "How did you know to come look for me? How did you know I wasn't . . . "

"I wasn't going to lose my son like I lost my wife." His voice is jagged and raw. "I would have burned the forest to the ground to find you. I would have driven a knife into the witch's heart. I would have ended all the world before I lost you."

I believe him.

He pulls me into an embrace, holding me hard against his chest as I shake and shake.

I'm safe now. I don't have to be afraid.

But I am.

Horribly, horribly afraid.

Father goes to fetch Awela from Brennan's Farm, and I crawl into my bed and try to sleep. All I can see are her yellow eyes, the blood dripping red from her hands.

Chapter Seven

OWEN

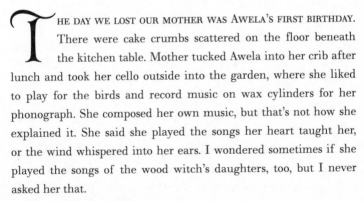

THE DAY WE LOST OUR MOTHER WAS AWELA'S FIRST BIRTHDAY. There were cake crumbs scattered on the floor beneath the kitchen table. Mother tucked Awela into her crib after lunch and took her cello outside into the garden, where she liked to play for the birds and record music on wax cylinders for her phonograph. She composed her own music, but that's not how she explained it. She said she played the songs her heart taught her, or the wind whispered into her ears. I wondered sometimes if she played the songs of the wood witch's daughters, too, but I never asked her that.

Perhaps I should have.

I liked hearing Mother play. I played some, too—she'd given me my first lessons when I was so small the cello dwarfed me, my hand barely big enough to wrap around the bow. I enjoyed playing, but I'd never be as good as her. Her whole soul was filled with music; mine brimmed with stars.

That day I was up in my room, reading one of my father's scientific journals about a telescope being built in Saeth that would be powerful enough to look deeper into space than ever before. My mother's music drifted up from the garden.

She stopped playing suddenly, in the middle of a phrase. It was strange enough that I glanced out the window in time to see her drop her cello onto the cabbages to stride with purpose toward the Gwydden's Wood.

"MOTHER!" I cried, flinging the journal onto my bed and bolting downstairs.

Alerted by my shout, Father joined me on the stairs, and the two of us burst outside just as the hem of my mother's dress vanished among the trees.

"Eira!" my father cried. He ran after her.

"Father! Father, *wait*!"

"Stay with Awela!" he called back to me. "Keep her safe."

And then the forest swallowed him, too.

I paced in front of the house, more shocked than frightened. I trusted my father to bring my mother back. I didn't fear the Gwydden then, not any more than a child fears a monster from a story.

But when Awela woke and there was still no sign of either of our parents, I was afraid.

And when the sun set and clouds rolled in and Awela cried for her dinner and they hadn't come back, dread gripped me in its lion's jaws. I fed Awela leftover birthday cake and lumpy porridge, because it was the only thing I knew how to cook. I ran outside to save Mother's cello when it started to rain. I shoveled coal into the stove when the early spring night grew swiftly cold.

I put Awela to bed, trying to remember all the songs my mother usually sang to her. I swept the cake crumbs off the floor. And then I collapsed in front of the fire and wondered if I was an orphan.

I must have dozed, because when the door banged open sometime during the night, I jerked awake to find my father stumbling into the house.

He looked like he had been to Hell and back again. His clothes ragged and torn, dried blood caking both his arms, his neck and face covered in scratches. There were leaves caught in his dark hair.

"Father?" I whispered.

He collapsed to the floor and wept, his whole body shaking. "She's gone," he choked out, over and over. "She's gone."

The next day he started building the wall, working feverishly from sunrise to sunset, hardly sleeping, hardly eating. He worked until his hands were scraped raw, until his skin was gray with mortar. He didn't stop until he'd finished it: a mile long and five feet high. It was meant to protect us from the Gwydden, but I saw what it really was: a memorial to my mother. The evidence of my father's guilt and shame, because if he'd built it earlier, like he'd always meant to, he might not have lost her at all.

I never asked him what he saw in the Gwydden's Wood, how he managed to escape, if he'd found my mother, if he'd seen the Gwydden or her daughters.

A part of me had always wanted to believe that my mother was alive, that she'd escaped somehow.

Now, I have no such illusions.

My father saved me.

But he couldn't save her.

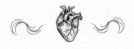

Father stays home with Awela and me the rest of the day and all of the next. I'm glad he's here. I don't know how to give Awela the attention she needs when my head is splitting apart trying to forget yellow eyes and silver-white skin. Trying to block out the screams of the train passengers, the snap of their bones, the tree siren's song, pinning me helpless to the ground.

At least in the light of day, there's the garden to weed and the meals to cook and the futile task of attempting to keep Awela out of mischief. When night falls, there are the stars to chart with my father, a pot of cinnamon tea to drain down to dregs. But after that, when I crawl into bed and try to sleep—there is nothing to keep that day in the wood from playing itself over and over behind my eyes, an endless parade of blood and leaves ringed with a violet-flower crown.

It is impossible to distinguish the moment my thoughts morph into nightmares, for my sleep is the same as my waking: yellow eyes and silver skin, blood dripping red onto the ground.

But in my dreams the tree siren doesn't let me go. In my dreams she never stops singing, not even when she rips my heart from my body, not even when she breaks all my bones and leaves me gasping up at the wheeling sky, the lifeblood pouring out of me. Even in death, I hear her song.

She kills me again and again, her teeth sinking into my throat, her branches impaling my chest. I drown in dirt and leaves and blood.

I wake up screaming, my heart racing like a wild hare, my body slick with sweat.

I don't try to go back to sleep. I pull on a robe and climb up to the observatory, opening the dome and adjusting the telescope. I take comfort in the planets and stars, in telling myself the old stories of the constellations.

Astronomers speculate that the constellations as we see them now didn't always look the same—that they have shifted, little by little, over time. In a few thousand years, I might not even recognize the Twysog Mileinig—the Spiteful Prince—or the Morwyn, the Maiden. Maybe future astronomers will rename these constellations, create new myths to go with them. But I can't imagine the Spiteful Prince being anything other than the thief who betrayed the Morwyn and stole her crown. He escaped up into the heavens, where he made himself into a constellation to hide from her. She wasn't deceived; she followed him there, and now every year she chases him around the ecliptic, stretching out her hand for the crown, never quite catching it.

Nonsense, of course. But it was one of my mother's favorite stories.

It hurts to think of her. I shift the telescope to a different part of the sky, and doze off in the chair trying to forget anything ever existed apart from the stars.

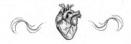

Father goes back to his work at Brennan's Farm, and I go back to minding Awela and the house every day, trying to regather the pieces of myself that fractured apart in the Gwydden's Wood.

It's hard. It's so, so hard, and try as I might I can't quite fall back into the rhythm of it. I'm restless and uneasy, my eyes traveling always to the trees over Father's wall. They hang lower with every passing day, trailing leaves rattling over the stone. It feels as if the wood is watching me. Waiting.

I don't trust it. And I don't trust myself around it.

So as much as is humanly possible, I try to keep Awela indoors.

Her response is to learn how to unlatch the door and let herself out, and after that I *do* take her outside, so I'll at least always know where she is.

Because I don't trust Father's wall, either.

Spring deepens into summer, and Awela helps me pick the first batches of strawberries from our garden. Most of the ones she picks don't make it into her basket, and she's soon covered in sticky red juice. I wash her with water from the pump, and she laughs and wriggles and screams as I scrub her clean.

"Come inside, little one. Time for lunch," I tell her.

"Want stay siiiiide!" my sister wails.

And I can't quite deny her, so I make a picnic for us, and we eat on the blanket in full view of the warm sun. A cool breeze curls out from the wood and over the wall, smelling of earth and growth and that acrid scent of dead things. I push away the memory of yellow eyes and blood dripping from silver skin.

Exhaustion weighs on me. Nightmares chased me to the observatory again last night—as they have every night since my father rescued me—and Awela woke earlier than usual. She eats half her lamb and potato pasty and licks the gravy from her fingers, then clamors for her milk. I lounge on the blanket and she leans against my chest as she drinks, curling her small body into the hollow of my shoulder.

The trees whisper and the bees hum in the garden. The blanket is soft beneath my cheek. My eyelids drift shut.

For the first time in weeks, I sleep deeply, dreamless. Some part of me is certain Awela hasn't left the shelter of my arm, that she has fallen asleep, too.

But when I wake with a start, the afternoon is half gone and I am alone, Awela's bottle empty and abandoned beside me.

For a moment, I don't understand the sudden, paralyzing fear that seizes me. Then I raise my eyes, and see the hole in Father's wall.

No. *No.* This isn't real. I'm dreaming.

I jerk upright and bolt to the wall. The ground bulges with the lump of a tree root, with the tumbled stones it shifted as it grew—somehow—in the short time I was sleeping. The hole is big enough for a child to squeeze through. A child wearing a dress the same color blue as the scrap of torn cloth caught on the jagged edge of one of the stones. The trees rustle eerily, though there is no wind.

I can't breathe. *This is a dream.*

But I drag my finger along the broken stone, and suck in a breath at the prick of pain, at the blood beading up.

Something else catches my eye just beyond the wall, incongruous with the undergrowth.

It's one of Awela's shoes: scuffed brown leather, the strap undone.

I shimmy over the wall and drop down on the other side and snatch it up.

I'm caught in one of my nightmares. This can't be real. *This is a dream.*

But it's not, oh God it's *not.*

I'm shaking hard. I can't stop. *Please*, I plead, *please let this be a dream. I can't go back in there. I can't.*

The trees whisper around me, the ground undulates with more hidden roots, moving like living creatures under the earth.

Terror suffocates me. Paralyzes me. But I can't let my sister be swallowed by the wood. I won't. I will find her. Save her, like my father saved me. And then all three of us will go away from here. Far, far away. We'll never come back.

I'm still shaking as I shove Awela's shoe into my pocket, and step under the trees.

Chapter Eight

MONSTER

THE SOULS ARE TOO HEAVY.

I cannot bear them any longer.

There is a patch of earth at the foot of an ash. It is dappled with sunlight, thick with moss.

I kneel in the earth, tug the orb from my neck.

I bury it.

The souls will run through the veins of the earth,

into the heartless tree.

They will be strength for my mother.

Food for her.

I am lighter,

when the orb is gone.

Light enough

to dream.

I must go back to her.

I must kneel at her feet

and receive a new orb.
I must go and kill for her,
and fill it up again.
I do not want to collect more souls.
But my mother bids me.
I
am
her
creature.
I must obey.
But not yet, not yet.
There is peace here.
Solitude.
Silence.
I stretch my feet
into the earth.
I stretch my arms
into the sky.
I dream
I am once more
a tree.
Part of the earth and
part of the stars.
I drink rain,
wind.
The deer bow to me,
birds nest in my branches.
There is no blood here.
No sound
of screaming,
no bones
no souls

no music.
But there is a voice, high and bright in the air.
It
wakes
me.

Chapter Nine

OWEN

THE WOOD ENGULFS ME. THE AIR IS DENSE AND COOL IN HERE, that scent of dead things stronger. Dark branches thick with rustling leaves blot out the sky. Fear burrows under my skin like a thousand stinging nettles. I've come unarmed into the Gwydden's Wood like the greatest of fools—I don't even have wax to plug my ears.

I try to push away the memory of yellow eyes and silver skin. The scent of blood and snap of bones.

I force myself to walk on.

"Awela," I call softly. I meant to shout, but the wood swallows my voice. "Awela."

There's no answer. I try not to wonder how long she's been wandering in the forest. I try not to wonder if she's already dead.

The trees are quiet, but I feel them watching me. Listening. They're ash trees, gnarled and old, the undergrowth a tangle of ivy and rotting leaves. The ground is never quite still: The earth moves in humps and hollows, roots writhing impossibly just below the surface. It scares me almost more than the trees—I don't want to be pulled under the earth, suffocated, swallowed. With my last breath, I want to see the sky.

I pick my way slowly over the ground, watching my footsteps, straining for any sign of my sister. I'm terrified I'll go the wrong direction, that I'll be too late to save her because I went right when I should have gone left. Everything in me screams to turn around, to bolt back to safety.

But I'm not leaving Awela at the mercy of the wood.

An icy wind stirs through the trees. They seem to bend their heads over my path. Branches snag my sleeve. I yelp and leap forward, a gash ripping in my shirt. Cold air touches my skin. I walk faster.

I find Awela's other shoe a moment later, caught in the rotting leaves at the foot of another ash. I shove it into my pocket. Hope sparks—she can't have wandered too much farther on bare feet. I'm going to find her. We'll be home in time for tea.

I pass through a pocket of violets, dark as poison against the forest floor. Awela's hair ribbon is caught in a bush; it's frayed almost to nothing, too tangled to pull free.

"AWELA!" This time the word rips out of me, thunderous in the dead air. Branches creak and stir. The trees are listening. Watching. Waiting. The ember of hope inside me dies.

Silver skin and dappled hair. Yellow eyes. A violet crown. The images clamor into my mind. I can't shove them out again.

But there is no music in the air. My will is yet my own.

I walk faster, the ground eerily still again. I strain to see Awela behind every tree. But I don't.

Somewhere outside the wood the afternoon is waning. The light fades bit by bit; the air grows cold. Father will be home soon. I have to find Awela. I have to bring her back before he comes into the wood after us. I don't think the trees would let him go a third time.

I'm nearly running now, crunching over twigs and fallen leaves. The noise of them is somehow muffled and deafening all at once. I come to another patch of violets, or is it the same one? I'm certain it can't be, until I see Awela's frayed ribbon, trembling on the bush.

Fear grips me. The light is nearly gone. I can't find Awela in the dark. I can't even find my way home. The siren will sing. She will trap me with her music and break me with her silver hands, and cast me aside for the earth to swallow.

"AWELA!" I scream.

But there's no answer. I hurtle deeper into the wood, crushing the violets underfoot. Their scent clings to me, so sweet I want to gag.

I race against the setting sun and my own throbbing panic, the trees clawing at me, twigs scratching my neck and face. Even if I knew the way home, I'm not going back without my sister. I'm not leaving her to die in this Godforsaken place.

The light is nearly gone when I burst through the trees into a small clearing, a single pale birch alone in the midst of it. The remnants of the sunset are splashed red across the patch of sky, and it's bright enough to see the blur of pale blue at the base of the birch tree.

I bolt toward it, a cry tearing from my throat. *"Awela!"*

The birch tree *moves*.

Oh God.

Not a birch tree.

The siren is crouched over my sister, green and yellow hair dragging across Awela's motionless form. She's crowned with roses.

I lunge for Awela, with no other thought than to snatch her from the siren's grasp. Roots burst up from the earth, knocking me backward, wrapping around my leg and pinning me to the ground.

I blink and there's another siren, tall and silver-white, yanking the first siren away from my sister. They hiss at each other, the first with roses in her hair, the second violets. They are like, and yet not like, monsters of the same blood.

"Leave it," seethes the siren with the violet crown, the siren who slaughtered every person on the train. "Leave it to me." Her voice is a gale of wind through dead trees.

"I found it first," hisses the other. "Its soul is mine."

"I will bring it to our mother. A peace offering."

"You are late returning. She will be angry."

The siren with the violet crown snarls. Her teeth gleam like bones. "That is why I must have the child."

"It will not save you."

Wind tears through the clearing, whipping the sirens' hair about their shoulders, leaves about their knees. All the while, Awela does not move, and I can't breathe, can't breathe, because *what if she's already dead?*

"You are in our mother's favor," says the siren with the violet crown. "What is one soul to you?"

"I see why our mother despises you. You are foolish. Weak." The siren with roses in her hair rakes her claws down the other's bare arm. Dark liquid bubbles up from the wounds. Then the rose-crowned siren turns away, and vanishes into the wood.

The root around my leg releases me. I scramble to my feet. I bolt toward my sister.

The siren with the violet crown wheels on me, swift as a snake, and grabs me by the throat. She holds me choking and writhing, my feet hanging in empty air. I claw at her hands, try to pull them off, but they squeeze tighter and tighter. I can't breathe, can't breathe. *Oh God.* Spots blink bright behind my eyes. Blackness crowds the edges of my vision. I'm choking. I can't even scream.

She releases me without warning, and I slam onto the ground, sobbing for breath.

She looms over me, silhouetted against the wood, a monster in her truest form. The violets tremble in her hair. Dark liquid drips from the sores in her arm.

I gasp, shaking. I gulp air but it's not enough. The pain in my throat is unbearable. I shake and shake. Tears pour from my eyes. She's going to kill me. She's going to kill Awela. And when our father comes looking for us, she'll kill him, too. We'll all be nothing but bones, scattered and swallowed beneath the forest floor.

"Why have you come?" she hisses at me. "Who are you to rob me of my prize?"

"Please." The word scrapes raw past my bruised throat. "Please spare her. Do what you like to me, but don't hurt my sister. *Please.*"

"Sister?" The tree siren kneels beside me, the wind stirring through her long hair.

In the sky above the clearing, the stars appear, one by one. They cast her in a luminous silver light, and it softens her. Makes her look less monstrous. But that frightens me even more.

"She's just a child," I rasp, "hardly more than a babe. Please let her go."

The siren tilts her head. Her eyes glitter. "What do you offer me in exchange for her life?"

My heart wrenches. I shove up to a sitting position, forcing myself not to recoil from her proximity. She smells of deep earth and new growth. She smells of violets. "My own life."

She sneers, a curl of her lip. "You cannot give a soul for a soul."

"It's all I have." My eyes fix on Awela's small form, the steady rise and fall of her chest. Somehow she's sleeping in the horror and the dark of the Gwydden's Wood.

"Who are you?" the siren demands again. "Why did you follow me here?"

I stare at her, still feeling the echo of her hands squeezing the life out of me. "I didn't follow you. I followed Awela."

Her eyes narrow, the wind rising wild. It whips her hair about her face, sends a gust of dead leaves rattling past us. "You were there before. In the wood. The last soul from the iron machine." Her face hardens in the silvery light. "I let you go, and I should not have. I will not let you go again."

It's so hard to breathe, with the fear slamming through me. "I'm not asking you to. Let my sister go. Let me take her home to our father. Then you can do anything you wish with my soul."

She regards me coolly. "You should not have come here."

From the depths of the wood comes a sudden thread of music, a song that coils up my spine and pulls me ramrod straight—the other siren. I'm climbing to my feet without realizing it, turning toward the song.

The tree siren hisses, and snatches my wrist in her rough, un-yielding fingers. "You are *weak*," she scoffs. "As weak as the rest of them. Easy prey for *my* sisters."

I try to jerk out of her grasp, but she catches my other arm and wrenches me close. She's taller than me by nearly a foot, and clothed in leaves that are sewn together with translucent thread.

"I thought you were stronger than the others," she hisses into my hair. "But you would go to my sisters like a moth to a flame, no matter it will burn you."

My heart beats erratic and wild; it pulses in my neck, in the places her rough fingers press into my wrists.

"Should I let you go to them?" She tilts her face down, exposing the curve of her strange silver cheek, the glint of her eyelashes, the harsh line of her mouth. "They would not hesitate to rip your soul from your body, or the child's either."

I try to shove down my terror but it roars through me, ravenous. "Why do you hesitate?" My voice shakes.

Her face hardens. "I have not yet received a new orb from my mother. There is nothing to put your souls into. I must drag you both to her court instead, and it is far, and I am tired."

Something in the cadence of her voice belies her. It startles me into speech. "That is not what you said to your sister."

She hisses again, flings me bodily to the ground. I land hard on my right shoulder.

"Take your chance with my sister, then!" she snarls.

The music seethes on the wind; it pulls at me, jerking me to my feet. I take a shaky step toward it against my will. I fight the pull, but it's not enough. I take another step. "Please don't hurt Awela." A sob rips out of me as the music forces me forward. "Don't take her to your mother. Please let her go. She's just a child. She doesn't deserve to die in the dark. Please." My body takes another unwilling step. "Please."

Oh God. I'm going to die in the wood after all. My death wasn't avoided. Only delayed.

The music reels me in, a fish on a line. The trees sway ahead of me, laughing and dancing, applauding my end.

I'm never going to see Father and Awela again. I can't even tell them goodbye.

Rough fingers grab my hand, yank me away from the looming trees and the beguiling music. The tree siren leans her face down to mine. "Be still."

She drags me over to the place where Awela lies. I wrap my arm around my sister, pull her tight against me. I'm shaking and crying. "Awela. Awela." I kiss her cheek.

My sister sleeps on.

"Close your ears."

That is all the warning the tree siren gives me before she opens her mouth, and starts to sing.

MONSTER

THE BOY STINKS OF FEAR AND SALT.
   He shakes like a rabbit in the snow.
   His soul is a tremulous thing,
yet it burns so very bright.
I sing and sing,
music to combat my sisters'.
They will hear it.
They will think that the prey they ensnared with their song
has fallen to me.
They will not hunt him in the dark.
They will not feed his soul into their own orbs.
He will be safe.
Yet he whimpers and shakes.
How fragile he is.
How easy it would be,
to break his body to pieces.

Chapter Eleven

OWEN

S HE RAISES HER HANDS, AND VINES GROW FROM THE GROUND IN A circle around the three of us, weaving together like canes in a basket. As the siren sings, the vines grow higher. They shut out the starlight, piece by piece. Fear eats at me. I cling to Awela, and try not to feel the tree siren's music twisting down into my soul.

Just before the vines seal us in completely, I lift my eyes to hers. I'm staggered to see her face bathed in starlight for one heartbeat, two, before the vines weave their last knot, and darkness swallows us up.

She stops singing.

I gulp ragged mouthfuls of air, numb with terror.

"Do you fear the dark?" she asks me. Her voice is biting. Cruel. "Or only the monster who lurks here?"

"What have you done?" My words come brittle from my raw throat.

"Saved you from my sisters. From the wood."

I think for the first time of the root that grabbed my ankle, that pinned me to the ground while this siren kept the other from taking Awela. "Why?"

She hisses a word in the dark, and fireflies slip through the cracks between the vines. They spark and glitter between us. Her face comes alive with a hundred darting shadows. She is so strange, up close. The skin on her cheeks curls and peels. Twiggy growth protrudes from her knuckles. Her yellow eyes make me want to crawl out of my own skin.

"I did not want my sister to kill the child."

This admission startles me. "Why?" I repeat.

For a long moment, she doesn't answer. She cocks her head to the side. "I heard her laughing in the wood. I have never heard such a sound among the trees. I did not want my sister to silence it."

I cradle Awela's head in my arms. How can she sleep, with so much horror spinning around her? But I'm glad of it. I don't know how I could explain. How I could keep her still. "But what about me?"

She peers at me, as if she can see through skin and muscle and bone, down to my very core. "I did not know a sister could be someone you might offer your soul for. My sisters are cruel, as I am cruel. Even if I had a soul to give, I would not give it for them."

"And yet you saved us."

She turns away. I think I've angered her, but I don't know why. Her silver skin shines in the light of the fireflies.

Beyond the bower she built around us, the tree sirens' music seethes on the wind. I hear it, but it can't touch me here. Can't put its hooks in, or make me dance like a puppet on a string. She protects me from that. Guards me. Why?

"Sleep now," she says. "Until morning."

I gape at her. I can't sleep. Not here, not shut in with a monster. "You will devour me."

Her pale brows draw together. Her skin creaks and cracks. "Sleep," she commands. Her voice is heavy with the power of her song.

I obey, as I must.

I sleep.

I do not dream.

Chapter Twelve

MONSTER

IN THE FIREFLY DARK, HE SLEEPS.

The prints of my hands bruise his throat. Almost, I killed him.
But I did not.

His soul burns so very bright.

My mother will rage, if she learns what I have done.

She gave me my heart. She could take it back again.

I fear her.

But

I

will

not

kill

him.

Chapter Thirteen

OWEN

I WAKE TO THE SCENT OF RICH EARTH AND WILDFLOWERS, MOSS pressed under my cheek. Awela is tucked tight against me. Sunlight seeps through the cracks in the bower the tree siren wove around us. The siren herself stands silent and still, her head turned away.

An overwhelming sensation of peace steals through me, so strong I nearly drift back to sleep, but then I remember my fear, and jerk to a sitting position. Awela whimpers in her sleep. I take her small hand in mine.

The tree siren looks at me. Her yellow eyes are brighter this morning, her pale eyelashes tinted ever so slightly green.

"You wake," she says. "Come. I will lead you from the wood before it wakes as well, and knows that you have lingered too long."

For a moment, she does nothing, just watches me. I realize the violets in her hair closed up sometime during the night, that they're beginning to open again. I think they must be part of her.

She raises her hands, her silver-white skin patchy and curling off of her in places.

She touches the branches that are woven around us, and they begin to unwind, shrinking down layer by layer until they vanish altogether. Beads of perspiration show on her forehead. An indigo butterfly lands in her hair, drinking nectar from the violets.

Still Awela sleeps, her small fists bunched in my shirt. "Why doesn't she wake?" I ask. I can't quite tamp down my sudden fear that she will sleep forever.

The Gwydden's daughter glances down at her. A breeze stirs through the wood, whispering past my ear and making the tree siren seem to shimmer.

"I did not want her to be afraid of my sister, so I caused her to sleep. When she wakes, she will think all of this nothing more than a strange dream. Come, now. The wood is watching."

I realize she sent *me* to sleep last night, too, but I am too bewildered to be angry.

She slips away, a white shadow among the trees. I pick up Awela and follow.

The siren makes no noise as she walks, and the forest seems to bend to make way for her. Awela grows heavy and my arms tremble with the effort of carrying her, but the siren does not stop, and I don't dare ask her to.

On and on we go, farther than Awela could have possibly wandered yesterday, farther than *I* remember walking. I don't recognize this part of the forest—nothing looks familiar. The scent of loam is rich, deep, chased with a sweeter aroma of violets and honey.

Just when I am about to collapse from the strain of holding my sister, there's a break in the trees, the glimpse of an observatory window, the scent of mint and basil growing in the garden.

The wall my father built, with no hint of the hole Awela squeezed through to mar its unyielding surface.

The tree siren stops at the very edge of the wall, and turns to look at me. The violets have wilted in her hair. She looks younger or sadder or both. I don't know why.

"What are you called?" Her voice is the high vibrato of a hesitant violin.

"Owen Merrick." I shift my grip on Awela. "What's your name?"

Her eyes narrow. "I am my mother's youngest monster. I do not have a name."

"All living things deserve a name."

"Even monstrous ones?"

I find I don't quite fear her, in the light of day, the same as I did in the dark wood. There is the memory, still, of blood dripping from her silver-white fingers, the snap of bone, the litter of bodies. But she saved Awela from her sister. She saved *me*. And that means something. It has to.

"Even monstrous ones."

"What would you call me, Owen Merrick?"

I think of her face last night, flooded in starlight in the moment before her bower sealed us in. The image confuses me, unsettles me, more than anything else. "I would call you Seren."

"Seren." The word is harsh on her lips, full of jagged edges. "What does it mean?"

"Wen?" says Awela sleepily, yawning and rubbing her eyes as she finally, finally wakes.

One moment more I stare at the tree siren. One moment more she stares back. "It means 'star.'"

She touches my forehead with one silver finger, and something cool rushes through me. Then she melts into the forest with the sound of wind in the trees, and the next moment Awela and I are alone.

I could almost believe it all a strange dream, except for the wilted violet lying bright on the forest floor. Awela squirms out of my arms as I crouch to pick up the flower and tuck it into my pocket. I don't want to forget her, and I have the strong feeling that without a tangible reminder, I will.

We're at the place in the wall where the hole should be, but there's no trace of it. It's as if the wood pulled out the stones to lure Awela through, and then put them back again. I think of roots writhing under the ground and I shudder.

I pull Awela up onto my back and tell her to hold tight to my neck as I climb over the wall and lower her safely to the ground. I scramble down myself just as Father steps from the house.

"Papa!" shrieks Awela, barreling toward him.

His hair is disheveled, his shirt and trousers rumpled. His hands are rough and raw, as if he spent the whole night beating them against rough stone. He cries out at the sight of Awela, scooping her up in his arms, weeping into her neck.

I join them and Father pulls me close. His whole body shakes. "I thought I'd lost you," he gasps. "I thought I'd lost both of you, just as I lost Eira. And the wood would not let me in. It wouldn't let me *in*."

"We're here, Father," I say. "We're safe."

I don't even register his words about the wood until I glance behind me. The wall is streaked with dark stains, and I look back to my father's raw hands.

It wouldn't let me in.

Awela wriggles from Father's arms and dashes into the house, hollering for bread and milk and strawberries. Father and I follow her inside.

Father tells me what happened over breakfast, though Awela is the only one who really eats anything. I sip tea and try to gather the pieces of myself, try to think around the cold silvery feeling in my head.

Father doesn't even sip his tea, just holds it, his large hands engulfing his mug. "You weren't here when I got home from Brennan's Farm. Either of you. I knew the wood had taken you—I could feel it. So I put wax in my ears and lit a torch. I tried to climb the wall, again and again. But the trees hissed and pushed me off. I tried to go around, but somehow the wall was always there—I couldn't find the end of it. I took a sledgehammer to the stone but it wouldn't break. And I knew, I *knew* you were trapped on that side of the wall, as I was trapped on this side. I heard the sirens singing. I thought they were devouring you. God help me, Owen. I thought you were gone." He bows his head into his hands, and an awful sob wrenches out of him.

"Papa!" Awela tugs on his arm, concerned. Her face is smeared with honey; bread crumbs cling to her chin.

He pulls her onto his lap, holds her so tight she shrieks and squirms free. She finds her blocks under the table and begins merrily stacking them on top of each other and knocking them down, again and again.

The clatter of them grates at my mind.

"What happened, Owen?" Father's eyes catch mine across the table. Already he seems more solid than he did an hour ago, more himself. But the barely scabbed cuts on his hands make me shudder.

The strange coolness in my head has grown into a pain that seems to slice straight between my eyes. My fingers find my temples. I want to scream but I don't know why.

"Owen?" He stretches out his hand to touch my shoulder.

"Awela got lost in the wood," I whisper. "I followed her. A tree siren protected us in a bower of branches. She brought us home." I frown. This doesn't seem right.

And yet.

What would you call me?

Seren.

Star.

"Owen?"

I jump, knocking over my tea mug. Milky brown liquid seeps across the table. My father grabs a rag and mops it up.

"You can't have met a tree siren." His face is hard, his voice strange. "You must have dreamed it. What really happened?"

My fingers go to the bruises at my throat.

Silver hands, crushing the life out of me.

A voice like a gale of wind through dead trees.

You cannot give a soul for a soul.

"What happened?" my father asks again.

The scent of violets.

Fireflies in the dark.

Seren. Star.

Something inside of me is screaming, but that cool sensation drowns it out. I shake my head. My shoulders slump. I tell my father the truth. "I don't remember."

Chapter Fourteen

MONSTER

E WILL FORGET ME.
I touched his mind.
I made sure.
I will be nothing more than a dream to him.
Dappled leaves,
silver bark.
This is how it must be.
But.
I
do
not
want
him
to
forget.

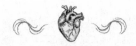

My mother reaches out for me.

    Her power pulses in the earth, in the trees.

    She commands me to return to her.

    I do not obey.

    I cannot.

    She will see the truth in me.

    She will hang an orb around my neck

    and force me to fill it with his soul.

    And

    I

    will

    not

    kill

    him.

    But I cannot forget him, as he has forgotten me.

    He is so helpless.

    So frail.

    Yet he would have given his soul

    to save the child.

    His sister.

    I do not understand.

    I want to understand.

    In the evenings I come to the edge of the wood.

    I peer over the wall at his house.

    I watch.

    Until the lights in his windows are put out.

    Until stars shimmer in the wide sky.

    Until the memory of his voice pours through me.

    I would call you Seren. Star.

I have never had a name.
But I desire one.
The desire consumes me.
How can I have a name?
I am nothing
but
a
monster.
Still I watch, through the long night and on into morning.
The sun rises, red as blood.
His door opens.
For a heartbeat I see him: slim form, dark hair.
I jerk back into the trees.
I am terrified
that he will not remember me.
I am terrified
that
he
will.
Seren.
Star.

Chapter Fifteen

MONSTER

I AM DREAMING WHEN THE PAIN COMES.
Searing agony, under my skin.
I open my eyes.
My mother.
Here,
in this quiet glade I chose
for my dreaming time.
Her claws are burrowed into me.
She slices me open from the inside.
"You wake." Her voice, cool with rage.
The relief, sudden and sharp, as she pulls her claws out of me.
I stumble back.
Pain dances bright behind my eyes.
Anger burns in hers. "I called to you. For twenty turnings of the
sun I have called, and you have not come."
Her antlers are stained dark with berry juice,

stark against the green of the trees.

Her claws drip amber,

sticky with my sap.

I

am

so

afraid.

I quail before her.

She knows.

She *knows*.

She made me.

She will unmake me.

He will never remember.

"Why have you not come?"

Wind snarls her green hair.

She wears a briar necklace,

blooming with roses.

She is heedless

of the thorns.

"ANSWER!"

Her voice is the bugle cry of a stag in spring.

I bow before her.

"Forgive me, my queen."

She paces round me.

The grass bends under her feet.

"You are different from your sisters. You are more like your brothers. Reckless. Willful. Wild. You will not defy your queen without penalty, as they did not."

She banished my brothers

from her court forever.

I fear

what she will do

to me.

Her claws pierce my back.

She rips away a piece of my skin

and I fall to the ground

in agony.

My bark is a curl of silver-white on the grass.

Sap wells from the wound.

Pain burns me.

Dew leaks from my eyes.

My mother's voice: "It will grow back. The quicker for each soul you claim for me."

She unfolds her hand.

An orb lies there.

Empty.

Hungry.

Cold.

I do not want it.

"The men come to lay their iron in the north. Find them. Slay them. Send their souls into the heartless tree."

I

do

not

want

the

orb.

I do not take it.

Claws, under my chin.

Forcing me to look up at her.

"If you do not obey me, I will strip away every other part of you. I will leave you for the beasts to devour in the dark."

She does not know about the boy.

She does not know.

He is safe.
Safe.
Pain pulses through me.
But there is also
relief.
I take the orb.
I hang it around my neck.
I go north.

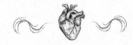

Every step is pain.
I press cool moss against the raw place.
I bathe in an icy stream.
It hardly cools the fire.
The wood is wide. I go very far from the boy's house.
I miss one night of watching him.
I miss two.
Now there is the clang of hammers. The grunts of men.
Lines of iron, crossed with wood. A track to replace the one I
wrenched apart.
I hide in the trees.
I watch them.
My mother's command trembles through me:
Slay them.
Send their souls to the heartless tree.
But I feel
the pulse of the boy's life in my hands.
I see
him shake as he tries to fight my sisters' music.
I hear

his voice echoing through me.
I would call you
Seren.
Star.
I cannot kill these men.
I do not want to.
I slip away,
leave them
to their clamor
and their noise.
I
do
not
want
to
be
her
monster.
I
will
not
be.

Chapter Sixteen

OWEN

I'VE FORGOTTEN SOMETHING IMPORTANT.

At least, I think I have.

In the light of day, when I'm cooking or gardening or minding Awela, I don't remember. In the dark of night, when I'm peering into the telescope and charting the stars with my father, I don't remember either.

But in the space between waking and dreaming, between dark and dawn, I smell violets, and the memories flood back.

A silver face. A bower of branches, woven with magic. The brush of cool fingers across my forehead. A resonant voice, sometimes deep like a cello, sometimes high like a violin. The spark of fireflies.

Even in daylight, when I think of the train wreck, of the passengers being slaughtered in the wood, the memory feels strange. Like it's not complete.

Three weeks have passed since Awela wandered into the forest; summer has turned the trees a deeper green, and I'm forever trying to chase the rabbits—the only creatures who don't seem to care that we live on the border of the wood—from the garden.

I make griddlecakes for breakfast, the batter stark white against the cast-iron pan. Awela is busy eating the strawberries we picked yesterday, dipping them in fresh cream.

"Vi-wets," she says, repeating it in her singsong voice. "Vi-wets, vi-wets, vi-wets."

"Be patient, little one," I tell her, my own impatience with her sharpening.

"Vi-wets!" she insists, pointing.

I look up from the griddlecakes. A sprig of purple flowers rests on the open windowsill.

I start. Is that a shadow, moving in the trees?

"Don't touch the stove, Awela!" I shout, and bolt from the house, the door banging noisily behind me.

I jerk to a stop at my father's wall, breathing hard. "Who's there? Who's *there*?"

There's no answer, just the wind in the trees, branches scraping the stone. I stand still, listening, peering across the wall and into the wood.

The smell of burning griddlecakes wafting from the kitchen window shakes me from my reverie. I race back to the house, hoping nothing's on fire.

Later, when Awela is napping and I'm sipping tea on the back stoop, I examine the violets, running the petals through my fingers, letting their scent wrap around me.

I shut my eyes and force myself to concentrate, to think past the needle of silver pain in my head.

I remember the grip of rough fingers, choking the life out of me. A song, coiling out of the wood. A strange hand on my wrist. A silver face in the starlight. Fireflies. A dreamless sleep.

Do you fear the dark? Or only the monster who lurks here?

I open my eyes.

I've crushed the flowers in my hand. Their scent has seeped into my skin. I think perhaps as long as I smell violets, I will remember her. The tree siren. The Gwydden's daughter.

She was here. Why?

I leave my half-drunk tea on the stoop and pace up to my father's wall, the wood stirring just beyond. For a moment, two, I pause, deliberating. The memories are slippery around the edges, hard to hold onto. Already they slide away. I don't want them to. I want to know why I can't remember, why she left me violets on the windowsill.

I scramble up the wall and drop heavily on the other side.

I don't dare stray very far, not with Awela sleeping alone in the house, but I walk a little farther than perhaps I should. All the while I strain my eyes for violets, stubbornly fighting to remember why.

I find a single purple flower, crumpled amongst fallen leaves. Triumph sears through me.

"Are you there?" I call. "Gwydden's daughter, are you there?"

There is no answer, but it feels as if the wood holds its breath, waiting for me to say more. The pain in my head sharpens as the memories fight to leave me.

"Who are you? Why did you leave me the violets?"

Wind coils past my ears. The scent of wildflowers is suddenly strong.

"A mistake." The voice is like a violin, rich and throaty with vibrato. "Forget me. Do not come again."

The scent vanishes. The trees grow still. I know I am once more alone.

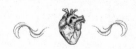

In the deep part of the night, when my father and I have laid aside our star charts, he goes to bed and I do not.

Violets, I tell myself, as I have all day. *Violets and fireflies.* Everything else has slipped away again. I want to remember. I *need* to. The desire consumes me and I let it, even though I know what it means—if I want answers, I have to go back to the wood.

It's foolish. Reckless.

But I take a lantern and a knife. I pace up to the wall and stare at it, my terror warring with my desperate compulsion to *know*. Somehow it's enough to dull my fear. I scramble over the wall and pace under the trees. My heart is overloud in my ears. I grip the knife and lantern so hard my hands ache.

A cloud of moths swarms around me, attracted to my light. I watch them for a while as I walk, flitting shadows, leaves with wings. They dart away as suddenly as they appeared.

The wood is wakeful. Watchful. Roots buck and dip under the ground like living creatures. The trees whisper, writhe. Chinks of moonlight cast wavering patterns on the forest floor. My lantern chases them away.

Fear is a second heartbeat, resounding in my bones.

Violets and fireflies.

I have to know who left me the flowers. Who spoke to me from the trees. I have to know what really happened that day Awela wandered into the wood. So I walk on into the dark.

I have no warning beyond a flash of silver.

A hand presses over my mouth, silencing my scream. Fingers seize my arm, pulling me into the trees. I struggle, thrash. I drop the lantern.

Terror claws up my throat.

Leaves trail past my cheek.

All is horror. Shadow.

There comes a note of song. It catches at my soul.

I writhe in the siren's grasp, but she doesn't let me go.

Oh God.

Ahead of me looms the form of a giant oak. It splits open with a creak and a sigh, and my captor shoves me toward it, her hand falling from my mouth.

I try to wheel on her; I try to scream.

The tree swallows me whole.

Chapter Seventeen

OWEN

B LACKNESS ENGULFS ME, PRESSES ALL AROUND. I CAN'T MOVE OR breathe. I can't see. I wonder in a panic what death will feel like, or if there can even be a greater horror than this immobilizing, choking dark.

Sap drips somewhere near; branches rustle in the muffled distance.

The tree seems almost to hum, examining me with invisible fingers, trying to see what I am made of. The silver pain in my head works itself free, like a splinter drawn out with tweezers. Memories take the place of it, everything flooding back at once: the tree siren's hands around my throat. The bower of living branches. Awela tucked safe and slumbering in my arms. The siren's voice, punctuated with fireflies.

Do you fear the dark? Or only the monster who lurks here?

What have you done?

Saved you from my sisters and the wood.

I did not want my sister to kill the child.

A deep, dreamless sleep. A dawn I thought I would never see.

What would you call me then, Owen Merrick?

I would call you Seren. Star.

The brief touch of her fingers as she stole the memories away. The violets on the windowsill to remind me I had forgotten.

Searching the wood for her, without really understanding why.

Her hands, one viselike on my arm, one pressed brambly against my mouth, shoving me into the oak. Letting it eat me.

I don't understand.

I try to count the seconds I am frozen like sap in the heart of the tree. But terror claws behind my eyes and I feel myself sliding away.

Then comes a wrenching *crack*.

I tumble onto sweet grass, into the gray light of the burgeoning dawn. I sob for breath, choking and gasping, convulsing on the ground until my head has convinced my body that all is well. I live. I breathe.

Her silver feet are a handbreadth away. I look up to find her watching me, her eyes impassive. They are not quite the yellow I remember—they are the color of amber, of honey. There are dark marks on her arms, like someone took a knife to her. Violets bloom bright in her hair.

"My sister," she says. "Just ahead of you on the path. I could not let her see you. She would have devoured you whole."

I blink at her, still gulping air.

"I did not mean to leave you so long. I had to be sure she was far from here before I let you out again. You are a fool, to wander the wood alone."

I try to stop my hands from shaking as I push myself to a sitting position. I'm too winded yet to stand. "Thank you," I manage. "For hiding me."

She tilts her head to one side like a curious bird. "I am glad the oak did not kill you."

My staggering relief evaporates. "*Could* it have?"

"My mother's trees are powerful. It could have squeezed your heart and eaten your soul, as easily as I could."

I'm still struggling a little to breathe. I gulp air, not foolish enough to think I'm even remotely safe with her. "And will you? Eat my soul?"

Her face goes blank, cold, more tree-like than I have ever seen it. "I should have killed you when first I saw you."

"But you didn't. You saved me. You saved Awela, too—you didn't let your sister take her. Why?"

I remember the answer she gave me before. I try to reconcile it with the brutal monster who slaughtered all the passengers on the train: *I heard her laughing in the wood. I did not want my sister to silence it.*

To my utter shock, the siren crouches beside me, so we are eye level with one another. Her leafy hair is tangled, messy, and the wounds on her arms are deep, barely clotted.

"You offered your soul for hers."

"Awela is my sister. I love her. Anyone would have done the same."

The siren shakes her head. "They would not. Humans beg for their own lives. Not for others. I have seen it. Again and again."

Memory flashes through my mind: the sound of screams and breaking bones; blood on silver hands. I remember what she is, and am suddenly aware of her nearness. She could crush me like a gnat. I push myself to my feet, put distance between us. I stand well clear of the oak.

She rises, too, steps past me. I draw a sharp breath: A large patch of her silver-white skin has been stripped from her left shoulder, halfway down her back, exposing raw, pulpy flesh the color of sap.

She jerks the wound out of my sight when she realizes I'm staring. Anger vibrates off of her.

"I'm sorry," I say quietly.

Suddenly she is in front of me again, lowering her head to my eye level, close enough I can see the ridges and whorls in her bark-like skin, close enough that the scent of violets and sap makes my head wheel. "Why are you sorry?"

My heart beats erratic, quick. "Why did you save me?" It's a question, but it's an answer, too.

Her eyelashes shimmer in the early morning light. A violet petal falls from her hair. "You have broken me, boy. You have changed me. Now my mother and my sisters—despise me."

"Did . . . did they do that to you? Because—because you saved me?"

She draws back. Cold, once more. Untouchable. "It does not matter," she says. "It cannot. Now go. You are not safe in the wood."

"Siren—"

But she turns and sweeps away without another word. The trees and the underbrush part to make a path for her. I blink once, twice, and then she's gone.

Gooseflesh rises on the back of my neck. I don't know how deep in the wood I am; I don't know quite how to get back. But I understand I'm on my own, that she's done saving me. Exhaustion and hunger nag at me. Father and Awela will wake soon—if they discover me gone, they'll panic.

I stumble my way back through the forest, miraculously coming upon my lantern, and my father's wall not long after, the stones muddy from last night's climb. I shimmy across to the welcome sight of the garden, beans ready for picking on their sturdy, coiling vines.

I needn't have worried. The house is quiet, Father and Awela still asleep.

A nuthatch perches on the garden fence, flashing his yellow belly and cheeping to his mate somewhere in the wood.

I stare at the little bird, battling the sense of loss that feels as if it will crush me. Trying to understand what I *have* lost.

Because I have what I wanted. I have my memories back. I know what the tree siren did for Awela and me, the debt we owe her. The debt *I* owe her three times over, for all the times she let me live. I can't ever repay her.

You don't need to, I tell myself. *Whatever she did for you, she's a monster. You don't owe her anything.*

And yet.

Is she still a monster?

I heard her laughing in the wood. I did not want my sister to silence it.

You have broken me. You have changed me.

The wind stirs through the trees across the wall. The nuthatch wings away. I hunch my shoulders and go inside, just in time to greet Awela, who barrels happy and hungry from her bedroom and into my arms.

Chapter Eighteen

MONSTER

H E WAS WALKING IN THE DARK OF THE WOOD.
My sister—so near him.
He did not know.
He did not see her.
She would have killed him.
Swallowed his bright soul.
So I hid him
in
the
oak.
He is safe.
But he is gone.
I want him to come back.
I do not know why
but I do.
I want him to look at me.

I want him to look into my eyes
and not
be
afraid.
I want him to see me
as something more
than
a
monster.

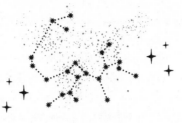

Chapter Nineteen

OWEN

THE DAY PASSES SLOWLY, AND I AM IMPOSSIBLY RESTLESS.
I studiously avoid looking out the kitchen window as I start tonight's cawl, chopping leeks and cabbage and potatoes and dumping them all into a pot to cook slowly over the stove. I don't want to see the wood, beckoning me from across the wall. I don't want to think about the tree siren. I don't want to think about how when she released me from the oak, I looked up into her face and realized she was beautiful.

And what does that matter? I think. *Monsters can be beautiful.*

I force myself to remember the train wreck, all the death and horror she caused. But those images slide too soon away, and all I can see is her silver face in the light of dawn, violets trembling in her hair. All I can see is her protecting Awela from her sister, weaving a bower of branches around us, guarding us from the malice of the wood.

You have broken me. You have changed me.

Has she changed? Is that even possible?

She saved Awela. She saved *me*, again and again.

Now my mother and my sisters—despise me.

But none of this matters. It can't. Because *my* mother was lost to the wood, and whether or not this tree siren had anything to do with it, it's part of what she is. It always will be. Awela and I are safe and whole, and for that I am grateful. That is the end of it.

I'm done with the wood. I have my memories and my answers. There's nothing for me out there.

And yet.

You have changed me.

I'm listless through dinner. Distracted charting the stars with my father.

He goes to bed, and I do, too. I pull the covers to my chin. Close my eyes. *She's a monster!* I scream inside my own head. *It doesn't matter that she's beautiful.*

You have broken me. You have changed me.

I know it's inevitable, but I lie here as long as I can bear it, longer, before at last I get up and shove my feet into my boots.

You have changed me.

I have to know if that's true. I tell myself that's the only reason I step from the house and pace up to my father's wall.

I can't quite justify scrambling over it, so I sink to the ground, my right shoulder pressed up against the stone. I sit there as the summer night grows deeper, as the chill of the earth and the wall shiver through me.

I sense the moment she's there, on the other side. There's a change in the wind, a subtle difference in the way the leaves rustle over the stone. The slightest hint of sap and flowers.

"Tree siren," I say to the wall.

"Boy." Her voice is muffled by the stone.

The grass ripples in the breeze, and I forget what I want to say to her, why I thought it necessary to have a wall between us when I said it.

Monsters can be beautiful.

"Why did you leave the violets on my windowsill?" It's not what I meant to ask.

For a while there's silence from the wood, though I know she's still there. I would have felt it if she'd gone.

"I wanted you to remember me," she says at last.

"Why?"

The wind picks up, branches swaying wildly over the wall. Somewhere deep within the forest a wolf howls at the moon.

"I did not want you to think me only a monster."

Her confession makes me uneasy, far too like the thoughts that won't leave my own head. I force out the words I came here to say: "Thank you for saving me and my sister. But I'm not coming back into the wood anymore. I shouldn't even be this close to the wall."

"Are you afraid of me, Owen Merrick?"

The wind whips wilder and wilder, and I have the funny idea it's picking up on her mood. My name on her lips makes me shiver. "Yes." It's the truth, even though I don't quite fear her in the same way as before.

"Do you always run from the things that you fear?"

I don't know why she's asking me this, if she wants some sort of confession in return. That isn't something I can give her. I stand up, and on the other side of the wall, she does the same. I forgot how tall she is—her face is visible overtop of the wall, her hair tangled with leaves and petals in the wind.

"I am what my mother made me," she says. "But I do not wish to be. I am—different than I was."

My uneasiness sharpens. Her words are seductive—they're what I want to hear. But that doesn't make them true. "I have to go."

"Stay." There's a longing in that one word, a loneliness that knifes into me.

I shake my head. "I can't."

"Then come again tomorrow."

"I can't," I repeat. "I shouldn't have come tonight. Goodbye, tree siren."

But for a moment, I don't go. For a moment, I linger.

She tilts her head to the side, brushes a strand of hair out of her eyes as the wind tugs a petal free, sends it spinning to the ground. "Seren," she says. "My name is Seren."

Chapter Twenty

SEREN

I ASKED HIM TO STAY.
He
did
not
stay.
I told him my name. The name I chose, the name he offered me.
But he gave no answer.
He went away into the dark.
He says he will not come back.
I want him to come back.
Why?
He should not. The trees are watching. They will bring tales to
my mother. Perhaps they already have.
He would be in terrible danger.
But there is something growing
deep inside of me.

Something
that calls out to him.
I am different,
than I was.
I do not want my mother's song,
my mother's souls.
I want—
I do not know.
But I want something more
than the death that she offers me.
I want something more
than her voice, her power.
I want something more.
I want something mine.

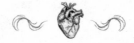

I wait for him all day.
It is foolish.
He said he would not come.
But I wait.
Night swallows the sun. The stars appear, fierce and white.
I watch his house. The silver dome opens. Its strange arm
pierces the dark. Its long white eye peers into the stars and I wonder:
Why does it look?
What does it see?
I wait for him.
Will he come?
My heart beats
hummingbird quick.
My eyes strain into the darkness.

He will not come.

But if he does, I must hide from him. I must not speak to him again.

I must not look

to find inside of him

a reflection of myself

that is not

wholly monstrous.

His door creaks open.

His footsteps pad across the earth.

Lightning crashes through me.

He is coming, and I must hide.

But when he comes,

when he scrambles

over the wall and

into the wood,

he finds me.

Standing here.

Waiting

for

him.

I say: "You said you would not come."

He says: "I did not mean to." He is restless. Uneasy.

But he is here.

His face

is touched

with starlight.

I ask him: "Will you come with me?"

He says: "Where?"

"Away from the wall. Into the wood."

He wars with himself.

Fights the pull of me.

As I ought to fight

the pull of him.
He says: "Why?"
"I am uneasy, near the wall."
"I'm uneasy in the wood."
"I will not let it hurt you."
His body is tense as a hare,
ready to spring away at any moment.
"Will you hurt me?"
The question sears
like my mother's claws under skin.
"You know I will not hurt you."
His jaw goes tight. "I don't know that."
I hold out a hand to him.
It is hard
to keep
from trembling.
I say: "Come with me."
If he denies me
I think I will splinter apart.
He watches me as he gives me his hand.
I fold my fingers over his.
Rough bark
against smooth skin.
He is fragile and
it frightens me.
I do not want to scratch him.
So I let go.
I step into the wood. I command the trees to make way for us.
They obey.
He walks beside me in the forest dark. He stumbles over trailing
roots.
   I bring him to a clearing, not far away:

a little hill, open to the sky,

to the stars.

It will make him feel easier, perhaps.

A window to his world,

encircled within mine.

I lead him to the top of the hill. I sink onto cool grass.

He sits, folding up his long legs. He stares at me across the air that divides us.

He says: "What are you?"

I say: "You know what I am. You saw me for what I am."

Darkness comes into his face.

Memory.

Fear.

He says: "You slaughtered them all. Women and men. Children. You took every soul on that train, save mine."

There is horror in his voice.

But

he does not

shrink from me.

"Why did you spare me? On the train. With Awela. In the oak. *Why did you spare me?*"

Anger radiates from him

like summer heat.

Something cracks deep inside of me.

I should not

have asked him to come.

I should not

wish for him to see me

as something

I

am

not.

I say: "I do not know."

He rakes a hand through his hair.

He curses in the dark.

But

he does not leave me.

Below the hill the trees pulse and shiver. Listening. Listening.

He says: "The wood has taken everything from me. It stole my mother away. It broke my father. And were it not for your mercy, Awela and I would be dead. Why did you spare me? What do you want? Do you truly expect me to believe that you wish to be more than a monster? That you *are* something more?"

There is iron in his words.

There is longing, too.

I tell him: "I have not killed since that day."

This is the truth that pulses inside of me.

That wants to spill out.

I needed him to know this.

I did not know I did till now.

He looks at me, looks at me. "The stories say there are eight of you. That the Gwydden poured her evil and her malice into a ring of birch trees and created monsters. Tree sirens, to do her bidding, to devour anyone who dared step within the shadow of the wood. But that can't be all. The Gwydden couldn't have given you a soul. Evil cannot create life."

"Can it not?"

Wind breathes over the hill. It brings the scent of iron.

There will be blood, tomorrow. More souls for my sisters to take for my mother.

More and more.

Until there are none left.

"My mother could only give her children what she herself possesses: a heart. I told you before. I do not have a soul."

This shakes him.

I wish I were brave enough

to take his hand in mine

and not let go.

But my bark is rough.

It would cut him.

He says: "You reason and act and feel. You had mercy on Awela, on me. How can you not have a soul?"

There is a taste like ashes

in my mouth.

"I do not need a soul to kill. I do not need a soul to refrain from killing."

"Then what is to keep you from killing again? What is to keep you from killing *me*?"

I stare at him.

I could never kill him, not now.

Not even if my mother compelled me.

I might shatter to pieces from rebelling against her

but that would be better

than watching the light

go out of his eyes.

I think

I shall drown

in his eyes.

"I am not going to kill you. I am not going to kill anyone. Not anymore."

I am too aware of my heart

beating and beating inside my chest.

I wonder why

my mother gave me one at all.

What use is it?

His eyes meet mine.

I am a sapling again,
undone by sun and rain.
He says: "I believe you."
In this moment,
it
is
enough.

Chapter Twenty-One

OWEN

S HE WALKS WITH ME TO THE WALL AT THE EDGE OF THE WOOD,
silver and silent, the wind teasing through the flowers in her
hair. Something is different now, something I don't quite
understand. My fear of her is still there, vibrant in the air between
us, but it isn't as strong as it was two hours ago. We stop at the wall,
and she turns to look at me.

"Will you come again tomorrow?" she asks.

Her gold and silver hair whips about her face; her honey-colored
eyes shine in the darkness. *Even monsters can be beautiful.*

"Is it safe?" I return.

"I will keep you safe."

That isn't quite the same thing. "Why do you want me to come?"

For a moment she watches me. Then she dips her head, her eyes
flitting away. "Because I am lonely. And because you are . . . kind. I want
to know more about your world. About you. I want to know why you
make me desire to be more than the monster my mother created."

I take a breath, trying to think past the intoxicating leaves-and-violet scent of her. "I'll come," I say.

I'm rewarded with the flicker of her eyes and a flash of a smile. Then she's gone into the wood, and I'm scrambling over the wall, dizzy with trying to reconcile my lingering horror of the monster who slaughtered the train passengers with the silver-white creature I've just parted from. With . . . Seren.

I sneak back into the house and crawl into bed, and the dawning realization of what I've done makes me shake. I went willingly with a tree siren into the wood. I promised I'd go back. She says she hasn't killed since the day of the train crash and she says she won't kill me. I *believe* her. How can I be such a fool?

Because she saved Awela, says my stubborn mind. *Because she saved* me, *again and again.*

My restless thoughts fade somehow into sleep. I dream of leaves and stars, tangled together in the tree siren's hair. I dream the sea is made of violets.

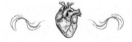

"Owen."

There's a note of severity in my father's voice I'm not used to hearing. I can sense his eyes on me, but I don't lift my own to meet them. Instead, I jot down the last star in the Morwyn constellation on the chart, then squint through the eyepiece of the telescope to observe the relative positions of the stars around the Morwyn.

"Owen, look at me."

I sit back in my chair and obey.

"I know you went into the wood last night."

A knot twists in my gut. "I didn't—"

"I saw you climb back over the wall." He stares me down, daring me to contradict him.

"I—" I scramble for an excuse and come up empty.

He shakes his head, not angry so much as . . . grim. Resigned. "The wood has got its claws in you. I mean to rip them out."

"It doesn't—it doesn't have its claws in me."

"Then tell me why you went over the wall last night! Tell me it was the only time you've ever done it. Tell me you don't mean to do it again."

I open my mouth and shut it again several times in succession. I can't lie to him. And I can't tell him about Seren. He would take an axe over the wall and hunt her down. He would kill her, and he'd be justified in doing so. My throat hurts. I don't attempt to explain.

Father nods. "It's time to resume our conversation about your future. I haven't pressed it since the train crash, since Awela wandered into the wood. You've been . . . different since then, Owen. I wanted to give you space. Clearly, that was a mistake."

"Father—"

He holds up his hand and I snap my mouth shut. "I was in the village yesterday," he continues. "King Elynion is recruiting soldiers into his army, looking for the next generation of guardsmen—there was a notice hung up at the inn."

I flick my eyes to the star chart, trying to ignore my rising unease. King Elynion's standing army is a legend in Tarian. They live and train just outside Breindal City, and being one of his soldiers is a huge honor. The king's personal guards are selected from among the standing army, too—many a career has been made that way. There hasn't been war in generations, but the army is ready in case Gwaed, the country on the other side of the Carreg Mountains, decides to reignite old grudges—or in case invaders come from across the sea.

"You're sending me away," I say quietly.

His jaw tightens. "I'm keeping you safe. You don't have to be a soldier. The village butcher is needing an apprentice. Or you could ask at the telegraph office. The inn. The baker's. Anywhere that includes room and board."

"But Awela—"

"Awela will be old enough for boarding school in a year. Until then, Efa has agreed to watch her during the day, starting next week. You need to find yourself a position by then."

I shudder at the thought of working for the butcher, elbow deep in blood, shut away from the sky. "I'm not going anywhere."

"You don't have a choice. I see how the wood draws you. Why else did you climb over the wall? How long until it lures you in and you never come out again?"

I want to be angry, to shout something ugly back at him, but all I can think about is sitting with Seren on a hill under the stars, promising her I'll come again. Being drawn to her and not even fighting it. Father is right. He can't trust me. I can't trust myself. I hang my head. Avoid his eyes.

"Go to the village tomorrow," he says. "Find a position. We'll all still see each other very often, and when I can persuade the king to hire a new astronomer, we'll go to Breindal City. Leave the wood behind forever."

Panic writhes through me. I'm numb with the thought of leaving Father and Awela, with the loss of honey-colored eyes and silver skin.

"And Owen?"

I raise my glance.

"If you even *attempt* to climb over that wall again, I will lock you in your room and not let you out for the remainder of your time living here. Do you understand?"

I nod. I don't trust myself to speak.

When the star charts are filled and Father and I have withdrawn to our respective rooms, I sit staring out my window for over an hour. The same traitorous thought worms through my head in endless repetition: I didn't actually *promise* my father I wouldn't go back into the wood.

I did promise Seren.

And I know, despite everything Father said to me, despite the awful, foolish recklessness of it, I'm going to keep that promise.

When the house has fallen wholly quiet, and I'm sure Father is asleep, I sling the strap of my portable telescope over my back and shimmy out the window. I nearly fall and break my neck, but something keeps me clinging to the ivy on the rough stones. I leap down safely by the kitchen window, and creep past the garden, along the length of the wall to a spot that (I hope) is not as visible from the house as my usual one.

I clamber over.

Seren is waiting for me in the same place she was last night. She turns as I thump to the ground, and the sight of her floods my whole body with heat.

She moves toward me like a silver ghost. "I did not think you were coming."

"I promised." I don't tell her that I've just jeopardized my relationship with my father, that if he has his way I won't even be here this time next week. I don't tell her I'm the greatest of fools.

She smiles.

We walk together up to last night's little hill, and I find that my lingering fear of her has somehow entirely gone. The simple fact of her existence fascinates me. Intoxicates me. As nothing has in all the world except the stars. The wind whispers over the leaves that trail down the length of her silver-white form. Her beauty takes my breath away.

She sinks to the ground and I kneel beside her, shrugging off the telescope strap. She glances at it, then at me.

My cheeks blaze. "You said you wanted to know more about my world. About me. I thought I'd show you the stars."

Seren's silver-green brows slant down, scornful. "I've seen the stars."

"Not like this." I find a flat spot in the grass and set up the telescope, adjusting the mirrors, focusing the lens. Seren watches me without a word.

The wind is warm tonight. It smells of sun-baked earth and that sharp, tangy scent that hangs in the air before a thunderstorm. Clouds dot the sky away to the east, but above us the stars shine clear.

"Here," I say when the telescope is ready. "Come and look."

She scoots close to me, her woven-leaf dress trailing across the ground. Her arm brushes mine. It's smooth, except for the places where her skin curls backward like peeling bark.

She peers through the eyepiece of the telescope, and for some moments is wholly silent, wholly still. I try not to see the clouds massing quickly over the tree line, try not to feel the keen bite of disappointment at the thought of rain driving us from the hill I have unintentionally begun to think of as ours.

At last she sits back from the telescope. She seems almost to *glow*. "The stars are very beautiful," she says, awe in her voice.

I grin. "You see? You do have a soul. A monster wouldn't care about the stars."

It's the wrong thing to say. Her face closes, and she turns away from me. Above us, the clouds blot out the sky; the air is heavy with the scent of rain.

Below the hill, the trees stir and whisper. Leaves rattle. Branches creak.

Seren flings her head up. "Owen, you must go."

"What? Why?"

"The wood knows you're here, and someone is coming. Maybe my sisters. Maybe my mother." She jerks to her feet and grabs my hand, pulling me up with her. "You must go. At once."

"But the telescope—"

She yanks me down the hill and I stumble after her, the rough part of her hand scraping painfully against mine. The clouds break just as she tugs me under the trees. The rain scarcely touches us here, but I can barely see her in the shadows, in the dark. We run together, back to the wall.

At the border of the wood, the rain sheets down, drenching me in an instant, turning Seren's skin a darker shade of silver. She lets go of my hand. For an instant, she stares at me in the rainy dark. "Come again tomorrow. I will make sure it is safe. Goodbye, Owen."

Behind her, the wood is teeming, howling. She turns to face it. Disappears into the trees.

"Goodbye, Seren," I say after her.

I clamber back over the wall, creep around the garden and up through my window. I strip off my wet clothes and hide them under the bed, so Father won't see.

In the morning, I take Awela with me into the village to see about a job in the telegraph office.

Chapter Twenty-Two

SEREN

RAIN DRIPS COLD
between the thrashing trees.
My oldest sister stands among them,
the sister with
roses in her hair.
The boy's telescope is in her hands.
She looks at me as she bends it,
as she snaps it like bone.
She flings the pieces behind her
into the dark.
"The wood has been telling tales, little sister."
She strides toward me.
She stops a leaf's width away.
Her breath is cool on my face. "Did you think the trees would
not tell that you brought a boy into the wood? A boy whose soul you
did not claim for our mother?"

Her fingers close around

the empty orb at my neck.

She smells of roses,

of fear.

"Your disobedience has not gone unnoticed. Do not dare to believe
you are safe from our mother, that you are free to do as you please, like
our brothers once presumed. They were not. You are not."

She lets go of the orb.

It settles hard

in the hollow

of my throat.

Rain seeps through the thread of air

that divides us.

I say: "Why are you here? I do not want you."

She says: "I am here to save you, little fool. Come, we have work
to do."

She snatches my hand.

She drags me through the trees.

Deeper into the wood.

I let her.

Because she pulls me

away from the wall,

away from Owen.

He is safe,

at least

for now.

She pulls me on,

until we are so deep into the trees

the rain does not touch us.

Dawn breaks beyond the wood.

The rain fades.

There comes the clang of hammers,

the grate of voices.

An axe bites wood.

A tree falls to the earth.

I jerk away from my sister.

She watches me. "The Soul Eater has sent them. They poison the wood. Mother needs their souls. The trees need their absence. Sing with me, little sister. Let us destroy them."

I shudder at the name of the Soul Eater,

the monster even monsters

know to fear.

But I told the boy:

I am not going to kill anyone. Not anymore.

I tell my sister: "I will not."

She seethes with anger.

She grabs my hands.

She snaps my fingers off,

one

by

one.

Agony bursts

behind my eyes.

I cradle my hands

to my chest.

She will kill me,

if I do not sing.

I

do

not

want

to

die.

I have no soul.

When I am gone,
there will be no part of me
left to remember
that I lived,
that I looked at the stars
with Owen
on a hill.
But I will not sing.
I will not be the monster
my mother made me.
Not even to fight the Soul Eater.
My sister sings.
Her song coils through the wood
and the men drop their hammers.
They turn to her.
Some sob.
Some smile.
She flicks her eyes to me.
She takes away my choice.
Her power is greater than mine.
Strong enough to force my mouth open.
To pull the song
unwilling
from my lips.
I sing.
I cannot stop.
The men come and come,
like flies drawn to honey.
But I do not go to her.
I do not help her
as
she

kills
them
all.
Blood drips from her hands.
Red,
like the roses in her hair.
She hisses at me as the bodies fall,
as the wood grows quiet,
as the screaming is cut off.
She stops singing.
She lets me stop, too.
She commands me: "Collect their souls."
Dew
pours
down
my
cheeks.
"I will not."
She drags one claw across my face,
deep enough for sap to well up.
"Do you think yourself above us? Do you imagine yourself to be
something more than what our mother made us to be?"
"I am more. I have named myself."
"Monsters do not have names."
Pain pulses
from my ruined hands.
"I do not want to be a monster."
She sneers at me
as she rips the orb from my throat,
as she collects the dead mens' souls
and leaves their bodies
for the earth

to swallow.
Then they are all of them gone
and the wood is empty
of souls,
of life.
Wind stirs through the trees.
It washes away
the scent of blood.
My sister kneels on the ground,
relinquishes the orb to the power
of the heartless tree.
Strength for the wood and our mother,
Strength to aid her fight
against the Eater.

My sister turns to me once more. "I will not help you again. If you value your life, you will remember that you are our mother's monster. Go to her. Receive a new orb. Fill it up with souls you take yourself."

"I will take no more souls. I will no longer be her monster."

"Then you are a greater fool than even our brothers. You do not deserve the heart our mother gave you."

My sister leaves me
in the empty wood.
I stare at twisted iron.
At the lumps in the earth
where the slaughtered men lie.
I did not kill them.
But
that
is
not
enough.

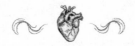

I go to the place I was born.

    The ring of birches.

    There are other trees here now,

    growing in the place of me and my sisters.

    They are tall.

    Silver.

    Strong.

    I sit at the feet of the oldest one.

    I lean back against its trunk.

    I try to draw strength

    from this place that usually comforts me.

    But I find none.

    My fingers will grow back, little by little.

    I will be once more whole,

    though perhaps not quite the same

    as I was.

    I cannot go to Owen tonight.

    He will ask about my ruined hands.

    If I tell him what I've done

    he will recoil from me.

    He will remember

    what I am.

    He will climb over his wall

    and

    never

    come

    back.

    Beyond the wood, the sun sinks.

    Soon, the stars will come.

Soon, Owen will climb over the wall
and I will not be waiting.
It is better, this way.
Better if he never sees me again.
The last of the light fades from the wood.
Beyond the trees, the stars are spinning.
I will stay at the feet of the silver birch.
I will not go to him.
I will not.

Chapter Twenty-Three

OWEN

I GET THE JOB AT THE TELEGRAPH OFFICE, BUT IT DOESN'T COME
with room and board.

I tell Father so at supper, which is roasted lamb and fresh
green beans from the garden.

He raises his eyebrows at me across the table.

I force myself not to squirm. "It'll be better like this—I'll be
away from the wood all day but home in time to cook for you. To
chart the stars with you."

He takes a bite of lamb. Chews it slowly. "Owen, that wasn't
what I told you to do."

"Please, Father."

Awela is sucking the beans from their pods and merrily spitting
them onto the floor. I can't believe he really intends to send her away
from us. I wait for Father to say he knows I went over the wall again
last night. To carry out his threat to lock me in my room.

But he doesn't say anything. Maybe I was careful enough.

Maybe he didn't see. "And if I'm staying the nights, it can't hurt for Awela to sleep here, too. Please, Father? Can't we all stay together?"

There's a thundercloud on his brow. I've never feared my father—it never really occurred to me before. But I sweat now under his gaze.

I have one last tactic to try. I blurt it out before I can think better of it. "Let's not worry about the wood right now. What did Mother always say? 'Don't borrow trouble from tomorrow.'"

Father's face closes. He crumples in on himself like a dropped handkerchief.

I loathe myself, instantly regretting my words. "Father, I'm sorry. Please—"

"Don't apologize. Your mother is always before my eyes, you know. Always at the very top of my heart."

My throat clenches. "Mine too." I don't dare press the issue. We go back to our dinner.

I get nothing else out of him until Awela is in bed and we're up in the observatory again, unrolling star charts and uncapping ink bottles.

"You'll stay away from the wood?" he asks me, taking the chair in front of the telescope.

I spin the brass rings of the armillary sphere and try to ignore my thundering pulse as I lie to him. "I'll stay away."

He nods, adjusts the telescope, and looks into the eyepiece. "Stay, then. I never *wanted* you and Awela to leave, Owen. I just want to protect you."

Guilt churns in my gut. I dip a pen in an ink bottle and hand it to my father. "I know."

He makes a mark on the chart. "I trust you."

I pour us each a cup of cinnamon tea. "I know."

We chart the rest of the stars in silence, then take the narrow stair down from the observatory. Just outside my bedroom door, my father catches my arm. "Remember your promise," he says. "To stay away from the wood."

"I remember," I tell him.

And I do. It's all I think about as I sneak out my window and crawl past the garden and climb over the wall.

Chapter Twenty-Four

SEREN

HE IS WAITING BY THE WALL.
The sight of him
makes my heart swell
like wood in water.

I hide my ruined hands in my gown of leaves.

I do not want him to see.

He has a large oblong box strapped to his back. It makes his shadow overlarge in the light of the rising moon.

Behind me, the trees whisper and hiss.

They are watching. Listening.

They will tell my mother we are here.

I say: "Come. Quickly."

He follows me into the wood. The box thumps against his back.

Trees reach out craggy fingers. Roots writhe under the ground. They mean to snatch him. Ensnare him. Choke the soul from his body, since I will not.

I say: "Stay close."

He curls one hand tight around my arm. Fear sparks off of him, hot and bright. But his trust in me is greater.

He does not let go.

The souls my sister slew today clamor in my mind.

He should not trust me.

We reach our hill. I climb to the top; I kneel in the grass.

He crouches beside me. Watchful. Tense.

The trees clatter and creak.

They are angry.

They mean to claim him for themselves.

But I will not let them.

I plunge my ruined hands deep into the hillside.

The earth reaches out for me,

breathing in the lifesap

that flows through my veins.

New fingers grow from my hands,

and from them I send out roots,

pushing them up and up, toward the sky.

I sing the shoots to life.

I call them higher, higher.

They reach up all around us.

They sprout branches,

unfurl tender leaves.

I sing and sing,

until the trees are tall enough to screen the wood below.

I stop

before they blot out the sky.

I make

our ceiling

stars.

I open my eyes

and draw my arms from the earth.

My mother's trees were angry.

So I grew my own.

I did not know

I was strong enough.

All this while, Owen has crouched beside me, silent.

Now I look to him. His eyes are round with wonder.

He says: "Magic."

I say: "Growth. My trees will shelter us for as long as we wish."

He studies me

in silvery light.

His throat bobs as he swallows.

"They are beautiful. Impossible. Like you are."

In the wood, my sister killed them all.

I

watched

and

did

nothing.

He calls me beautiful and

I cannot meet his eyes.

I say: "What have you brought?"

He sets the box in the grass and opens it.

He eases something out,

a tall thing, coming nearly to his shoulder.

He says: "It's called a cello—it used to belong to my mother.

Shall I play it for you?"

I say: "Yes," though I am not quite sure what he means.

The cello fascinates me.

Its body is made of a shiny wood

that seems to honor the tree

it once was.

It is curved and beveled, taut with strings.
He takes a stick from the box,
then perches on top of it,
puts the cello between his knees.
He draws the stick across the strings.
Music blooms on the hill.
I am transfixed.
He plays
the heart of the wood.
He plays
my heart.
Dew
runs
down
my
cheeks.
I feel the music inside of me,
engrained in sap and bark.
It swells like thunder,
whispers like leaves in a stream.
It is rich as honey, as earth.
He sways with the music.
The cello is
his voice
his heart
his soul.
He halts the movement of the stick.
He lays the instrument in the grass.
He kneels beside me,
close
enough
to

touch.

"Seren. You're crying."

"I am not human. I cannot cry."

"And yet." His gentle fingers touch the dew on my face. "What's wrong?"

I cannot tell him

that my sister killed them.

I cannot tell him

that I did not stop her,

that I sang them to their deaths.

I cannot.

I cannot.

I wish the music of the cello

dwelt inside of me

instead

of my mother's

monstrous song.

He takes my hands in his.

He smooths the knobby bark on my knuckles.

I say: "I do not want to be a monster. But that is all I'll ever be."

He says: "A monster wouldn't have spared me, or my sister. A monster wouldn't look at the stars in wonder and be moved by a badly played cello."

A crack splinters my heart.

He is so very close now.

He smells of ink,

of cinnamon.

I want

to trace his eyes with my fingers.

I want

him closer.

But. "I cannot be what you wish me to be, just because you wish it."

"What do *you* wish to be?"
He stares at me
and I stare at him
and it feels as if
all the world
holds its breath
waiting
for my answer.
He is beautiful and fragile.
His soul is so strong.
I say: "Something new."
He smiles. "Then that's what you will be."
He lets go of my hand.
He picks up the cello.
He plays and he plays
and I try
to wind his music up inside of me,
enough to fill the hollow place
where the soul I do not have
ought to dwell.
I want to keep him here forever
in my fortress of trees.
But when dawn touches the sky
with rosy fingers,
I sing a gap between the branches,
a tunnel of safety
all the way to his wall.
I
let
him
go.

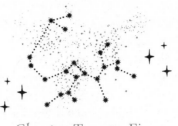

Chapter Twenty-Five

OWEN

THE JOB AT THE TELEGRAPH STATION TAKES MORE BRAIN POWER than I anticipated. I'm made to memorize a code comprised of long and short clicks and to learn how to translate it into actual words—that's for the telegraphs coming *in*. The ones going out are the reverse. I'm no stranger to detailed work, but the demanding monotony of my new duties mixed with the scarce hours of sleep I get every night has me longing to chase a muddy Awela through the garden and wash dishes while she sleeps.

The telegraph office is a narrow, windowless building near the inn, jammed with two small wooden desks—imported from Saeth or elsewhere, I imagine—and two sets of telegraph equipment. There's always one other operator working at the same time as me. I'm surprised to find that Mairwen Griffith works the evening shift, and comes in just before I leave every day.

"Owen Merrick!" she exclaims the first time she sees me. "I thought for sure you'd been eaten by the wood. You never come to the village anymore."

I don't know what to say to this. Her dark eyes and shiny hair have my insides sliding all over themselves, and I can't help but notice her daring outfit of trousers and high-collared blouse. Rumor has it she wears them when she rides her newfangled bicycle.

"Not eaten," I tell her in a stroke of brilliance.

She raises a laughing eyebrow at me and settles into her desk.

I finish my shift in an awkward puddle of sweat, but the instant I step from the telegraph office, I forget all about her.

Because there's only a handful of hours dividing me from Seren.

I have it down to a science now. Dinner with Father and Awela. Putting Awela to bed. Charting the stars. Waiting in my room until midnight, sneaking through my window with whatever I've put aside to show Seren tucked into my satchel or strapped to my back—I was wary, after losing the telescope, but I'm much more careful now. Crawling past the garden, climbing over the wall to where Seren waits in her tunnel of branches. Walking with her to our hill, where her trees shelter us from the wrath of the wood, from the watching eyes of her mother and sisters. Showing her the things I brought her, happy with her joy. Forgetting and forgetting and forgetting that she was ever a monster. That she ever could be.

One night I bring her fresh strawberries from the garden. "To eat," I explain, pulling the top off one of the berries and popping it into my mouth. I wonder belatedly if it's indecent to offer a girl who is at least half tree part of a plant to eat.

But she mimics me, chewing slowly. "It is very sweet." She smiles, and grabs another one.

After that, I try to bring her strawberries every night.

I bring star charts and books. The astrolabe from the observatory. A pair of my mother's shoes I find stuffed in the back of a closet. She doesn't even try the shoes, just shudders and hands them back to me. "How would I feel the earth?" she demands, as if I really should have thought about that before offering her something so offensive.

But the charts and books and trinkets fascinate her. She wants to learn to read. I teach her the alphabet and leave her newspapers and a few books. Within a week she can read simple sentences; in another week, complex ones.

Every day before dawn I sneak back into the house to sleep a few hours before dragging myself up in time to go to the telegraph office. The schedule is grueling and unsustainable, but I can't give up my nights with Seren. I'm terrified every one will be my last—that the Gwydden will tear a hole in Seren's guarding trees and devour us both, that my father will catch me sneaking over the wall. But I can't stop. I don't want to stop.

It's been nearly three weeks since Seren raised her screen of trees around her hill and I played my mother's cello. Not even Mairwen Griffith can distract me anymore. She makes a point to talk to me every afternoon when she arrives for her shift, her dark hair pinned up in a bun, or sometimes loose and curly about her shoulders. She comes in on her day off and asks me to have dinner with her at the inn. Once, I would have leapt at the chance, wishing I'd been brave enough to ask her myself. But now I give her request hardly a thought before I politely decline and walk home.

Because Seren is waiting.

I've almost begun to think that it will always be this way, that I will spend every night for the rest of my life amidst trees and stars.

Tonight I lug Mother's phonograph out of the garden shed, where I hid it before Father got home. I heft it carefully over the wall, then through the tunnel of branches and up the hill. I'm breathing hard by the time I lay it down in the grass, unlatch the top of the case and remove it. Sweat runs into my eyes and prickles between my shoulder blades. Seren watches as she always does, expectant and curious.

I fit the horn into the phonograph, then carefully slide a hollow, wax-covered cylinder onto the mandrel, a cylindrical component of the phonograph that's made of solid metal. I turn the crank on the side of the box, winding the device up, then set the stylus onto the wax cylinder. Music blooms from the phonograph's horn.

Seren leaps back in shock, and I straighten up, pleased with myself. It's a partial recording of a symphony Mother brought with her from her university days. Violins and cellos swell into the night, chased by a lone clarinet and the kettledrums' pulsing heartbeat.

Seren is transfixed. "Magic," she whispers at last. "*This* is magic."

I glance at the screen of trees around us, and shake my head. "Not magic. It's music and science."

"It's beautiful."

I smile, forcibly ignoring my jittering nerves. I hold out my hand. "Will you dance with me, Seren of the wood?"

She tilts her head. "I do not understand."

"I'll show you."

She takes my hand, her skin rough-smooth-sharp against mine. I pull her near me, gingerly resting my other hand on her waist. Leaves whisper over my fingers, soft as rose petals, soft as Awela's ruined hair ribbon. Beneath, smooth silver skin. I hardly dare speak. "To the time of the music, see?" It's a waltz, the lilting rhythm easy to feel, a weighty downbeat, two lighter upbeats, again and again.

She seems almost instinctually to understand. She moves as easily as the wind coiling round us, a part of the wood, a part of the waltz. The hand not folded in mine finds my chest, her knobby fingers splayed out, tiny leaves sprouting up from her knuckles.

"Your heart beats," she says. "Just as mine does."

I take my hand from her waist and brush my fingertips over her heart. I feel her pulse, erratic, quick.

Her eyes search mine as we dance on the hilltop, and I wonder what questions burn inside of her, in the hollow of the soul she claims she does not have. I move my hand back to the safer residence of her shoulder, but my eyes never leave her face.

The phonograph scratches and screeches as it comes to the end of the cylinder—it's only able to play for four minutes. For a moment more we keep dancing, to the music of the wood, the grass, the sky. We stop abruptly, mid-stride. We break apart. I feel strange and small, less than myself. Does she feel this way, too?

Mutely, I kneel beside the phonograph, move the stylus back to the beginning of the cylinder, turn the crank. The symphony starts over, crackly and beautiful in the summer night.

I rejoin Seren, and this time it's her who reaches out her hand to me, her asking if I want to dance.

We do, again and again. I restart the symphony five times, six, and then it doesn't matter anymore, and we don't need music to dance.

We're still dancing when dawn comes, and the rosy flush of it is reflected in her silver face.

Chapter Twenty-Six

SEREN

H IS HEART BEATS
beneath my fingers
as the music spins into the night
like spider silk
and I
never
want
it
to
stop.
I live for these nights:
for stars on a hill,
for Owen's gentle heart.
I hate the days:
my sisters' shrieking music,
blood and death and soul upon soul

taken for my mother,
power for her war against the Eater.
But I cannot have the nights
without the days.
Dawn comes.
He slips away.
I wonder
if this will be the day
that
I
lose
him,
or if we will have another night
under the sky.

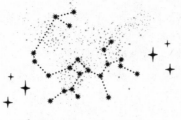

Chapter Twenty-Seven

OWEN

FATHER IS WAITING WHEN I CLIMB OVER THE WALL.
His arms are folded across his chest, the muscles jumping in his jaw. The sunrise touches his features with red light.

Mother's phonograph is strapped awkwardly to my back, and Father's eyes light on it briefly before fixing on my face. "Give it to me." His words are cold, short, sharp.

I shrug out of the strap and hand him the phonograph, my sudden, wild fear hardly dimming my lingering elation.

My father hurls the phonograph at the wall. It splinters apart, the pieces falling limp to the grass. It's all the warning I have before he seizes my arm and drags me back to the house.

I have never, in all my seventeen years, seen my father this angry. He yanks me through the kitchen, past a confused Awela, who's eating porridge, and up the stairs to my room. He flings me inside, shaking with fury.

"How many nights, Owen?" He speaks quietly, every word

edged with iron.

It would be better if he shouted.

"I—"

He punches the doorframe and the wood splinters. "HOW MANY NIGHTS?"

Shouting is *not* better. I gulp and stare at him, clenching my hands into fists. "I—"

He takes a breath. Swipes his hand across his forehead. There's blood on his knuckles and moisture in his eyes.

"All of them, sir," I say.

"You've been climbing out of your window."

"Yes, sir."

He sags against the doorframe. "The wood *took* her. It *took her away from us*. And you—why? Why do you go there every night, Owen? What could possibly be worth lying to me? What could be worth spitting on your mother's memory and endangering yourself, over and over again?" His voice is raw and wild.

"I'm not spitting on Mother's memory. I would *never*—"

"TELL ME WHY!" Father roars.

I suck in a jagged breath. "There's a—there's a—" How can I tell him? How can I tell him I danced with a tree siren until dawn, when Mother was slaughtered by one? I've spoken about my mother to Seren many times, but I've never *asked* her if she had anything to do with my mother's death. I've never dared.

"Tell me," Father repeats, quiet again.

"There's a girl. In the wood. She—she can't leave or the Gwydden will kill her and—and she's the one who found Awela. She protected her. Protected both of us."

He studies me. I wonder if he's parsing the truth from my lies.

"Do you fancy yourself in love with this girl?"

The question is like a punch to the gut. "What? No. No. She's a—" I clamp my lips shut on the word 'monster'. "She's just a friend." I blink and see her smiling in the starlight, feel her smooth-rough hand in mine, smell the sweet, strong scent of her. Fear of a different kind wakes up inside of me. Makes me shake. Because she's *not* just a friend. She's—I don't know what she is.

Father's jaw works. "Then she isn't worth risking everything for."

There's a clatter from downstairs that makes both of us jump—Awela has been left to her own devices for far too long. I make a move to the door but Father bars my way. "You're staying up here until I decide what to do with you."

The disappointment in his voice hurts. "I'm sorry, Father."

"If you climb out that window again, you will be." He shuts the door in my face and drags something heavy against it to block me in. His chest of books from his university days, probably.

I sag onto my bed, my traitorous eyes looking out the window, down to the wood. Wind stirs through the verdant leaves, and I wonder, as I have very often, where Seren goes during the day. She's never told me. For half a moment, I entertain the notion of climbing out the window and going to find her, but I dismiss it at once. That wouldn't help anything, and I'm not about to abandon Awela.

I'm exhausted. Without my meaning it to, my head finds my pillow. I sleep.

It's late afternoon when I wake again. Father has left me a plate of food on my nightstand: a slab of cold ham and a slice of bara brith. I inhale both and step over to my window, where I find Father has been busy while I was sleeping: He's cut away the ivy that used to wind up the stone, successfully eliminating my path down to the garden. My stomach clenches: He really means to keep me from the wood. From Seren.

I pace the length of my room, three strides between the window and the door and back again. I could probably batter my way through the door—I suspect I'm stronger than Father gives me credit for—but that wouldn't accomplish anything. Better to wait until he forgives me, or at least relents enough to let me out.

I dig a few dusty books out from under my bed: one of Father's scientific journals, and a collection of poems Mother loved. I started reading the poems a while back, planning to memorize a few to impress Mairwen Griffith.

Do you fancy yourself in love with this girl?

Father's question sparks unbidden in my mind. I've been trying not to think about it. Because *of course* I'm not in love with Seren. *Of course.*

But then what exactly am I doing? Why *have* I risked so much for her?

She's lonely, I tell myself. *I feel sorry for her. And I'm just trying to repay my debt.*

But that's not it at all.

She's fascinating, my mind whispers back. *As fascinating as the stars—more. She's brilliant. She's beautiful. I want to be near her.*

My heart throbs uncomfortably. I go back to pacing.

There's noise downstairs as Father and Awela come in. I wonder if I'm to be allowed down to supper.

I'm not. The sun sets. The first stars come out. The house grows quiet again—Awela must be in bed.

Father's steps creak past my room and up the stairs to the observatory. It's remarkably unfair that he means to keep me from the stars, too. I halfheartedly shove my shoulder against the door. It doesn't shift.

I pace and pace. I turn up my oil lamp and try to read, but I can't concentrate. Hunger and restlessness gnaw through me. My eyes wander continually to the wood. I poke my head out of the window. I could *attempt* to climb down without the aid of the ivy. I might make it—I also might break my neck. I curse.

I'm about to surrender what remains of my dignity and batter on the door until Father comes and lets me out when I catch a flash of light in the corner of my eye.

I turn to the window. Another streak of light flashes across the sky, followed by a third. Meteors. I'm surprised to see so many—it's not late enough in the summer for the Lleidr Meteor Shower, which happens every year. I itch to discuss it with my father, to see what he makes of the anomaly.

And then it seems the whole world fills with light.

Meteor after meteor illuminates the sky, a hundred at a time, more. It looks like it's raining stars.

I gape, so stunned I hardly hear the scrape of the trunk in the hallway, the creak of the door.

Father claps his hand on my arm. "Come up to the observatory. Quick."

We pound upstairs, but we needn't have hurried. The meteors flash and die, flash and die, streaking through the constellations, painting the sky with their fierce, impossible light.

We stand shoulder to shoulder, staring out at the shower of stars, silent in our joint awe.

I think, perhaps, that it's the end of the world.

But little by little, meteor by meteor, the shower lessens, until there's only fifty at a time, then twenty, then ten.

One last meteor streaks across the sky, its tail burning long and white. It dies at the horizon, and the night is still.

I take a breath, the first I'm aware of since the meteor shower started.

Father turns to me, his face awash with conflicting emotions. "Shall we do the charts?"

But I'm staring at the sky. I don't need to look through the telescope to know that the stars have—

"Father." I nod to the window.

He looks. He grows very still. "Bring out last night's charts, will you?"

I oblige him, even though we both know it's not necessary. I take them from their designated case and he unrolls the one he wants. He frowns at it. We both do.

"What about the charts from last week?"

I bring them to him.

He spreads them all out on the table, comparing them desperately against each other, trying to find some reason for what is staring at us so baldly from the night sky.

The stars have *changed.*

The Morwyn constellation, comprised of almost two dozen stars of varying brightnesses and distance from our planet, has *moved.* She's no longer chasing the Twysog Mileinig, the Spiteful Prince. Her constellation has swallowed his up; his is a mass of broken stars, the crown the legends say he stole from her burning in her midst. And all around the Morwyn hang stars I have never seen before: a cluster of eight bright ones, near her right side; many, many dimmer ones strewn about her feet and left side, and scattered around her crown.

It's absolutely impossible.

It breaks every natural law.

Maybe some unnatural ones, too.

I stare at my father. He stares back, letting the charts roll up again.

"How?" I say.

He shakes his head. "It would take immense power. Impossible magic. The kind of magic that makes worlds, or breaks them."

My eyes go to the observatory window. To the Morwyn, winking at us from her new position in the dark expanse of sky. "Do you think this is the work of the Gwydden?"

"Her magic is in trees, not stars. Not even the Gwydden could be so powerful."

I'm not so sure. Seren destroyed an entire train without even trying too hard, and the Gwydden *created* her.

"Father—" I swallow. Start again. "Father, I have to go back to the wood."

His face hardens. "Why?"

"Because she might know something about the stars."

"The girl who lives in the forest."

I nod.

He looks at me, waiting for me to elaborate.

I tell him the truth. "She's the Gwydden's youngest daughter."

His eyes go sad. "I knew the wood had its hooks in you. I didn't know quite how deep they went."

I don't even know how to begin to explain. I look at him helplessly. "She's not what you think. She did save Awela, that day in the wood. She's saved me, countless times. And she's—she's not a monster. Not anymore."

He sags before me. "I can't just give you my blessing to climb back over the wall, Owen."

"I know. But if Seren has any insight into *that*"—I gesture vaguely at the sky—"she'll tell me. And then we can prepare for whatever it means. For whatever is coming."

"Seren," he repeats.

"Seren," I say.

He sighs, rubs at his temples. "Go, then. I want to believe you'll be wise. I want to believe you'll be safe, that she truly means you no harm. But if nothing else—if nothing else, I'll believe you if you promise to come back."

My throat tightens, and tears burn at the back of my eyes. "I promise."

He pulls me into a swift hug. "I'm sorry I was so angry."

"You had every right to be." I squeeze his shoulders, and draw back. "What are you going to do?"

He shakes his head in bewilderment. "Chart the stars' new

positions as best as I can, and then send a telegram to Breindal City in the morning. I suspect the king will want the charts early this month."

"I suspect he will." I turn to leave the observatory, but pause in the doorway.

"Be careful, Owen." His voice breaks.

"I'll see you soon," I promise.

I go to find my tree siren under a wholly new sky.

Chapter Twenty-Eight

SEREN

THE
stars
are
falling.
They streak and shine
like silver rain
as my mother's power
burns through the night.
Fear snags at me like burrs.
Still they fall, so bright they hurt my eyes.
I knew my mother was strong.
I did not know
she
was
this
strong.

She is changing the sky.
Changing the stars.
Her rage against the Soul Eater
written out for all the world to see.
The stars rain on.
They drip and shimmer.
They spark and die.
I do not understand
how there can be any left.
Little by little they slow, they stop.
The night grows still.
The world
is different
than it was.
I look up into a new sky,
into stars that trace the shape
of my mother's power.
I understand
how very small I am.
How unimportant.
How weak.
My mother created me in a moment.
In another, she could destroy me.
"Seren?"
I turn and he is here,
in the light of new stars.
He carries a lantern,
and there is something in his eyes
that was not there before.
He says, "What does it mean? The stars—they've *changed*."
I want
to touch him,

to feel his heart beat beneath my fingers.

I want

him to look at me

like he thinks I am worthy

of something beyond being

splintered to pieces

and fed to the fire.

I say: "My mother has come into the fullness of her power. She is ready now."

"Ready for what?"

Around our hill,

the trees I made to shield us

begin to shriek and crack.

They do not answer to my mother,

so she kills them from afar.

This can no longer be our sanctuary.

I say: "Ready to devour your world."

He stands solemn and unflinching. "I will not let her."

"You cannot stop her. No one can."

He steps close to me.

He raises tentative fingers

to coil around a strand of my hair.

He says: "Not even you?"

"I am the weakest of all of my sisters."

He touches my face and

I feel every point

of his fingers.

He says: "You are the strongest of them all. How else could you have become more than what your mother made you?"

"I am not more."

He cups my cheek. "You are."

I am unnerved by the look in his eyes. I pull away.

Below us, my trees pluck up their own roots
and shrivel under the stars.
We are exposed.
My sisters might come at any moment. My mother might come.
There will be no more meetings on this hill.
There will be no more meetings at all.
This is the night
I
will
lose
him.
"Owen."
He looks at me
and I
ache.
"I must tell you something. But then you must promise to go
home. It is no longer safe here. I cannot protect you."
A vein pulses in his temple.
He takes a breath.
He does not promise.
"Tell me."
"I remember your mother."
His whole body stiffens and stills.
His eyes go wild.
"My mother took her as a slave. Bound her to the heartless tree."
He struggles to be still. He gulps air. "What does that mean?
Why are you telling me this?"
The wind is angry. It lashes over the hill. "It is right that you
know. I did not wish to keep it from you."
"Are you—are you saying she's still alive?"
I do not know how to answer.
"Seren." His voice cracks. "Is she alive?"

"She belongs to my mother. Her soul is gone—she is nothing more than an empty shell."

His jaw tenses. "How can she exist, without a soul?"

The question is a thorn,

hot and sharp beneath my skin.

"*I* exist."

Wind rages between us, spitting leaves into Owen's hair.

He stares at me.

I say: "You must go home now. Before my sisters come to hunt you."

He says: "Take me to her."

I peer at him. I am puzzled.

"Take me to my mother."

"Why? You cannot save her. You cannot free her. She is gone."

"Take me to my mother!" His voice is wild and high. "All this time I thought she was dead, and now you tell me she's *not*. I have to see her. I have to save her, if I can. Can't you understand that?"

"I cannot take you. It is dangerous. Foolish."

He drags a hand across his face. "Please, Seren."

"Your mother is past saving. Even if she were not, she is in the heart of my mother's court. You could never reach her there."

"Take me."

"My mother would kill you."

"Then protect me."

"I cannot protect you from her."

The wood writhes and whispers below the hill.

It watches.

Listens.

"You must go home, Owen. I am sorry."

His shoulders hunch. He looks away. "If you won't take me, I'll go myself."

"You cannot."

He wheels on me; his eyes spark fire. "Stop me, then."

He strides down the hill,
through the remains of my dead trees,
into
the
heartless
wood.
In a moment,
I will follow.
In a moment,
I will reach into his mind
and make him forget everything.
Our hill.
His mother.
Me.
It is the only way to protect him.
But oh, I do not want to.
Dew leaks from my eyes
and
drips
down
my
chin.
It will be better this way.
I will remember our nights on the hill
for both of us.
I shatter at the first note of my sisters' song.
It slides through the wood,
whispers through leaves and branches,
shimmers like silver in the air.
It
will
ensnare

him.
I run
down the hill and
through the trees.
He is there in the distance,
his lantern flashing like
a star.
My sisters' song twists into him.
He drops the lantern.
He turns.
He runs.
Toward the music,
toward my sisters,
toward
his
death.
I cross
the distance between us
in four pulses
of my heart.
I crash into him,
knock him to the ground.
He screams and thrashes.
The music inside of him
robs him of his will.
He
is
not
himself.
I throw my body on top of his.
I sing a command to the wood.
Living branches grow from the forest floor,

winding overtop of us,
shielding us from sight.
But they do not silence
my sisters' song.
He fights me, fights me.
I am stronger.
I hold him down.
I press my hands
over his ears.
Still he struggles,
though I can see
in his eyes
he does not wish to.
Tears slide down his cheeks and
my
heart
hurts.
I stare at him
one moment more
and then I bend
my face to his
and touch his lips with mine.
They are warm
and soft
and taste of tears.
The fight
goes out of him.
Beyond the concealing branches, my sisters' song slowly fades.
But I do not take my mouth from his.
He looks at me
with emotions
I have no name for.

He lifts one hand
to stroke my hair,
to caress
my cheek.
He traces
the curve of my neck
with gentle fingers.
I take my hands from his ears and see
I have been
too rough.
I have cut the sides of his face.
He bleeds.
I wrench off of him.
The branches unwind,
vanish back into the earth.
All that covers us now
are the trees
and my mother's
devouring
stars.

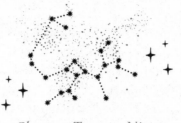

Chapter Twenty-Nine

OWEN

"I DID NOT MEAN TO HURT YOU," SHE WHISPERS.

I gasp for breath, faintly aware of the pain pulsing in my cheeks. I touch them, and my fingers come away wet with blood. But that is nothing compared to the agony of the tree sirens' song, blazing through me like a thousand stinging ants. And it is nothing compared to the feel of her body, pressed against mine, her lips on my lips, her power tethering me to the earth.

I am undone by her kiss.

I am undone by *her*.

And yet.

My mother is *alive*. Seren knew it all this time. And she never told me.

"I did not mean to hurt you," she says again. Tears slide down her cheeks.

My gut clenches. "That doesn't matter." I wipe the blood away with the backs of my hands. I can still feel the echo of her mouth on mine. "You saved me. *Again*."

She shudders in the wind that rips through the wood. She steps near me, closes the distance between us.

"I'm still going. To find my mother. To try to save her." I square my jaw. I know how futile it is—if Seren doesn't help me, I'll die long before I reach my mother. But I still have to try.

Seren touches my temples, her fingers quick and cool. Her eyes fix on mine, and I remember the silvery magic that made me forget her, what feels like so long ago now. "Help me find her. Please." I swallow past the lump in my throat, telling my heart firmly to be *still*. "Don't make me forget you."

She jerks her hands back. A petal falls from her hair. "It is the only way I can be sure you will be safe."

I cup her face in my hands, my fingers smoothing her cheeks. "I don't want to be safe if it means forgetting you."

"I do not want you to forget me," she whispers.

"Then don't make me. Help me find my mother."

Around us, the wood laughs and rattles. Roots writhe under the ground. Trees lean toward us, reaching craggy fingers.

"I will take you to the heartless tree," she says. "I will take you to find your mother. But you must understand, Owen. We cannot save her. We cannot restore her to what she was. Her soul is gone— she is empty of herself. The best you can hope for is that she will remember enough of her former life to know you, enough that you can bid her farewell."

My eyes burn. "There has to be some way——"

"There is not. Can you believe me?"

I don't trust myself to speak, so I nod.

"Then come. We must go quickly, so the wood does not have time to bar our way." She offers me her hand.

I take it, her rough-smooth-sharp fingers encircling mine.

We walk together through the wood. I retrieve my lantern,

abandoned when the tree sirens' music caught me. It's still full of oil, and I light it again. It flares yellow. Shadows play about Seren's face, making her look unearthly and angular in the darkness.

"What is the heartless tree?" I ask her, to distract myself from the teeming wood, the crash and rattle of a thousand branches.

"My mother's first creation. Before she knew how to make hearts, she gave the heartless tree life. It has no will of its own, but it is very strong. It is where she keeps the souls. The souls feed the tree and the tree feeds the wood and the wood feeds my mother. It is how she harnesses her power. How she focuses it."

"Perhaps I should take an axe to the heartless tree."

Seren shudders. "That would kill us all, I think. All but her."

We walk on through the night, and Seren never lets go of my hand. Just before dawn she orders me to sleep, and I am too weary to refuse. Once more she causes a bower of branches to enclose me, and I fall into swift, dark dreams.

When I wake, we continue on. I worry about my father, waiting for me to come home. To fulfill my promise. I hope he knows I still mean to. But if he were here, if he knew I was going after my mother, he would understand. If he knew, he would come with me.

The wood is different in the daylight, shifting shades of green and brown, of wildflowers in unexpected places, of spiders spinning webs in hidden shadows. It still teems with power, but it is beautiful, too. Perhaps the beauty makes it more dangerous, because there are long moments when I begin to feel safe.

Seren is as much a part of the wood as I am not, moving soundlessly through the trees, melding into them. Birds flit about her shoulders, bees drink from the violets in her hair. Deer bow to her, and a fox rubs against her legs like a cat.

I am bumbling and awkward next to her, every step seeming to disturb the peace of the forest. Yet the trees let me pass, as if Seren has asked them to do her a favor. Branches don't reach out to grab me, roots don't writhe beneath my feet. With her, I am safe.

But as we walk, even though she is always beside me, her hand tight about mine, it feels as if she is slipping further out of my reach with every step we take. Our nights on the hill are gone. I know that. And whatever awaits us at the heartless tree, whatever has truly happened to my mother, that will be an ending, too. I don't see how Seren and I can have anything more than this. We have been caught in a dream, and we're about to wake up. I am losing her. It breaks me, piece by piece.

And yet—

How can I lose her? She was never mine.

How can I love a thing that has no soul?

How can I love her at all? When did I attach such a weighty, impossible word to the Gwydden's youngest daughter?

But what else could it be?

Dancing on the hill, four minutes at a time. Starlight and telescopes and strawberries.

Her hands pressed against my ears, blocking out the deadly music of her monstrous sisters. Her silver lips touching mine. She tasted of rain and grass and earth. Of heat and ice and wind. No matter how I try, I cannot push the memory of that kiss from my mind.

We walk all day. A few times, Seren presses nuts and berries into my hands, and waits for me to eat them before leading me on. In the slanting light of the afternoon, we come upon a ring of birch trees, stark white against the browns of the oaks and ash around us. Seren's steps slow, and she turns to walk among the birches.

I follow.

She stops in the center of the birch ring, and kneels on the forest floor. I realize, without her telling me, that this is the place she was born. I brush my fingers along the birches, their silver-white bark like her skin, and yet unlike, too. They are not alive. They have no hearts.

Seren lifts her face to mine, and I am gutted to see the tears shining on her cheeks. "I am not a tree," she says. "I am not a woman. What am I?"

I kneel beside her, wrap my arms around her shoulders, feel her heartbeat against mine. There is nothing I can tell her, no answer I can give, because I don't know the answer. I don't even know if there is one. But I can hold her while she cries. I can stroke her hair and wish that I could make her happy. I can believe, deep down, that she *does* have a soul, no matter how much she denies it. Because how can she not?

You only want her to have a soul so she won't be a monster, says a voice in my mind. *You don't want to love a monster.*

She is warm and solid in my arms; her tears fall damp on my shirt. I almost tell her that I've changed my mind; she doesn't have to face the horror of her mother for me.

But I can't do that. I can't resign my own mother to whatever torment she suffers as the Gwydden's slave.

So I don't say anything. I wait until Seren grows calm again, until she pulls away from me and wipes the tears from her eyes.

"Come," she says, rising to her feet. "My mother's court is close." She swallows, all at once tremulous. Uncertain. "You remember what I told you before."

"That we can't save her. I know."

The ring of birches where she was born whispers and weaves around us, but there is no wind that I can feel. Her gaze knifes through me. "Do you believe that, Owen Merrick?"

I don't believe it—how can I? But. "I believe you." It will have to be enough.

Chapter Thirty

SEREN

H E DOES NOT BELIEVE ME.
   I can see it
   in the way he holds himself,
in the set of his shoulders,
in his unwavering stride.
He means to save his mother.
Even
if
it
kills
him.
Last night, I should have taken his memories.
Now I have not the courage.
I could lead him to stray forever in the wood.
I could tell him my mother has shut me out of her court.
In time, he would forget about his mother.

In a hundred years,
perhaps
he would grow
like me
and perhaps
I would grow
like him
until we are both
not quite human,
not quite tree,
not
quite
monster.
But I gave him my word.
I will not break my promise.
There is blood on the wind.
Can he smell it?
Has he ever felt it
sticky on his hands?
The wood hisses around us.
The Soul Eater's men lay more iron
and the trees are angry.
I say: "Keep close."
He steps near me.
We walk shoulder to shoulder,
my hand around his.
Grief claws up my throat.
I am not his kind.
I am a tree,
a monster.
He is human.
I want to kiss him again

but
I dare not.
I would give
anything
to shed
this monstrous form,
to have a soul
planted inside of me,
that would put down roots
and grow.
The wind smells of lightning, of rain.
It spits leaves into our faces.
The scent of blood grows stronger.
My sister steps into our path,
blood-dark rose petals dripping from her hair.
Owen's pulse throbs in his wrist.
His fear is a wild thing.
His courage is stronger.
My sister says: "So this is why you hid him from us. You bring
him to our mother as a prize. Or is it an offering, to atone for your
sins?"
I hiss at her. "He is neither prize nor offering. His mother is the
slave of the heartless tree. I have brought him to see her."
My sister stares. This is not the thing she expected me to say.
I command her: "Let us pass. Leave him be."
She throws back her head as she laughs. "Is he your *pet* then?"
She steps toward us.
She grazes her fingers down Owen's cheek.
He flinches
as her claws
draw blood.
I yank him away from her.

She says: "Are you angry, little sister?"

I say: "Let us *pass!*"

"Or what? You will devour me?"

"I will make you wish I did."

She laughs again, a screech of crows. "Little fool. Our mother knows you are coming. She waits for you."

"Then come with me to greet her. Help me draw her away from the heartless tree, so Owen may bid his own mother farewell."

She scoffs. "It has a name, does it? You think it as worthy a creature as me, as you? If I sing to it, it will come gladly; it will *beg* me to devour it. It has no more value than a *worm*."

"He is a living soul. He has the highest worth."

Displeasure sparks between her eyes. "Your game has gone on long enough. Kill him now, or I will, and drag you both before our mother."

"When our mother has defeated the Eater, her wood will cover all the world. There will be no more humans. No more souls to take. Let me have this one. Let me do with it what I will. What harm is there for him to speak with his mother, before all his kind are devoured?"

She spits at me. "There is something wrong with your heart. There is sentiment in you. There is weakness."

Rain falls, cold through the trees. Owen's hand is warm in mine. His strength gives me strength.

I say: "Our mother will be angry with me for being away so long. For not coming when she called. She will punish me. She will be cruel. Perhaps that is prize enough for you to let him go."

I feel Owen's eyes on my face.

He does not like

that this is the price for him to see his mother.

He does not know

that I brought him here willing to pay it.

My sister says: "I will come with you, if only to see our mother
rip you apart. I will laugh. And then I will come and devour him
anyway."

It is all I can hope for.

I say: "Let me show him the way. Then we will go to our mother
together."

She smirks at me in the falling rain. "Go. I will be waiting."

She melts into the wood.

Once more, Owen and I are alone.

I cannot meet his eyes

as we walk

through dripping trees.

His unrest pulses through me

as surely as his heartbeat.

He says: "Will your mother kill you? For helping me?"

I say: "She does not know about you. You are not the cause of
her anger."

"What, then?"

"It is because I have taken no new souls for her in many weeks.
It is because I did not come to her when she called."

He pulls me to a stop and

at last

I look at him.

His face is

creased with worry,

drenched with rain.

He says again: "Will she kill you?"

"I do not know. Perhaps. Does that change your mind?"

He blinks water from his eyes. "I have to see my mother. But I
don't want it to mean your death."

"Death will come for me, whether you see your mother or not."

His jaw clenches. "I will kill the Gwydden if she touches you."

Pain splinters through my heart.

He would not say such things to me

if he knew

what I have done.

I tug him through the trees,

close to the heart of the wood.

We stop at a weathered oak.

I say: "The heartless tree is just beyond, on the bank of the river. You will find your mother there. Say your farewells and then——"

Almost, the pain is too great to bear.

When these moments are past,

he will

revile me.

When these moments are past,

I will be again

a monster.

"When you have said your farewells, run into the wood. As fast as you can. I will find you, if I am able, but if not—if not, I will ask the wood to guide you, to protect you all the way back to your wall."

I can only hope

the wood

will obey me.

I breathe him in. "Thank you."

"For what?"

Longing and fear and grief pour out of him.

I want to encircle him in branches,

protect him forever

from the wood and my mother

and the truth

of what I am.

I say: "For strawberries. For books and music and dancing. For not fearing me, if only for a little while."

"I do not fear you now." He cups my face in his hands.
I tremble
at his touch. "You should never have stopped being afraid."
I step back from him and
it
is
agony.
I say: "Remember. You cannot save her."
I leave him by the oak
and go to find my sister.

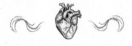

She waits for me, not far away.

Amusement tilts her mouth up. "You have told the boy farewell,
then. Shall we to your death?"

"You need not be so gleeful."

"I only wish the rest of our sisters were here, to see you brought
low."

"Do not breathe a word of the boy. You promised."

She laughs. "I did not, but I shall hold my tongue until it pleases
me not to."

We pace together
into the heart of our mother's domain,
through corridors of ash trees.
Branches arch far over our heads,
an ever-shifting canopy
that blots out the sky.
Bones litter the ground, offerings from the earth to its powerful
queen.

The scent of blood grows

stronger,

wilder.

I am glad.

It means my mother is not at the heartless tree.

It means she is here, waiting for us.

My mother

is the thing

that smells of blood.

She stands

stiff and straight at the end of the ash tree corridor

under a darkly writhing sky.

Lightning crackles beyond her,

gilding her with power.

A body lies lifeless at her feet, the husk of a boy younger than Owen.

His face is frozen in agony.

Hers is luminous.

Fury wells inside of me.

I stare at the boy's face

and picture Owen there,

broken at her feet.

Our mother watches us approach.

Her eyes are narrowed to slits.

Her antlers branch out from either side of her head, tipped in
fresh blood.

The

boy's

blood.

It drips crimson onto the ground.

Beneath her feet the earth whispers and writhes.

Above and all around, the trees bow to her.

They are awake and angry,

ready to do her bidding.

My sister and I stop three paces before her.

My sister bows.

I kneel, pressing my forehead into the ground,

a breath away

from the boy's ruined body.

Claws dig into my neck, force my head up.

"I have called you for a full life of the moon, and now you come?"

"Forgive me, mother."

She hisses and rakes her claws down my shoulder, tearing off the strip of newly healed bark.

My sister is as good as her word.

She laughs.

My mother flings me to the earth and wheels on her. "And why are *you* here, daughter?"

"To see my youngest sister made to mind."

My mother bares her teeth.

My sister flinches, but holds her ground. "She has learned her lesson, you see. She comes to you on her knees, ready for a new orb."

Pain sears through me

as my mother rips another patch of bark

from my back.

She pulls the violets from my hair

one

by

one

and flings them to the grass.

She grinds them under her heel.

I curl in on myself, dew pouring from my eyes.

I think of music on the hill.

Of dancing with Owen.

Of looking at stars through a telescope that lies ruined somewhere in the wood.

I try not to think of him going to the heartless tree.

Of him trying to save his mother.

Of his soul, bright and shining,

left to wink out

with all the others.

My mother's breath is icy in my ear. "I should take your heart from your body, since you are of so little use to me."

I shake.

I find I cannot bear dying,

now that my death is so near.

My sister says: "She can yet be your soldier. You will need her in the coming war."

I listen to the beat of my heart,

to the pulse of the earth.

I wonder why my sister cares to save me.

Perhaps she will have nothing to laugh at

when I am gone.

Rain lashes down. Hail stings like ants.

My mother drags me up by my hair. "Your sister asks me to be merciful. Do you also wish for my mercy?"

I tremble in her grip,

my back screaming in pain. I whisper: "Yes."

Her smile

is a cruel twist

of her mouth. "Do you know what I will do to you, if you defy me again?"

She drags her claws down my face.

She slices deep enough

to make sap spill out. "I will rip you to pieces, and make a bonfire of your bones."

I can only nod.

The pain is too great for anything more.

"Now, daughter. There is a human somewhere near. Prove your loyalty to me. Kill him, and bring me his soul."

She draws an amber orb from within her robes.

She hangs it around my neck. "Go."

I stumble back from her, nearly falling.

She says to my sister: "Other daughter, go with her. Make sure she obeys."

My sister bows. "Yes, my queen."

My mother eyes me with contempt.

The rain has washed the blood

from her antlers. "You are fortunate I have a whole wood to waken, an army to raise to stand behind me when I go to face the Soul Eater. Otherwise, I would not be so merciful."

She sweeps away.

The ash trees bow behind her.

Chapter Thirty-One

OWEN

THE HEARTLESS TREE GROWS ON THE BANK OF A SMALL, SWIFT river, just as Seren said it did. I'd imagined it would be strange or terrifying, but it is just a tree, dark and old and thick, with rattling leaves and great humps of roots stretching out below the earth.

At the base of the tree, a woman crouches, digging in the dirt with her bare hands. I know her, even in the rainy half-dark. Even though she looks like the ghost of herself.

A cry rips out of me. I run toward her, stumbling on slick leaves and mud. She lifts her head as I reach her, as I kneel beside her and tug her into my arms. Ragged, guttural sobs wrack my body.

She pulls back from me, peers into my face. "I know you." Her voice is not what I remember. It is hollow, empty. Her eyes are, too. Her hair, once pale and bright, hangs limp and matted at her shoulders. She's dressed in rags.

"It's Owen, Mother." I grip her shoulders, gently, for I fear she might break. "I'm going to take you home to Father and Awela. Awela's grown so big! You'll be so proud of her."

I will her to remember, but her eyes remain vacant. She blinks at me. "Owen," I beg. "I'm Owen, and you're Eira, and you're married to Calon Merrick. You play the cello and you love to garden and you have the sweetest singing voice in all the world. Please, Mother. Please remember."

She digs her fingers into the sides of her head, agony writing itself in lines across her face. "I remember I was not always as I am now. I remember I was once something more than her slave. I had a will of my own. But all she's left me is my heart, and it no longer beats for anyone but her."

"Please. *Please.*" Tears pour down my face. "Irises are your favorite flower. You always said you fell in love with Father because his head was in the sky and yours was in the earth and together you made a horizon. Please." My heels grind deep into the mud. The rain is cold, and a chill shivers into my bones.

"The stars fell," she says. "They fell and they fell, and the sky is changed. The Gwydden's time has come. Soon, it will all end." Her eyes focus suddenly on mine, a spark of her old self. "I protected you all as long as I could," she whispers. "The Gwydden took my soul. She bound me to herself, bound me to this tree. Bid me watch over it and the souls that it contains. It is glutted with them, but it is never satisfied. I draw blood from its body. I make orbs for her daughters to hang around their necks. Blood to draw the souls, the souls." She grips my shoulders with a fierceness that should not come from her frail body. "I am bound to the tree, and so I could use its power. I used it to remember, and when I could remember no more, I used it to protect the souls that once were dear to me."

Realization slams through me. "*You* kept me safe on the train tracks while Father was searching for me. *You* kept Father out of the wood when Awela and I were safe with Seren."

"I've been watching over you," she whispers. "And it's over now. The stars are changed. She will swallow the world. Stop her, if you can. And remember me."

"I'm here to *save* you," I choke out.

Her eyes go vacant again, and she crouches back on her heels. "I followed the tree siren into the wood." Her voice has a singsong quality to it, like she's repeating a nursery rhyme. "The siren with violets in her hair."

"No."

"Violets, violets, violets!"

Numbness steals over me, swallowing me whole.

"She said my soul was strong. She brought me to her mother. Her mother stole my soul, my soul, my soul. She bound me to the tree."

Rage rises inside of me, a monster I cannot control.

"Mother—"

"She stole my soul, but she cannot have my heart. It is finished now. You don't need me to protect you anymore." Her face changes, that last spark of herself coming once more into her eyes. She touches my face, smoothing her thumb over the stubble on my cheek. "When did my little boy become a man?"

I choke back a sob.

"I am glad I got to see you once last time."

"I'm going to save you."

Pain sparks in her face. "I am long past saving. But there is yet one last thing I can do for you."

"Mother—"

She presses her hand against my chest, and I gasp as pain flashes through me, as it sinks fiery into the core of my being. It pulses once, twice, and then it's gone. I stare at her. "What *was* that?"

"One last spark of power. To guard you from her. So she can never take your soul, the way she took mine." She kisses my temple, then crouches back on her heels. "My soul is gone forever, but she cannot have my heart anymore."

She claws suddenly at her chest, screaming in pain as her nails meet skin and dig deeper. Blood blooms in my vision.

"My heart belongs to you," comes her voice, thin and distant. "To Awela. To Calon. Tell him—Owen, tell him I'll always be burning in his sky. Goodbye, brave one. I will love you, always." She gives one last piercing, inhuman screech, and then in the haze of blood and rain, I see what she's done.

She's torn out her own heart. She holds it in her hands as her body goes still on the forest floor.

Animal cries rip raw from my throat. I don't understand. She can't be gone, not like this. She can't be lying there dead, her own heart in her hands.

And yet.

Her heart turns to ash as I watch. The rain washes it away. It cleans the blood from my mother's hands, cleans the dirt from her face. I take her hand.

I feel like a stranger in my own body. I weep and I scream and I'm scarcely aware that I'm doing it.

She shouldn't have died like this. She shouldn't have died here. She shouldn't have—

"Owen, come away." Knobby fingers jab under my armpits. Hands lift me to my feet. I'm fighting the hands, the arms, the viselike grip that won't let me go.

My mother's body turns to ash, like her heart did.

She's wholly gone, the rain grinding her into the earth.

"Owen, come away."

I'm dragged from the river and the heartless tree. I stop resisting after a little while, exhausted and hollow, all the strength sapped from me.

I'm released then. I crumple to the ground like a broken toy.

I look up into Seren's face.
I followed the tree siren into the wood.
The siren with violets in her hair.
I lunge at her.

Chapter Thirty-Two

SEREN

I CATCH OWEN'S WRISTS.

I hold him back from me.

He howls in the rain and the dark.

He struggles in my grasp. He shouts: "LET ME GO!"

I release him,

and he falls

into the mud.

The rain is driving, cold. The wood drinks it up, roots stretching down into damp earth.

Owen convulses on the ground.

He weeps.

I crouch beside him

but there is nothing I can do.

He is broken

and I

am the one

who has broken him.

I should never

have brought him here.

Should never

have told him his mother was alive.

And now—

"Owen."

He roars: "GET AWAY FROM ME!"

I jerk back.

Somewhere close by my sister is waiting, watching to see what I will do.

It is all a game to her, his soul like any other.

But it is not.

It

is

not.

I say: "She was already dead. She was just a shell. My mother took her soul long ago, and when your mother plucked out her own heart, there was nothing left to bind the husk of her together. So she faded. But she was already dead."

He wheels on me. His eyes flash. "You would know, wouldn't you? *You're* the one who killed her!"

"Owen, come with me. Let me take you home to your father and sister. Let me get you warm. Please."

Rain runs in rivulets down my cheeks; my bark soaks it in.

Pain screams through the raw places in my back, the gouges in my face.

But it does not hurt as much

as the hatred in his eyes.

He screams: "How could you spend all those nights with me? How could you, knowing you did *that* to my mother? How could you look up at the stars and *dance* with me and *kiss* me when

YOU KNEW WHAT YOU HAD DONE?"

He scrabbles for something on his belt as he lunges to his feet.

A metal blade gleams in the rain.

He holds it out toward me and

the point quavers.

I say: "The heartless tree must always be bound to someone, someone to channel the power, to fashion the orbs. But humans do not endure, and every so often, my mother sends me or my sisters to take a new one, someone whose soul is strong enough to bear it. Your mother was strong. The strongest I have ever seen. That is why, when my mother sent me to find someone new, I chose her."

"You're a trickster. A monster. A demon from Hell. I never should have believed your lies."

"I have never lied to you, Owen Merrick. I am my mother's creature. Her monster. Her slave. I always have been."

My words are

molded leaves

in my throat. They choke me.

Fresh tears pour down his face. "But that's just it, Seren. You're not her slave. She doesn't control you—your will is your own. You are only a monster because you choose to be."

His words slice through me

like an axe through wood.

"I never knew I had a choice until you."

He says: "Then choose, but I want no part of it."

"Owen—"

He is suddenly beside me, his blade at my throat. "I will never forgive you for what you did to my mother. If I ever see you again, I will kill you."

He is so close

I feel

the heat of him.

And yet he is further away than he ever has been.

Grief is a river.

It

engulfs

me.

He curses and jerks away, hurling the blade at the ground.

It lands with a *thunk* in the soggy dirt, buried to the hilt.

For one moment more, his eyes meet mine. He says: "Don't follow me."

He turns and tugs the blade from the earth.

Then he's gone.

I sink to my knees. The scents of moss and leaves and blood overwhelm me.

But my sister

does not let me mourn in peace.

She grabs my hands, yanks me to my feet.

There is scorn still in her face, but there is something softer, too.

I think it is pity.

"You are the greatest of fools, little sister. You cannot love one who is not your own kind. You should not love at all. That is not why our mother gave you a heart."

Dew mingles with the rain on my face. "Why did she?"

"Perhaps because that is where her own power came from, in the time before she lost her soul."

"Are you going to take me to her? Or will you kill me here in the mud?"

Her lip curls. "You are not worth killing. Go. Go far and fast away from here, for our mother will not have pity on you."

She yanks the amber orb from my neck. "I will fill it for you. I will tell her you are dead. Your death will come soon enough, when the Eater is gone and the wood has swallowed the world."

"Sister—"

She spits at me: "I am not your sister. I could never share blood with such an unworthy creature. Now *go*."

I stumble into the wood.

Misery and numbness come in waves.

It is not a mercy, for her to let me live.

Perhaps she knows that.

Perhaps that is why she did.

His voice repeats in my mind,

over

and

over

again,

like the recording on his magical phonograph.

You're not her slave. She doesn't control you—your will is your own.

You are only a monster because you choose to be.

Choose.

Choose.

The night grows very dark.

The rain clings

like ice

to my hair,

my skin,

my gown.

You are only a monster because you choose to be.

I never knew I had a choice until you.

Choose.

But how do I choose not to be a monster?

I cannot atone for the souls I slew,

for the blood I shed on the forest floor.

I cannot undo what I did to Owen's mother.

Choose.

I am what my mother made me to be.
I cannot shed the form she gave me
like a snake sheds its skin.
Can I?

Chapter Thirty-Three

OWEN

I RUN BLINDLY THROUGH THE DARK, SOAKED THROUGH WITH RAIN, branches clawing at my shoulders.

I followed the tree siren into the wood.

The siren with violets in her hair.

I burn with anger. It propels me on and on, makes the trees shrink back from me.

She said my soul was strong. She brought me to her mother.

I want to claw my eyes out, but even if I did I would remember Seren, gleaming silver in the rain while my mother's blood poured red onto the earth.

She bound me to the tree.

All the nights I spent with her on the hill. Every time I looked at her and forgot she was a monster. Every time I wished her to be more than she was, that I *thought* she was more—

She as good as murdered my mother, and I'd thought—I'd thought—

Do you fancy yourself in love with this girl?

Her mouth on mine, her body on mine. Her smooth-sharp hands pressed against my ears, blocking out the horror of her sisters' song.

The same song that *she* sang when she lured my mother to her death.

Her betrayal cuts deeper than any knife.

And yet it gutted me to leave her alone in the dark.

I loved a monster.

Now I must pay the price.

I'm not sure how I make it to the edge of the wood and Father's wall, just as dawn lightens the world around me. Maybe it's the lingering remnants of the magic Mother wielded to keep us safe. Maybe it's Seren, commanding the wood to leave me be. Or maybe I am simply not important enough for the wood to bother with.

I scramble over the wall. The lantern is lost somewhere among the trees—it would be just if the oil spilled and caught fire, if the wood burned all to ash. But I don't think there is any justice to be had in the Gwydden's Wood.

I drag myself past the garden, up the steps to the door.

A paper notice stares me in the face, nailed into the wood and stamped with King Elynion's seal. I tear it free, shaking so hard the words swim before my eyes. I force myself to be still.

A warrant for the arrest of Calon Merrick, on the charge of high treason, signed and witnessed on this day by His Royal Majesty Elynion, King of Tarian.

It's signed with an illegible scrawl, and dated yesterday afternoon. I read it three times, disbelieving. Father arrested for treason? Why? How? The king must have sent soldiers by train. They must have arrived around the same time my mother—

I force away the echo of her screams, the memory of her heart in her hands, before she turned to ash.

A new terror grips me. If Father was arrested, he would have been taken to the palace in Breindal City by now. But what about Awela?

I fling the door open and tear through the downstairs rooms, then race upstairs to search those as well. My little sister is nowhere to be found.

I pace the kitchen, telling myself to be calm, to *think*. Awela spends most days with Efa at the farm. She's probably there. I'll stop and check on my way to Breindal City. Because of course I'm going after my father. This all has to be some horrible mistake. Father could no more commit treason than Awela—he hasn't got it in him.

I'll take the train. Go straight to the king. Bring Father home.

A clap of thunder rattles the house, and I jerk my eyes to the kitchen window. Rain breaks anew from heavy clouds.

Breath rushes out of me. Suddenly, all I can see is a bloody heart in a rainy wood. All I can hear is my mother screaming.

I press my hands against my ears. "STOP IT!" I cry. "STOP IT! LEAVE ME ALONE!"

I collapse onto the kitchen floor as the horror of my mother's death repeats itself behind my eyes, over and over again.

And I weep for her. Because I am the only one who knows she's truly gone.

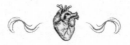

It doesn't take long to get ready—I shove food and a few changes of clothing into my pack, along with last month's payment from the king, and the star charts that document the sky before and after the impossible meteor shower. I pull on a clean pair of trousers and a fresh shirt, fumbling with the buttons. I jam my top hat onto my head and then shrug into Father's old oilskin coat. It's overlarge on me, and smells like him: ink, cinnamon, woodsmoke. My brain works at the knot of his arrest, trying to understand the incomprehensible.

It's midmorning, and still raining as I trudge to Brennan's Farm. I'm eager to see Awela, eager to promise her that all will be well very soon, that we'll be together again. We never have to go back to the house by the wood. I never want to.

I knock on the farmhouse door as rain cascades from the eave of the roof, and damp chickens cluck in annoyance from their pen beside the house.

Efa opens the door, but she's alone. Her eyes widen at the sight of me. "Owen! What are you doing here?"

"I've come to see Awela. Where is she?"

"Awela's not here. The king's soldiers took her away with your father to the capital."

"WHAT?"

She shrinks back from me.

I force myself to breathe. "Forgive me, Efa. Why would they take her?"

"I don't know. The same reason they arrested your father, perhaps. I wondered what had become of you. Why you weren't with them."

I can't even begin to explain, even if there were time. "Do you know why he was arrested?"

She shakes her head. "They'd bound his hands," she says. "Awela was crying. They wouldn't let me comfort her. They just took her away."

My gut wrenches. "Thanks for looking after her, Efa."

Tears slip down her cheeks. "If I'd known they would take her, I would have hidden her. I would have—"

"You did all you could," I say gently. "Thank you." I pull her into a swift hug.

She pats my arm and wipes her eyes. "Hurry. You don't want to miss the train."

I walk to the village in the sucking mud. Rain slips under my collar and drips from the brim of my hat. I blink and see vacant eyes and clawing fingers, blood and ashes.

I try to remember Mother as she was in life: full of laughter and music. Playing her cello in the garden, cursing when she realized she'd set her stool in the cabbage bed and mangled several of the plants. Baking bread in the kitchen, her belly round with Awela, her nose streaked with flour. Dancing with my father in the observatory to the music of the phonograph, their elbows bumping against the bookcase because it was far too small up there to dance. The wonder in her eyes when she first held Awela, though her face was pale and streaked with tears.

She shouldn't have ended that way.

She shouldn't have.

I make it to the village before the train, and duck into the inn to buy my ticket. Mairwen Griffith eyes me across the counter, accepting my fare and writing the ticket for me. Wisps of dark hair have come loose from her bun, and I remember how beautiful I used to think she was. How I imagined I might marry her.

But I don't think her beautiful now. Or maybe her beauty just doesn't hold the same charm it once did.

Silver skin and silver lips. The scent of violets.

I followed the tree siren into the wood.

The siren with violets in her hair.

I shudder.

"Owen? Are you all right?"

"Fine," I say.

She offers me the ticket, and I take it.

She studies me. "When you come back, will you have that dinner with me? I've been waiting quite a while."

"I'm sorry, Mairwen," I reply. "But I don't think I'm coming back."

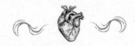

I settle into my seat, tugging my father's coat tight against my shoulders as the train lurches into motion. I take off my hat and put it on the empty seat beside me. The rainy countryside blurs past my window, and I hurtle toward Breindal City, toward my father and Awela and the king.

I try not to think about the last time I was on a train.

Part Two

STARS

He looked at his own Soul with a telescope. What seemed all irregular, he saw and showed to be beautiful constellations, and he added to the consciousness hidden worlds within worlds.

— Samuel Taylor Coleridge, *Notebooks*

Chapter Thirty-Four

SEREN

FTER MY MOTHER SANG A HALF-LIFE INTO THE HEARTLESS TREE,

before she created me and my sisters,

she made my brothers: the Pine Princes.

They are the only beings I have ever heard of

who defied her,

and lived.

I do not remember them.

I was only three winters old when they left our mother's court

forever.

She had not meant to make them so powerful.

When she made my sisters and me

we were only given the powers

of song,

strength,

growth.

But my brothers were created

with drops of her own blood.
Her power took root
inside of them.
I have never known what they did to defy her.
My sisters would not tell me.
I have never dared ask my mother.
I do not even know
if they still dwell within the wood,
or if they left it long ago.
But they are my only chance to change what I am.
My only chance of shedding this form,
of leaving behind
the monster
forever.
I head east, toward the wild reaches of the forest,
the only place my brothers could be hiding.
My back aches
where my mother stripped away my bark.
But it is Owen's words that torment me.
I will never forgive you for what you did to my mother. If I ever
see you again, I will kill you.
You are only a monster because you choose to be.
Choose.
The trees shelter me
from the rain
and I am left
in a roaring green world,
leaves crackly and dry beneath my feet.
I kneel on the forest floor,
plunge my hands into the earth,
reach out to the heart of the wood,
to my brothers.

Neither answers.

The wood turns its back on me,

rejecting me.

I feel it, waking at my mother's call.

It is strong.

Angry.

Ready to do her will.

I go on.

The forest hisses and mutters.

Branches reach, roots writhe.

I sing to the wood and

it listens,

lets me pass.

Here, the trees grow so close together

their trunks are tangled up, so that I cannot tell one apart from

another.

Moss thrives on exposed roots and worn stones,

russet brown, daffodil yellow.

The air is dense and still.

There are no birds,

no deer,

no creatures of any kind.

I have strayed into a part of the wood

that does not wholly answer to my mother.

Beyond the trees

the rain stops,

the clouds break,

the day brightens.

Light filters through the leaves,

casting dappled shadows on the ground.

The sound of rushing water reaches my ears.

I come into a clearing, where a waterfall crashes into a shining pool.

Colored rocks gleam
beneath the surface.
I kneel on the bank,
drink my fill.
When I straighten again, one of my brothers is there,
watching me across the pool.
He is tall and thin,
his brown skin raised with ridges and whorls.
Dark green hair spills past his shoulders.
His silver robe looks to be spun from spider silk,
and is girded with a strand of rowan berries.
"You seek us." His voice is deep and rich as the earth itself. "I
will take you to our dwelling place. Come."
He turns and strides into the wood.
I follow, crossing the pool. Cold water laps over my knees.
He leads me up a slight incline,
to a place where pines grow thick and strong,
scattered with copses of birch trees and elms.
We break through the tree line. A cliff rises sheer and straight
before us, blocking out the sky.
Butted up against the cliff is a stone structure thatched with
pine needles. Beside it march plants in neat rows.
I realize the structure is a house, the rows of plants a garden.
I ask: "Who lives here?"
My brother turns to me, a smile touching his face. "We do."
Ducking out of the low doorway come my other two brothers.
One has a beard of knotted moss,
the other a tangle of rowan berries growing out of his hair.
The one who led me here joins them.
I fall to my knees at their feet.
All three of them crouch down where I kneel.
The brother with the moss beard

touches my chin with his rough finger,

raises my face to his. "Little one. What is your name?"

"Our mother did not give me a name."

"Our mother does not like names. Names are power, you know." He smiles. "I am Pren. He is Cangen." Pren nods to the brother who met me at the pool. "And he is Criafol." Pren nods to the brother with the rowan berries in his hair. "We named ourselves. Not very cleverly, but the names belong to us and not to her. That gives us power for ourselves, do you see?" Pren takes my hands and raises me to my feet. Cangen and Criafol stand as well.

I say: "Perhaps."

Cangen says: "None of our other sisters sought us out. None of them found their names. But you have. That is why we heard you calling to us."

I draw myself up very straight. "I am Seren."

Cangen smiles. "And so you are. What request would you make of us, Seren?"

Fear twists through me,

but I have not come

all this way

for nothing.

"I met a boy in the wood. I spared his life. He told me I had a choice—that I choose to be our mother's monster. That I do not have to be. Do I? Do I have a choice?"

Rowan berries gleam in Criafol's green hair. "If you did not have a choice, you would not be here."

He gestures with one hand.

A branch grows up from the ground,

twists and flattens into a chair.

"Sit, little sister. Tell us everything." He waves his hand again, and three more chairs sprout up. My brothers sink comfortably into them.

I sit, too.

I tell my brothers about Owen,

about sparing him and his sister,

watching his house,

leaving him violets.

I even tell them

about dancing on the hill.

I do not tell them

that our mother stripped the skin from my back.

That my sister forced me to sing the railroad workers to their deaths.

That I am the reason his mother is dead.

Cangen, the brother who met me at the pool, says: "But what is it you wish from us?"

A sweet-smelling wind

blows down from the cliff,

wraps around me,

rustles the leaves in my hair. "I want to choose not to be her monster."

Pren says: "It sounds as if you already have." A yellow finch lands on his beard. He strokes its head with one finger. "What do you really want?"

I am not ready to answer.

I ask them a question instead. "What did you do to defy our mother? Why did she send you away?"

Criafol says: "She could not control us."

Cangen nods. "We could not overpower her."

The finch flits away. Pren says: "She wanted death. Wanted us to help her cover all the world with her trees, choke out all life that did not belong to the wood. But we had no wish to entangle ourselves in her petty quarrel with the Soul Eater."

"We tried to kill her." Cangen's eyes burn deep and sad. "We tried to take her heart, but we failed. We did not know it was protected."

I say: "Protected?"

Pren nods. "As long as her soul endures, her heart cannot be killed. Our power is great, but it is not that great."

"And so you came here." I gesture around the clearing. "To . . . garden?"

Criafol laughs. "We came to wait, until the end of her time, when we can roam freely through the wood again."

Their answers do not satisfy me.

I think perhaps they are cowards.

Their power is greater than mine,

yet they do not stand up against our mother,

do not help the humans.

They only hide.

"But you still have not answered my question." Pren peers at me, his beard bobbing against his chest. "What is it that you want from us?"

I say: "To wholly forsake the thing my mother made me. To become human."

Chapter Thirty-Five

OWEN

THE TRAIN RIDE IS LONG AND UNEVENTFUL, AND I ARRIVE IN Breindal just as the sun is setting. I disembark from the train, and step up to the ticket counter inside the station, where a white-haired old steward is yawning as he pulls down a metal grate to lock up for the evening.

"Excuse me," I say hastily. "Can you give me directions up to the palace?"

He scowls. "Just follow the road, boy. A babe could find it. But they won't let you in until morning. Gates shut strictly at seven." He slams his grate closed, effectively ending our conversation.

I don't have time to wait. I have to find my father and Awela *now*—I don't care about the gates being shut. The king is *going* to let me in.

Stars appear as I climb up the twisting city streets, toward the palace on its distant hill. They look dimmer here. Too much light and smoke from the city factories. I understand why the king sent my father to our house by the wood, to dark skies and clean air.

On the plains below the palace are the army barracks and training grounds. It's where I would have gone, if I'd listened to my father's advice and enlisted. I look south, toward Gwaed. According to the history books, there was a Tarian king some centuries back who took an army across the mountains and attempted to conquer Gwaed with no provocation. The Tarian army was defeated, and slunk back home. Gwaed suffered heavy enough losses that they made no pursuit, but relations between our two nations never quite recovered. If Gwaed decides to pick up the threads of old grievances and declare war, Tarian would be caught between an enemy army and the Gwydden's Wood. I don't think even King Elynion's army could survive that.

A pair of guards stand watch at the city's southern gates— beyond them is the only road up to the palace. Torchlight gleams on the rows of brass buttons marching down their uniform jackets, the brims of their caps shadowing their eyes. Both guards are armed with swords and muskets.

"Gates are shut," says the left guard gruffly. "Come back in the morning."

I fish my father's arrest warrant from my pocket, and hand it over. "I need to see the king."

The guard peruses it, then hands it to his fellow. "Come with me," says the right guard. He relieves me of the knife I put to Seren's throat just last night, then unlatches the gate and waves me through. He starts up the hill. I follow.

It's a steep climb. I'm panting and sweating by the time we reach the palace gates: tall arched doors made of stone, carved and painted in a green and gold pattern that is not immediately familiar to me. As the guard explains my presence to another pair of guards stationed here, my eyes make sense of the pattern: The green and gold are leaves and stars, intertwined with each other in an unending sequence. I wonder why our king, who has been at war with the Gwydden for longer than I've been alive, would adorn his palace with the symbols of her wood.

The city guard passes me off to one of the gate guards, who unlocks a small door inside of the gate and unceremoniously shoves me through.

I'm left alone in the palace courtyard, the gates at my back, high stone walls on either side thick with ivy. The palace itself looms ahead of me, an imposing structure that's all angles and arches, silhouetted against the rising moon. I shift the pack on my aching shoulders, and march up to the front door, where I show my father's arrest warrant to yet another pair of guards. They're both female and are young and old versions of each other, clearly related. The younger guard's hair is cropped to her chin; the older one wears hers in a long braid draped over one shoulder.

The older guard beckons me across the courtyard, and brings me through a door cut into the ivy-covered wall. We walk a few minutes down a stone corridor, lit by oil lamps, until she deposits me into a room that is clearly someone's office. A desk at the back is mounded with paper. A dilapidated bookshelf bows under the weight of far more books than it was meant to hold. A red ottoman boasts a tea tray mounded with dirty teacups and a smattering of half-eaten biscuits. From one corner, a brown and yellow cat peers at me suspiciously.

"Merrick's son," says the guard to the man sitting at the desk. He's thirty, perhaps, with dark hair and eyes, and what looks like a king's ransom in medals pinned to his cobalt blue uniform.

"Owen," I supply, as the guard salutes her captain and retreats.

"Owen. Yes. Sit down." He waves vaguely at the ottoman. "I'm Taliesin, captain of His Majesty's guard."

After an awkward moment and more gesturing from Taliesin, I relieve the ottoman of the tea tray, and take a seat. I hand the arrest warrant over. "There's been some mistake," I explain. "My father *works* for King Elynion. He would never do anything to betray our country. And I need to know what's happened to my sister. Is she safe? Is she here? I need to see her."

The captain puts his elbows on the desk, or rather on the thick stack of papers covering the desk, which he doesn't seem to notice. "Your sister is perfectly safe. But there's no mistake. Calon Merrick is in prison, awaiting his trial. I'm afraid his guilt is unmistakable, and he will face either execution or lifetime imprisonment, depending on the leniency of our king."

I try to shove down my flash of wild panic. "I don't understand. What is he charged with?"

Taliesin graces me with a condescending smile. "The details are known only to King Elynion himself, and your father, of course."

"Then how is his guilt 'unmistakable'?" I'm having a hard time not shouting.

Taliesin raises an eyebrow. "Do you accuse our king of lying?"

"Of course not! But my father's *life* is at stake. At least bring me to him. Let me talk to him. Let *him* explain it to me."

"I'm afraid that isn't possible. Your father is to see no one, lest he pass along his treasonous ideas."

"But what *are* they?"

Taliesin shrugs. "They're nothing for me, or for you, to concern ourselves with. Now, as to the matter of your father's house."

"Our *house*?"

He regards me with mild confusion, as if not remotely understanding my frustration. "Yes. Let me see." He shuffles through the papers on the desk for a moment, then pulls one out. "Your father's house, awarded to him by the king, is now forfeit to the crown. I'm afraid you will have to find some other place to live."

"WHAT?" I jerk to my feet, barely keeping myself from lunging across the desk at him.

Taliesin just hands me the paper, which I scan in a white-hot rage. It's hard to read when anger is making spots dance in front of my eyes, but I vaguely absorb its contents: the seizure of my father's house and possessions. I can't focus on the other things Taliesin said—can't think about "execution" or "life imprisonment." I feel myself separating—my mind going one way, my body frozen here.

"I'll take Awela then and go pack up the house," I say heavily, sinking back onto the ottoman. I think of Mother's cello in the closet, of the telescope and books in the observatory, of Awela's toys scattered about her little room, of her lace curtains, one of the last things Mother ever made. "I'll have everything sorted out by the end of the week. You have my word."

Taliesin frowns. "I'm afraid you don't understand."

If he says "I'm afraid" one more time, *I'm* afraid I may kill him. "What don't I understand?" I say through gritted teeth.

"The house *and all its contents* are forfeit to the crown. You can't go back."

"But our things—"

"Now belong to King Elynion," says the captain, enunciating each word loudly and slowly, as if he's speaking to a very stupid child.

I try to focus on breathing, try not to let the panic crawl into the edges of my vision. "Awela, then. Where is she?" I stare Taliesin down, daring him to keep her from me.

"The child is being looked after, but she is no longer your concern."

"She is my *sister*! Of *course* she's my concern. I demand to see her!"

"Owen." Taliesin sighs, steepling his fingers as he peers across the desk. "I'm afraid I must come to the point. As the son of a known traitor—"

"My father is not a traitor!"

"—you are suspect as well. If you will sign a document swearing you know nothing of your father's actions and are not in collusion with him—"

"How could I be in collusion with him? HE'S NOT A TRAITOR!"

"—then His Majesty is willing to offer you a post in the army. If you enlist, your sister will be raised as a daughter of the court, and never want for anything. She will of course not be told what befell your father."

"And if I do *not* join?" I hate this man with my whole being, and for a moment I wish I could drag him and the damned king into the Gwydden's Wood and leave them for the tree sirens. Memory flashes through me: my mother's heart, pouring her lifeblood onto molded leaves. Seren's eyes, her skin shining in the rain, violets tangled in her hair. I can barely breathe.

"If you do not join the army, Owen, I honestly don't know what will become of you. Your sister will still be looked after, but I can't think you'll ever be allowed to see her. Because what will you be? A beggar? A thief? Your sister must be protected from you and your father both."

I drop my head into my hands. "Please let me see her. She's lonely and scared. She needs me."

Taliesin scoffs. "She doesn't need you. Now give me your answer. Will you accept His Majesty's generous offer? Will you sign the statement that you know nothing of your father's actions, and enlist?"

I think of Father, head bent over his star charts, ink staining his fingers, his cup of cinnamon tea gone cold on the desk. I think of Awela, romping in the grass like a newborn lamb, her face stained with strawberries. I think of dancing on a hilltop to the music of a phonograph, four minutes at a time. I think of my mother turning to ash in a bloody wood.

"I appeal to the king," I say quietly.

"Speak louder, boy. I can't hear you."

I fling my head up, locking my eyes on Taliesin's. "I ap*peal* to the *king*. It's my right as a citizen of Tarian. You're bound by law to uphold that right."

The captain sighs, like I am the greatest inconvenience he's ever had to deal with in his life. Maybe I am. "Fine," he says, standing from his chair. "But I'm afraid you're not going to like it very much."

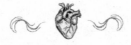

I'm not sure what I was expecting of the interior of the palace, but it isn't this: a foyer under a low ceiling, the walls covered in wood paneling, the carpet a deep mossy green. Taliesin leads me down a corridor lined with more wood paneling, carved intricately with leaves and vines. I have never seen so much wood in my life, and think fleetingly there must be a reason the Gwydden seems to hate the king so much. That's foolish, of course. She has no particular grievance with the king—she's centuries old and he was crowned only thirty years ago, when my father was a boy.

Glass lamps flicker from sconces on the wall, and it takes me a moment to realize they're not oil but electric, eerie and buzzing. I've always been fascinated by the concept of electricity, but now that I'm suddenly confronted with it, I find it more unsettling than anything else.

I'm surprised when the captain ushers me into a parlor off the main corridor. I was imagining we'd have to walk a long way to reach the king. He gestures at the claw-footed sofa facing an enormous pianoforte. "Wait here."

He steps back out into the hall, and shuts the door behind him.

I pace the room. Apart from the sofa and the pianoforte, there's a real wood-burning fireplace on the left wall with a narrow book-shelf beside it, and a window looking north. A clock hangs above the fireplace, the seconds ticking down. There aren't any electric lights in here, just an ordinary oil lamp on the end table.

I pace until my legs begin to ache, then trade off between peering out the window at the dim stars and perching on the sofa, neck craned around toward the door. I try not to look at the clock. An hour passes. Two. Three. Midnight approaches, and my stomach rumbles, reminding me I haven't eaten since the train. I wonder if the king forgot about me. I wonder if Taliesin even told him I'm here.

I grow stiff with waiting, my mind inventing terrible things: Awela locked in a prison cell, my father executed and buried in an unmarked grave, Seren, her silver fingers dripping blood, laughing as she steals my soul.

I ache for home, for the telescope in the observatory, for Awela sleeping soundly in her bed downstairs, for Father drinking tea at my elbow.

It's after four in the morning by the clock on the wall when the door at last, *at last*, creaks open.

I jerk up from the sofa, heart racing, and stare straight into the face of King Elynion. I know him from newspaper articles, from his portrait that hangs in the common room at the inn. He's far more imposing in real life. His piercing eyes are green, his beard is neatly trimmed, and his dark hair lies loose on his shoulders. He doesn't look a day over forty, and he's thin as a sapling.

Belatedly, I bow. My legs nearly give out.

"Well then, Owen Merrick. You have proved a very inconvenient ending to my day. Make your request and be done with it."

I gulp as I straighten up again, pleading with my body not to shake.

He folds his arms across his chest. "Well?"

"Your—Your Majesty." I chew on my lip. "I'd like to see my sister. And I'd like to know what my father is charged with, and to visit him as well."

The king frowns. He's wearing a green suit and jacket embroidered with gold thread, which glistens in the lamplight. I catch the scent of earth and damp leaves, and realize it's coming from him.

"No," he says.

I blink. "What?"

"No. You may not see your sister. You may not know what your father has done—if indeed you do not already know—and you may *certainly* not visit him. Is that all?"

It feels as if the room is closing in around me, and for a moment, I think I catch that same scent of decay that drenches the Gwydden's Wood. "Your Majesty, why can I not see my sister?"

"Because it is best for her if she forgets you and your father, and never remembers her life under the stars."

There's a roaring in my head. "Why?"

"So she does not grow up to commit the same treason."

"I don't understand what my father has done! Why won't you tell me?" My voice is high and strained—I'm *shouting* at the *king.*

He grabs my shoulders, his fingers digging into my skin. "It is by my grace alone that you are not currently languishing in a cell with your father. I believe my captain already presented you with my generous offer: Enlist in my army, train with my soldiers. Prove you are loyal to Tarian, to your king."

His fingers squeeze tighter still, and I gasp at the pain. "I *am* loyal. So is my father."

He laughs. "Tread carefully, Owen Merrick. Take the chance I give you. Enlist. Train. Prove you are no traitor. Perhaps one day I'll take you into my personal guard—maybe even let you see your sister again. But right now, there's too much at stake. So. Will you take my mercy? Or shall I throw you in prison and set the day for your execution?"

Spots dance in front of my eyes. Fear bites even deeper than the king's fingers, and I feel the intensity of my own helplessness.

"Answer me, boy."

I suck in a ragged breath.

He shakes me, hard. "Answer me!"

"I will take your mercy," I whimper.

He lets go of me, and I tumble to the floor. He brushes some speck of dust from his jacket. "Do not *dare* appeal to me again. Do you understand?"

"Yes, Your Majesty."

"Thank me for my magnanimity."

I'm trembling violently, and realize to my horror that tears are pouring down my face. I press my forehead into the carpet, groveling before him. "Thank you, Your Majesty."

I hear his step, the creak of the door, and I'm alone again.

It takes me some moments to collect myself. I wipe the tears from my eyes, untangle my limbs, stand. I can't stop shaking.

Taliesin appears at the door, holding a sheet of paper and a pen. The pen drips ink on the carpet. "I understand you have decided to enlist."

"Give me the damned paper," I growl at him.

He hands it over. I grab the pen and scrawl my name at the bottom of the page without reading a word.

Chapter Thirty-Six

SEREN

ANGEN SAYS GRAVELY: "WE DO NOT HAVE THE POWER TO SPIN you a soul. You understand that, don't you?"

"Then what can I do?" My voice cracks, breaks. "How can I forsake the monster I was created to be?"

"We can change your form." The sunlight gilds the rowan berries in Criafol's crown a liquid gold. "We can make you *appear* human. Essentially, you *would* be human, in all aspects but one. But your choices, your actions—those are up to you, as they have always been."

Hope grips me once more.

Fierce.

Bright.

Pren says: "Temporarily. We can *temporarily* make you appear human. Our mother's magic is stronger. We cannot thwart it forever."

I kneel before them,

bowing my head to the earth.

Dirt

scratches

my cheek.

I whisper: "Then make me human for as long as you can."

"Do not bow before us, little sister." Pren touches my face, lifts it to his. His expression is steeped in sorrow.

I say: "Please. I cannot bear to be the thing she made me a moment longer. Even if it is only for a little while. I want to know what it is like to be something else. *Someone* else."

All three of my brothers sigh, but they do not rebuke me.

Cangen takes my hand.

He lifts me to my feet again.

"It will hurt, dear one. The changing."

I think of my mother,

piercing my arms with her claws,

stripping the skin from my back.

I think of Owen's mother,

dead in the mud

because of me. "I do not care about the pain."

Cangen says: "Then come with us and be, for a little while, reborn."

Cangen walks with me. His rough hand encircles mine. Pren and Criafol flank us.

We return to the pool where Cangen first found me,

the waterfall crashing from the rocks above our heads,

sunlight refracting through the water.

Patches of rainbows glint,

dance.

I kneel on the edge of the pool,

my face

to the wood,

my back

to the waterfall.
Pren asks me, solemn: "Are you certain?"
I think of dancing with Owen under the stars
to the music of his magical device.
Of the hatred in his eyes
when his mother turned to ash.
Of
his
blade
at
my
throat.
You are only a monster because you choose to be.
This is me.
Choosing.
I say: "I am certain."
I bow my head.
My brothers begin to sing.
Their voices twine together in an intricate counterpoint,
around and between and through,
swelling louder and louder
until their song seems to envelop the wood.
The ground beneath me
shakes.
The waterfall behind me
roars.
Their music sinks into me,
slips under my skin,
through muscle and bone,
down to my heart.
It is slippery and silver,
sharp and cold.

Pain sears through me.
My skin cracks and
falls
from
my
flesh.
My bones bend and
bend and
bend
until they snap
in a blaze of agony.
I am enveloped in fire,
in a million stinging wasps,
in the flash of white-hot lightning.
I am falling,
drowning,
broken.
I am devoured
bit by bit,
torn apart
by ravenous teeth.
But through it all
I see
Owen on our hill.
I taste
strawberries and cream.
I feel
his mouth warm and soft on mine.
I slide sideways onto the earth, and suddenly I can breathe again.
The sky wheels wide and blue above me.
The pool laps quietly beside.
A voice says: "Easy. You must take it easy, at first."

Hands grasp my arms, help me sit up.

I focus on three craggy faces, one hung heavy with a mossy beard.

Criafol says: "Look into the pool. See what you have become."

I drag myself to the water's edge. I do not have the strength to stand, to walk.

I am strange and uncertain.

I feel heavy and light all at once, and I do not recognize the weight of my limbs, of my head, of my body.

Hair blows about my shoulders, unencumbered by leaves.

There is no scent of violets.

I look into the water, waiting for the ripples to dissipate, for the pool to grow still.

But when it does—

When it does, I do not recognize the face looking back at me.

It is a pale, round face, set with green eyes and framed by yellow hair. I hold up my hands, staring at them in turn: human hands, human fingers. My skin is strange and smooth. All of me is unfamiliar.

I turn to my brothers with tears on my cheeks.

Criafol says: "Why are you crying, little one?" He looks as though his heart might break. "We thought this is what you wanted."

"I do not want to go back." My voice is strange and high. "I do not ever want to go back to being her monster."

Droplets of water catch in Pren's beard. "This form is only temporary. We thought you understood."

"There has to be a way." I tremble. This body feels the cool touch of the wind in a way my other body never did. "I want a soul. I want to be mortal. To be truly human. I will do anything."

"Dear one." Cangen peers at me with sad eyes. "We do not have that power."

"There has to be a way." My vision blurs as the tears keep

coming, more and more, like I am a spring that cannot be quenched.

Pren sighs. "There is one way, but dear one, you will not like it."

"Tell me. I will do anything."

Pren looks at Criafol, at Cangen. Both of them shake their heads. "Please."

Criafol waves his hand. A dress of leaves folds over me, bringing a little warmth back into this frail body.

Pren says: "To become wholly as you are, you must give up the thing you hold most dear: You must carve out your heart, and bury it in the green earth. Then, and only then, do you have a chance to become human. To become mortal. To be given a soul that will endure even when your body is gone."

Anger sprouts vicious thorns inside of me. "If I carve out my heart, I will *die*!"

Pren shakes his head. "That is the only way that we have ever heard of. I am sorry, little one."

"How long do I have in this form?"

Criafol says: "We do not know. We hope for as long as you need."

I need forever.

Cangen's brows bend close together on his craggy face. "Where will you go? You will need food, clothing, shelter."

"I will go to him. I will go to Owen."

Pren says: "The boy has gone to the palace of the Soul Eater."

My human body shakes at the name of the only monster I fear more than my mother.

Wind races down from the cliff, coiling around my ankles, tangling in my hair. "Then that is where I must go."

Chapter Thirty-Seven

OWEN

TALIESIN DEPOSITS ME IN ONE OF THE BARRACK DORMITORIES, A small room crammed with two sets of triple bunks and already occupied by five slumbering soldiers. I clamber into the middle bunk on the right wall—the only empty one—and find it's been stripped of both mattress and pillow. There's only a hard board between me and the bunk below, with not even a sheet to lie on. I use my pack as a pillow and attempt to sleep, but my mind is too wild with anger to let me.

I'm damned if I'm going to let the king keep me from Awela. Or leave my father to languish in prison for treason he didn't commit.

I think back to that last night I spent with Father in the observatory, meteors raining down from Heaven like it was the end of days. The shifting constellations. The changing stars.

Father told me he was going to send a telegram to the king to inform him about the anomaly.

And then he'd been arrested.

It can't be a coincidence, but it doesn't make any sense. Anyone could look at the night sky now and know it was different than it had been last week. It wasn't something to get thrown into prison for.

Was it?

Do you know why he does it? the king's man asked me all those weeks ago. *Why he pays your father for these charts every month?*

Was this it? Was the impossible transformation of the stars the thing the king had been waiting for? Watching for? That doesn't make any sense, either. No one could possibly have known that that meteor shower was going to happen. I saw it myself and I still hardly believe it.

I roll onto my side on the hard bunk. I'll play the king's game, I'll be a soldier—I don't have any choice. But I'm also going to find Awela and uncover the truth about my father. If I can't convince the king of his innocence, I'll find a way to break him out of prison, and the three of us will flee to Saeth. We can start a new life there. Away from the king and the war and the wood. Away from all of this.

I jolt awake to the sharp call of a trumpet and the muttered curses of my bunkmates. I can't have slept more than an hour, and my eyes feel like they're full of sand.

In the light of a single overhead lantern, the five other soldiers tug on their uniforms, somehow managing to not bump into each other in the limited floorspace. They're all about my own age, a couple of them maybe even younger, and they take no notice of me.

They all stumble out the door, and I roll over in the awful bunk, deciding I may as well get some more sleep—Taliesin left me with no instructions, and I secretly hope no one knows I'm here.

But half a moment later, the older female guard from last night comes in, and scolds me roundly for still being in bed. She introduces herself as Commander Carys, and makes me turn in my clothes—including the extra sets in my pack—in exchange for an army uniform: blue trousers, white shirt, blue jacket. There's boots, too, a matching blue cap, and a heavy sword belt. She stands there with her arms crossed the whole time I'm getting dressed, which I do as quickly as possible, flushing hotter and hotter with every moment that passes. The uniform is staggering and stifling; it makes me feel claustrophobic.

Carys orders me outside when I've got it on, and I have my first view of the barracks in the daylight: ugly, sprawling buildings made of mud bricks. She points out the four training fields, a gun range, a riding arena, a mess hall, and a bathhouse, which she informs me I won't be able to use until I get my first paycheck, as each visit costs a whole silver penny. I'll have to use the pump in the courtyard until then.

Then she tells me to report to one of the training fields, where the commanding officer makes me run laps with a handful of other new recruits.

The uniform is heavy and suffocating, and I'm not used to running. I'm used to sitting in Father's observatory painstakingly filling in the star charts, or weeding the garden while Awela digs for worms. Not even the smallest part of me belongs here. But I've nowhere else to go, and I refuse to give up my proximity to my father and sister.

So I force myself to keep running. I collapse on the field after five laps and am brought directly to the medical tent.

The nurse on duty is a dark-skinned woman with shrewd eyes and a blue cap pinned to her tightly curled hair. She gives me water from a canteen and tells me to drink it slowly.

I do, my eyes flitting about the tent, listening to the shouts and pounding footsteps drifting in from the training fields. It's a relief to be in here, away from the brutal glare of the sun. I wish I never had to leave, but only moments later, the nurse says I can go.

"Work up to the drills slowly, you hear?" she tells me with a shake of her head. "I'd wager you've never run a mile in your life. You shouldn't try to do ten all at once."

My cheeks warm. I mumble thanks and duck back outside.

After that I report to a different training field for sword drills, which are conducted by the younger female guard from last night. Her name is Luned, and she's Commander Carys's daughter. She has me and a dozen other recruits practice guard stances, footwork, and raising and lowering heavy wooden swords in thrusts and parries until I'm certain my arm is going to fall off. It only gets worse when we trade our swords for muskets, and are made to load, tamp, aim, and fire at hay bales draped in brightly painted canvas. My ears ring with the noise of the guns, and my left shoulder *hurts* from the recoil of the musket ramming into me again and again.

By the time Luned dismisses us for lunch, not only am I fairly convinced I'm dying, I almost want to. We're fed lentil stew and days-old bread in the mess tent, and I itch to be back home in the kitchen, yelling at Awela to stop flinging her porridge in all directions while I chop lamb and veggies to put in our cawl.

In the afternoon, there's riding drills and marching drills that fill the time until dinner. Afterward, a majority of the soldiers tromp off to the bathhouse, while the rest of them play cards in the mess hall, bemoaning the fact that there isn't time to go down into the city and be back before the gates shut for the night.

I drag my weary body up the hill to the palace, following a worn track from the training fields that leads to the kitchen courtyard. It's as good a place to start looking for Awela as any—I'm not about to attempt the front door.

A harried-looking serving woman is plucking chickens just inside the courtyard gate. "If you're sniffing about my girls, you can go right back down to the barracks, young man," she informs me curtly.

I'm rather offended at her implication. My face warms. "I'm not sniffing about at anyone."

"Then you were sent up to help?" Her whole face brightens.

"We're so short-staffed, and the king *will* have his feasts every night. There's a mountain of potatoes to peel. Go on."

Before I have a chance to protest, she shoos me inside, where I find she was *not* exaggerating. A pale-skinned serving girl stands at a huge wooden counter in the center of the room, dutifully peeling the potatoes that cover nearly the entirety of it. This seems to be some kind of back room to the kitchen proper, which I glimpse bustling past another doorway. The serving girl looks up as I come in, and her eyes grow huge. Her hand slips with the knife, and she yelps, blood welling red on one finger. She stares at the cut and turns almost green. She looks like she might pass out.

"It's just a little blood," I say hurriedly, grabbing a clean-looking rag and pressing it against the cut. "It doesn't look that deep."

She sucks in shallow, panicked breaths as I tear another rag into strips and tie one of them tight around her wounded finger. She leans against the counter and, slowly, returns to her normal color.

"Are you all right?" I ask.

She nods mutely, still staring at me with her large eyes. She's pretty in a pale sort of way, with blonde hair pinned badly underneath her maid's cap, and a generous allotment of freckles covering her nose. Her blue uniform and crisp white apron hang overlarge on her skinny frame.

"I can help for a few minutes," I say, grabbing a spare knife and starting in on the potato mound, "but I'm really here to sneak into the palace. I'm looking for someone. Could you show me to the servants' entrance?"

She nods again and picks her own knife back up.

We peel together in silence for longer than I mean to, and the light outside the window begins to fade. We've made barely a dent in the potatoes.

"Thank you for helping," she tells me, when I tell her I have to go. "I can bring you through the kitchen now."

She does, leading the way through a huge rectangular room, where cooks and servants vie for space amongst four iron stoves and a half-dozen work stations. Thankfully, they're too busy to notice us.

"That way," she instructs, pointing to the narrow stairway that winds up from the kitchen.

I smile at her. "Thanks. I'm Owen, by the way."

"Bedwyn," she returns, with an unnecessary bow. "And thank you for binding my hand. I—I don't like blood."

I shudder at the unbidden memory of the train passengers, slaughtered in the wood. Of my mother, cradling her heart in her hands. "I don't either," I reply, and climb the stairs.

I want to search the palace for any sign of Awela, but it proves more difficult than I'd thought. There are servants and nobility roaming the halls, and I'm terrified of bumping into the king around every corner. I do my best, darting down hallways and hiding behind large potted trees, the sight of which make my skin crawl.

It seems the king is obsessed with the Gwydden and the wood— there's evidence of her influence everywhere, from murals and tapestries depicting the wood itself to floor tiles patterned with leaf designs, and, of course, the potted trees. Each floor seems to be going for a slightly different section of the forest—oaks on one floor, elms on another, birches on another still. These last ones make me shiver.

Every hallway flickers with more of those eerie electric lights. The whole palace hums with them, giving it an unnerving energy that feels like insects crawling up my spine.

I wind my way nearly to the top floor of the palace without finding the slightest hint of Awela's whereabouts. But at least now I have a general idea of the layout, and can focus my search better tomorrow.

The stars have been out quite a while by the time I crawl into the horrible bunk in my dormitory. My exhausted body drops immediately into sleep, and I dream I hear Awela screaming.

I wake to the sharp blast of that damned trumpet, and drag myself from the bunk to do everything all over again.

Another day passes in an excruciating haze, and the second night's search of the palace ends in disaster. I'm caught on the birch tree floor, and the guard who finds me drags me all the way to Taliesin's office for judgment. Taliesin seems exasperated to have to suffer my presence again so soon after our last meeting. He barely looks at me as he waves a dismissive hand and orders me to be whipped.

Chapter Thirty-Eight

SEREN

GRASS AND SKY BLUR PAST THE TRAIN WINDOW.
I dig my fingernails into the seat cushion.
I try to banish my fear.
The whole car rattles and shakes,
like it will break apart at any moment
and spew me out onto the earth.

"First train ride?" It is the woman across the aisle. She has skin
as pale as mine, with smooth dark hair and a book open on her lap.

I look at her without speaking. I nod.

She tells me with confidence: "You'll get used to it. We're perfectly safe—it's not like we're headed into the Gwydden's Wood!
Although between you and me, I wouldn't take the train to Saeth
these days for anything."

I grimace at her with what I hope is a smile.

I turn away.

I press my face against the train window. The glass is cold.

I never thought I would be at the mercy
of the humans' iron machines
as they were once
at my mercy.
Yet here I am encased in one,
like sap in a tree.
My brothers told me the way to Owen's village.

They gave me coins they had found in the wood years ago, enough for the plain gray dress I am wearing, enough for a train ticket.

Not enough for shoes, or the food this frail body craves. My human stomach growls, loud enough for the woman across the aisle to hear.

"Haven't you brought a sandwich?" She is incredulous.

I shake my head.

"Well, here, you must have one of mine. I made too many."

I do not accept or decline, but I find her settling into the seat next to me, drawing food out of her bag.

I take it, because my body demands me to.

I eat, and think about strawberries.

I sip something sweet from the cylindrical container she offers me.

While I chew, she says: "What sends you to Breindal City? I'm visiting my sister. She's in the army, you know—she just made commander! I am excessively proud of her. My talents lie in a completely different direction. I make sandwiches and knit sweaters and keep our old mother company, and here she is off protecting Tarian!"

She chatters on and on. She does not seem to require an answer to her initial question. This suits me.

But after a while she stops recounting every detail of her life and studies me. Her face softens. "You seem to have come upon a hard time, my dear. Do you have somewhere to stay in Breindal?"

I shake my head.

"You'll be looking for work, then. You should try up at the palace—they're always needing new servants. According to my sister, so many of the maids have gone to join the army, they're shockingly short-staffed. Just mention Carys's name at the door—that's my sister—and tell them she's sent you. They're sure to hire you right away." She pats my arm. "But I'll let you sleep now."

Her kindness humbles me. Tears prick hot in my eyes. "Thank you. For the advice. And the sandwich."

She smiles. "Don't mention it, my dear. Don't mention it." She goes back to her own seat.

I lean my head against the window, my eyes sliding shut.

The motion of the train lulls me to sleep.

When I wake, it's pulling into the station.

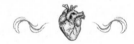

The chaos of the city overwhelms me.

The noise, the press of people, the *stench*.

It is steeped in filth and smoke,

with buildings squeezed so tightly together they seem to leer over the street.

I am lost among them.

My companion from the train warned me that there would not be time to get to the palace tonight. She suggested I take a room at an inn until morning. She even gave me money for it.

I tried to refuse, but she just shook her head and folded my hands tightly around the coins. "You need them more than I do, dear." Then she gave me careful, detailed directions, and we went our separate ways.

Even with her directions, I get lost.

I can read, thanks to Owen's lessons on our hill, but I cannot make any sense of the street signs. And there is just so much *noise*.

I can hardly breathe.

But I stumble upon the inn at last, and hand over the coins to the woman in charge.

My head pounds and my feet hurt from my long walk on the hard stone streets.

She frowns at my lack of shoes, but ushers me up a creaking narrow stair to a little room on the top floor anyway.

She snaps: "Dinner's downstairs," and goes away again.

The room makes me panic even more than the crowded streets.

How do people *live* shut indoors all the time?

How do they breathe?

At least there is a window. I figure out how to open it. I poke my head out into the night air. It is heavy with smoke and unpleasant smells, but it makes me feel a little easier.

My human body is too tired to go downstairs again. It drags me to the narrow bed.

I lay my head on the pillow, shut my eyes.

I sleep.

In the morning, the cross innkeeper begrudgingly gives me a bowl of something called porridge. It is sweet and good, but so hot it scalds my mouth.

I have a long, miserable walk through the city, all the way up to the gates that lead to the Soul Eater's palace.

My feet are cut and bleeding by the time I get there. The two men standing watch look at me suspiciously. "No beggars here, girl. Away with you."

I hold myself very straight. I try not to tremble. "I am not a beggar. I was told there is work, up in the palace. A woman called Carys sent me."

The name works just as my train companion promised it would.

I am let through the gate and taken up the hill, around the massive front doors of the Soul Eater's palace, to a smaller entrance around to the side.

It frightens me, being this close to the Soul Eater. But if Owen is truly here, I have to find him.

Protect him.

Get him safely away before my human form falls away and I am once more revealed to be a monster.

I am ushered through a wooden door into a small room.

Flames leap greedily in a stone hearth.

Heat curls off of it. I scramble backward until my shoulders press up against the wall.

The guard who brought me frowns. "What's wrong with you? Have you never seen a fire before? Sit." He waves me onto a low cushioned stool.

I obey, sitting as far away from the fire as possible.

The guard instructs: "Wait here." He disappears through another door that leads, perhaps, farther into the palace.

I am even more uneasy in here than I was in my room in the inn.

I cannot see the sky or feel the wind, and the fire burns and burns, reaching out its many wicked tongues. It laughs at the thought of devouring me. Even from across the room, its heat pulses on my skin.

The inner door creaks open, and a dark-skinned woman in a pretty blue dress comes in. Her black hair is pulled back into a severe bun. She is short and plump. She thunders: "Who let you in here?"

I stare at her, terrified.

"Well?" she demands.

"I—I came about a job. The woman on the train told me to come. Her sister is Carys."

The woman sighs. "Carys's sister will be the death of me. Can you actually work? You look like a breath of wind might blow you away."

I blink at her, confused.

She clarifies: "Can you clean things? Wash dishes and boil laundry and scrub floors?"

"Yes," I say, though I do not have even the slightest idea what that means.

"It pays room, board, and meals but nothing else. Does that suit you?"

I nod.

"Well then. It's not like I have a lot of applicants, so you're hired, I suppose." She sighs. "I'm Heledd, which is what you will call me. Now, first things first." She grabs a length of blue and white cloth that was draped over a chair, and hands it to me. "Put this on. You look like a wild creature in that thing you're wearing."

I obey, though stripping the dress I bought with my brothers' money feels somehow like shedding the last of my skin.

I pull the blue dress awkwardly over my head. The fabric is rough. It scratches.

Heledd fastens the back of the dress. "I'll go and find you some shoes—can't have you trotting about the kitchens with bloody feet. Back in a tick." She disappears through the doorway.

I sink onto the cushioned stool, tugging at the collar of the dress.

I breathe slowly, in and out, eyeing the fire with distaste.

I shut my eyes and reach out for the threads of Owen's soul—I will be easier when I know exactly where he is.

But I feel nothing, because I am human now.

I do not have the power of my monstrous body.

Heledd is back the next moment, with horrible black shoes she makes me put on, no matter how much I tell her they hurt.

She says dismissively: "You'll get used to them. Now follow me. You're needed in the laundry this morning."

She beckons me through the door.

I step into a narrow corridor in the Soul Eater's palace.

Heledd leads me down the hall. "What did you say your name was?"

I have thought of this. I cannot call myself Seren—Owen cannot know I am here.

So I give her another word he taught me instead.

"My name is Bedwyn."

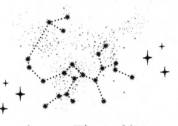

Chapter Thirty-Nine

OWEN

"YOU AGAIN," SIGHS THE NURSE IN THE MEDICAL TENT. "I didn't expect to see you back so soon." She spreads healing salve on my shoulders, but even her gentle fingers exacerbate the pain of the lash marks. My whole back feels like it's on fire—I had to be carried in here. "What did you do, anyway?"

"Snuck into the palace," I mutter into the cushion of the healer's bed. My throat is raw from screaming. "Got caught." And I'm no closer to Awela than before.

She laughs a little, but not at all unkindly, finishing with the salve and unwinding a length of white bandage. She wraps it carefully over one shoulder, across my chest, then crosses it in an X and does the other shoulder. "Why were you sneaking around the palace?"

I focus on breathing. "Looking for my sister." Awela's absence pinches at my insides. I haven't even *tried* to see my father.

"I hope they put you on kitchen duty tomorrow," she grumbles. "It's not like you can attend any of your training sessions *now*." She ties off the bandage and helps me ease into a sitting position.

I duck my head to hide the tear stains streaking my face.

"Nothing to be ashamed of." She smiles and taps my nose. "I have literally seen it all. Now. What *do* they have you doing tomorrow?"

"I'm on stable duty."

She rolls her eyes. "Not very efficient of them, but good luck to you." She presses a steaming mug into my hands, and I sip slowly. The tea is bitter, and I make a face.

"Willow bark," she says, "for the pain. Get some rest, now. I'll change your bandages in the morning. You'll feel a little better, then." She kisses my forehead like I'm her child, and helps me lie back down again.

I sleep fitfully in the healer's tent, unused to the shadows and noises. The healer wakes me in the morning, changes my bandages, and apologetically helps me to my feet. She hands me a packet of more willow bark. "Chew some if the pain gets too bad. Come again this evening for fresh bandages. If it were up to me, you'd stay."

I thank her and shuffle from the tent. Every step sends shooting pain up and down my back, but I make my stiff, slow way to the stables, where I am given a pitchfork and shovel and instructed to muck twelve stalls.

In my current condition, the work is agonizing. Blood and sweat seep through my bandages. Blisters begin to form on my hands. I chew strips of willow bark until the bitterness overwhelms me and I spit them out again.

I've only gotten through one stall when there's a step behind me, a light voice calling my name.

I turn to find Bedwyn there, holding a tray of food. Strands of pale gold hair slip out from underneath her maid's cap, curling slightly on her neck. Her eyes are green, I note, with flecks of sliver.

"Lunch," she says, nodding at the tray. "For you," she adds when I don't answer.

I recollect myself, accept the tray, and sink gingerly to a seat in the main aisle of the stable. "Thank you."

She doesn't slip away like I'm expecting, just watches as I eat. I inhale the food: a cheese and chicken sandwich, a glass of icy milk. Maybe being away from the mess hall on stable duty with my back torn to shreds isn't the worst thing after all.

I hand the tray back when I'm done, but she still doesn't leave. "Do you need some help? You helped me with the potatoes the other night."

"I'm supposed to do it myself."

Her eyes flit to my blood-soaked shirt. "You won't be able to finish."

She is not exactly wrong. "Won't they miss you in the kitchens?"

She shrugs and sets the tray down in the aisle again. "I don't think so. I'm new here and known for being quite stupid."

I smile. "You're not stupid."

"Oh, I am. The cook has told me I'm almost entirely useless. I have been banned from the kitchen and the laundry, and this morning I dropped a bucket of wash-water on a priceless rug. I only bring people things now. It's all I'm trusted with, and even then only just." She tilts her head and smiles at me. Her eyes dance as she gestures at the stalls. "So you'll have to tell me exactly what to do."

Bedwyn cleans the rest of the stalls herself—she doesn't even let me get up. She's surprisingly strong for a slip of a girl, and I find myself admiring her in a way that startles me.

She slides down beside me when she's finished, grimy and caked in sweat, but she smells faintly sweet. Like wildflowers opening in the sun.

"Do I know you?" I ask her, without meaning to.

Her smile falters a little. She shakes her head. "Only from the potatoes." Gentle fingers skim across the bandages on my shoulders. "I am sorry for your pain. They had no right."

I start to shrug, and wince. "They can do whatever they want."

"Did you find whoever it was you were looking for the other night?"

"No. And they caught me sneaking around, so I don't know how I'll even keep looking."

Her face pinches. "Who are you looking for? Not . . . not the Soul Ea—I mean the king?"

I look at her strangely. "I've had one meeting with the king, and that was quite enough for me."

She shudders, goes even paler than she already is. "I hate being so close to him. He frightens me."

"I'm not exactly fond of him anymore either, but why does he frighten you?"

"He's a monster," she says simply. Her voice wavers on that word.

My insides clench up. "I thought the only monsters were the ones in the wood."

It's the wrong thing to say. She jerks away from me, snatches the tray, hugs it to her chest. "The housekeeper will be missing me. I had better go now." Her gaze darts everywhere but to me.

I'm not sure how to make her feel at ease again. "Thank you for helping me. I couldn't have managed on my own."

Her eyes flit to mine. "I can search the palace for you," she offers. "I am only supposed to go where I am sent—" Her face tightens—something else she's clearly been reprimanded for. "But everyone thinks me stupid enough to keep getting myself lost. Who *are* you looking for?"

"My little sister. She's only two, and I think the king is keeping her shut up somewhere in the palace. I have to find her."

Bedwyn nods. "I'll look," she promises. She stares at me for a moment more, then quirks a little smile at me and is gone.

For a moment I just sit there, staring after her, and then I drag my aching body up and go report to Carys that I've finished with the stables.

She informs me I'll be back to my regular drills tomorrow, and then unexpectedly sends me straight up to the kitchen for dish-washing duty. I'm not expecting to be elbow-deep in soap suds when Bedwyn comes in, carrying a tray piled precariously with dirty dishes.

She's not expecting to see me, either.

She drops the tray.

Chapter Forty

SEREN

B EING HUMAN IS THE STRANGEST THING THAT HAS EVER HAPPENED to me. My body grows hungry and weary. My hands grow chapped and rough with work. My feet and back and arms ache from standing and walking and carrying. My mind is dizzy with remembering the layout of the palace, the instructions of the cook and the housekeeper, the names of the other maids, the names of *things*.

And every time I see Owen, I ache. That first night, when he helped me peel potatoes. This afternoon in the stables, his bloody back making me want to strangle the Soul Eater with my own two hands. I know it is the Soul Eater's fault. It has to be.

Now he is here in the dish room, on his knees, scrambling to pick up pieces of broken plates while I gape at him like a fish drowning in air on a riverbank. He's changed his shirt, but red still seeps through.

I force my body to move, to act. I kneel with him, minding the jagged edges.

"Do you have a broom?" he asks when we've collected all the larger pieces.

I nod to the closet in the corner, and he goes to fetch it, bending and sweeping up the rest of the mess, though I know it pains him. He winces with every movement.

"I have to get back to the dishes or my commanding officer will kill me," he says when he's finished.

"I was supposed to wash all that," I admit, staring helplessly at the dustbin.

He laughs. "Less work for both of us, then."

I join him at the sink, plunging my arms into the scalding soapy water. We work companionably side by side for some moments, him washing, me rinsing and then stacking the dishes neatly in their racks to dry.

"Why are you here?" I blurt after a while.

He looks at me. "My father was arrested on charges of treason. Both him and my sister were taken here. I'm trying to work out a way to free them."

Unease twists through me. I think of his sister. I am afraid I know why the Soul Eater wants her.

I want to tell Owen everything—confess who I am and why I am here. I want him to look into my eyes and see me for myself, and not revile me. I want him to dance with me again, like he did on our hill in the wood.

But I cannot tell him. I cannot ever tell him. Because the last time I saw him, his mother tore out her own heart and died on the ground like an animal. Because of my mother.

Because of me.

I will never forgive you for what you did to my mother. If I ever see you again, I will kill you.

So instead I tell him I will look for his sister as soon as I can slip away. I tell him to wait for me in the kitchen courtyard when the moon is high, and if I have news of her, I will meet him there.

He looks into my eyes. He smiles at me. Thanks me.

But only because he does not know who I am.

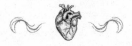

There are moments when I sense my power, lurking just beneath my skin, moments when I can reach the threads of my old life, remember the spark and pull of a human's soul. I can sense Owen's again. I have to concentrate, stand very still and *reach* in a way I did not have to when I was wholly my mother's monster. But I can feel it. I do not know if that means my human skin is already fraying around the edges, or if I have simply gotten used to this form.

Whatever it is, it will help me find Awela. When I slip from the kitchen with a tray of food meant to be brought up to a nobleman's sick wife, I stop in an out-of-the-way corridor, press my shoulders up against the wall, and *reach* for her. At first I do not feel anything, but I reach deeper, further. And there—the glimmer of her soul. She is here, somewhere. Owen was right.

Uneasiness worms through me. I grip the tray tighter, and take the servants' stair to the next floor. The feel of Awela's soul is still faint, but it seems a little stronger. I climb to the next floor, then the next. The pull of her soul grows bright and strong.

I am on the top level of the palace, a many-paned window at the end of the corridor looking west over the plains far, far below. There are no trees up here, like there are on every other floor; the walls are painted with birds and bright flowers. Violets spill out of tall clay pots. There is only one door, and the tug of Awela's soul pulses strongly behind it.

I am still carrying the dinner tray, and so I step up to the door and knock. A pale, white-haired old woman opens it. Beyond her a dark-haired child plays with toys scattered on the rug, her soul burning bright.

The old woman moves to block my view of Awela. "I didn't send for food," she says coldly. "And you're not the usual maid. What are you doing up here?"

"I took the wrong stair." I duck my head. "Forgive me."

She frowns and shuts the door in my face.

I go and deliver the food to the nobleman's wife, who shouts at me because I took so long and her dinner's gone cold. Then it is back down to the kitchen, where I expect Owen to still be washing dishes, but he is not—one of the regular girls is at the sink.

The remainder of the day passes slowly. Heledd gives me real tasks again, because I have not done anything too disastrous today, and there is no one else to do them. So I scrub floors and deliver food and polish silver with a stinking paste that lingers even when I have washed my hands four times.

At last I am given my own dinner, and when I am finished, I step into the courtyard to dump the potato peels in the slop bin to be brought to the pigs in the morning. Owen is there, leaning against the wall. I yelp when I see him, and drop the bucket of peels.

He laughs as he bends down to help me pick them up. "I'm not trying to scare you, you know."

My face warms as I scoop peels back into my bucket. "The moon is not even out yet."

The sun hangs low on the horizon, the last orange rays slanting through the courtyard. Owen shrugs. "If I had crawled into my bunk I would have fallen asleep and not come at all. Did you find her?"

I dump the rest of the peels into the slop bin. "How do you even know I had a chance to look?"

"Just a feeling."

The setting sun swathes him in orange light. He is so beautiful it makes me ache. "She is shut in a room on the top floor.

There is a woman with her."

"Can you bring me there?"

"I can, but the woman will not like it. She won't let us in—she will probably call the guards and—" My eyes flick to his shoulders. He's wearing another clean shirt, and there is no red seeping through anymore.

Owen waves his hand like he is batting a fly. "We'll find some way around her. Can we go now?"

"Now?"

"Might not have another chance."

He is right. The woman might be suspicious of me; if she tells the Soul Eater, he might move Awela somewhere else—or worse. Fear pulses sharp beneath my breastbone. "Come with me."

I lead him through the kitchen, then up the servants' staircase to the main floor of the palace. We duck behind a wall to avoid another maid, then skitter up a staircase.

Two staircases later, and we have to dart into a random room when we hear footsteps coming toward us down the hall. The foot-steps approach the room, and we exchange frantic glances and dive under the couch on the back wall.

We stare at each other in the musty semi-darkness. I take quick, shallow breaths. I am suffocating, too far from the earth and the sky. I shake. I swallow a scream. Owen takes my hand, his fingers warm overtop of mine. Our mingled heartbeats pound together in the soft underside of my wrist.

The nobleman sinks into a chair opposite the couch, a book in one hand, a glass of wine in the other. He drinks and reads, and does both things maddeningly slow. I grow stiff and sore as we wait for him to leave. Owen never lets go of my hand. His presence calms me, keeps me tethered to my human form.

Beyond the palace the last of the sunlight fades. Shadows swallow the room piece by piece. At last, the nobleman lays down his book and goes back out into the hall.

We wait one heartbeat, two, three. Then Owen squeezes my hand, and we crawl out from under the couch. He pulls me to my feet. We wait by the door another excruciating moment, but we do not hear anything outside of it. We leave the room behind us and barrel on down the hall and up the last few floors.

Owen is laughing again, a wheezy, breathless noise. But it is choked off when he sees the violets, spilling from their pots. Anger tightens his face. "He *would* have these cursed flowers up here."

My pulse throbs in my throat. I have no answer for him. "What now?" I say quietly.

He takes a breath, tears his eyes away from the violets. "We have to get the woman to leave. Can you tell her she's wanted downstairs? Or that you were sent to relieve her?"

I nod. "But there is nowhere for you to hide."

He glances at the flowerpots again. They are fairly large, and there are no lamps burning in the hall. The shadows should conceal him.

He grabs my hand, squeezes once, then crouches between two of the pots at the far end of the corridor. I would not know he was there if I had not seen him hide.

I step up to the door. Knock.

The woman creaks the door open and scowls at me. "Don't tell me you got lost again, girl. What do you really want? I've just got the child to sleep."

"Heledd sent me to relieve you." The lie slides out easily. "She said you are to have a few hours off."

The woman's face lights up. "It's about time! I'm lucky anyone remembers to send food up, let alone give me a moment away. I'll be back by morning, but not before." She pushes past me without another word, mumbling something about finding a proper drink.

Her footsteps clatter on the stairs, and fade slowly away.

Owen appears at my side. "Thank you," he says seriously.

He goes in alone. I sink to a seat by one of the violet pots to wait for him.

Chapter Forty-One

OWEN

MY SISTER IS SLEEPING IN A LITTLE BED UNDER A WINDOW, hugging a stuffed bear tight to her chest, a blanket pulled up to her shoulders. It's a charming room, filled with books and toys, a child's tea set, a mock sword. But it still angers me—has she been kept here since my father's arrest, never allowed out of doors?

I hate to wake her, but I do, sinking down onto the bed beside her, gathering her into my arms.

She opens her eyes and squints up at me. "Wen?" she mumbles.

"I'm here, Awela."

She hugs me tight and cries into my neck. My own tears drip into her hair. "Are they treating you well, little darling?"

She doesn't understand the question enough to answer it, just bunches my shirt in her little hand and asks for Father.

"We can't see him just yet, dearest."

"PAPA!" she screeches.

When she's screamed herself out, she wiggles from my arms and goes to show me her toys: blocks and dolls and wooden beads on brightly colored strings. I admire them all, wishing I could scoop her up and take her home and all would be as it was before.

"Why is the king keeping you here, little one?" I wonder aloud. "Just to punish my father for some imagined slight?"

Awela bursts into tears.

"Awela, what's wrong?"

"King!" she sobs, shaking her head. "No king, no king, no king."

My stomach drops. "The king has been to see you? Why?"

But of course she can't tell me. I hold her until she's grown calm again, yawning against my chest.

I try to think—I should have planned better. I should have found a way to break my father out of prison so the three of us could flee the palace tonight. Leave Tarian forever. I can't take Awela and leave my father behind. But how can I leave her *here*?

I tell myself it's enough that I've found her, for now. It has to be. I have nowhere to take her. Nowhere to hide. I *have* to leave her here.

She's nearly fallen asleep on me, and I tuck her back into bed. I tell her the story about the woman who becomes a star, sing her her favorite lullabies. Her eyes shut tight. Her chest rises and falls beneath her blanket. She's grown, I realize, and it makes me angry. The king has no right to shut her up in here. No right to keep her from her family. I don't know what he wants with her—I don't know what he's *done* to her—but I'm going to find out. And I'm going to find a way to get both her and my father to safety, as soon as possible.

I sit with Awela for longer than I mean to, nodding off in the chair beside her bed.

Bedwyn wakes me, a gentle touch on my shoulder. "It is nearly dawn," she says softly. "The woman is coming back."

I swallow a curse. I don't know *what* Taliesin will do to me if he finds out I've been up here all night.

"Go down the stair, quickly," Bedwyn tells me. "Hide behind one of the birch trees, and wait for her to pass you. Then you should be able to get down the rest of the servants' stairs, out through the kitchen courtyard, and back to your room before sunrise."

I nod. It's as good a plan as any. "Thank you," I tell her again.

She flashes a smile at me.

I'm shocked I make it back to the dormitory without being seen. There's no time for sleep. The morning trumpet sounds just as I'm crawling into my bunk, so I make it seem like I'm crawling out of it instead. I dress with the other soldiers, and drag myself to the training grounds.

Days pass. Weeks pass. My back heals and my body grows stronger and stronger, until it's nothing to me to run ten miles in the full glare of the sun, to perform hours of sword drills, to load and fire my musket again and again, and hit the target almost every time.

I learn the names of my bunkmates, and even befriend two of them. Baines immigrated from Saeth with his family when he was a baby. He has a bunch of older brothers and is determined to distinguish himself in the army—get his parents to notice him for the first time in his life. Baines has dark brown skin, and is built like a bear, ridiculously strong from a lifetime working his parents' farm. I'm certain he's never fainted in his *life*.

Rheinallt, on the other hand, hails from northern Tarian, and he's trying to get *away* from his parents. He's the exact opposite of Baines, tall and thin and so pale he must have some Gwaed blood in him somewhere. When he gets old, he'll look exactly the same as he does now—his hair is already white. Although Rheinallt joined the army to be a field physician, he's required to have the same military training as the rest of us. He doesn't have to be either a soldier *or* a doctor, really—he's the heir to his family's lucrative inn, but he didn't want to inherit, and enlisted instead. Baines and I tease him about it relentlessly, especially at mealtimes.

"I bet you had roast pork and bara brith for breakfast, lunch, and dinner every single day—and you traded it for *this*," Baines will say. The "this" he refers to is always some sort of sloppy thing it's best not to look at while you're eating.

"And my whole life plotted out for me," Rheinallt grumbles.

"Plus if we ever go to war, you could *die*!" Baines adds. "Couldn't have that excitement at the inn."

"Hey, one of the patrons might have murdered him," I put in. "It really is safer here."

Rheinallt punches Baines in the arm and flicks slop in my face, and then we're all friends again.

I never tell them where I'm from or why I'm here, but they must have found out from someone—maybe Captain Taliesin—because one evening in the mess tent, it's me being teased instead of Rheinallt.

"Ran away from the wood, did you?" says Baines. "Afraid of the witch and her daughters? They're not even real." He stabs a piece of questionable-looking meat with his table knife, and eats it off the point, chewing slowly.

"Afraid of a fairy-tale monster," Rheinallt adds, waggling his pale eyebrows. "Is that why you're here, Merrick? To learn how to fight so you can go back and kill her?"

I jerk up from my seat and leave the tent without a word, pacing out to one of the training fields and climbing onto the fence. The sun is already down, the last red glow of it faint in the sky.

They come after me.

Baines pokes my arm. "We're just having a bit of fun."

"Lighten up, will you?" Rheinallt pushes me off the fence and into the dirt.

I lunge at him, my fist connecting with his jaw.

Rheinallt curses. He wipes blood off his chin. "God, Merrick. What's wrong with you?"

Baines just stares at me, clearly shocked at my outburst.

I flex my fingers. I shouldn't have done that—brawling's against the rules, and if Baines or Rheinallt rat me out, I'll be assigned to stable duty or spend another night in the medical tent nursing fresh lash marks. "I lost my mother to the wood," I tell them. "I saw a tree siren wreck a whole train and slaughter all of the passengers. Don't tell me they're not real."

Rheinallt touches his jaw with gingerly fingers. "You never told us that."

I shrug.

There's a respect in Baines's eyes that wasn't there before. "What was she like? The tree siren?"

I blink and see Seren laughing on the hill, dancing with me to the phonograph, four minutes at a time. "She's a monster," I say. "That's all I remember."

They don't press me.

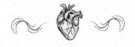

In the morning, when the three of us have reported to drills in one of the training fields, something's changed between us. Rheinallt is sporting a deep purple bruise on his jaw, but somehow, I haven't gotten in trouble for it. They clearly haven't said anything.

"Clumsy idiot," says Baines, clapping Rheinallt on the back with his huge bear hand. "Ran his face into the bunk in the middle of the night."

Rheinallt winks at me, and I can't help but quirk a smile in return. It seems that slamming my fist into his jaw has firmly cemented our friendship.

We run through sword drills, then practice with our muskets, loading and tamping and firing at targets halfway across the field. I'm getting to be a pretty fair shot. Baines is all right, too, but Rheinallt might be the best marksman in the army.

Luned, the young female guard who runs most of our drills, is certainly impressed with him. And I think it's mutual—Rheinallt can hardly keep his eyes off her. She's quick, strong, smart. I suppose she's pretty, too, her shorn hair whipping about her ears in the wind—I can understand why Rheinallt might admire her. But for whatever reason, Luned holds no charm for me.

In the afternoon, we do a new sort of drill—one with swords and unlit torches. It's unusual and annoying, and I don't see the point of it. Luned makes us do it again and again, two lines of soldiers facing off against each other with swords in our dominant hands, whilst wielding the unlit torches against rows of flour sack dummies in the other. After a few hours of this, I'm sweaty and sore and cross. Luned gives the order for the torches to be lit, and makes us run through the drill one last time.

The dummies flare up the instant heat touches them, and suddenly I'm choking and blinded as I fight, pushing through the line, panic clawing up my throat. Rheinallt is my last opponent, his pale form wreathed in smoke. We collapse in the dirt when he's bested me. Luned shouts at us to get up and help put out the fire.

When at last we're dismissed for the day, Rheinallt and Baines and I drag ourselves to the bathhouse, where we have a luxurious soak in heated water. Scented steam curls up to the peak of the roof. My aching body relaxes as the tension melts from my muscles.

"Drills are getting stranger," says Baines, leaning his bulking form back against the tiled edge of the bath. "And weirdly specific."

Rheinallt shuts his eyes. His pale hair floats around him in the water.

"What do you mean?" I ask.

"The king is preparing for something," says Rheinallt, eyes still closed. "Preparing his army for something."

I stir the water with one finger, watching it ripple out. "War against Gwaed?"

Rheinallt shakes his head. "Gwaed isn't a threat."

"What then?"

"Why do you think we're practicing with fire?" says Baines.

In that moment, I know. "He means to face the wood. He means to weaponize his army and—"

"And burn the wood to the ground," Baines finishes.

Rheinallt nods in agreement. "It's the only thing that makes any sense. He's been recruiting more and more soldiers. And the training is, as Baines said—"

"Weirdly specific," I repeat. "But the king *can't* face the wood. No one can. The last time he tried fire—"

"We all know Tarian's history," says Rheinallt, referring to the village the Gwydden slaughtered in retaliation for the king scorching her trees. "He must have a plan."

I think of the potted trees inside the palace, the patterns of leaves and stars on the gates. "Maybe he just wants to be ready. In case the wood grows all the way to Breindal City. So he can defend against her." Whatever my grievance with the king, I'd rather be on his side than the Gwydden's. At least he hasn't tried to murder me.

"Maybe," says Baines doubtfully. "But it feels like more than that. It feels *bigger*."

I think of my father, locked in a cell somewhere down in the prison. Of the meteor shower and the impossibly altered sky.

I never want to see the wood again. But if it's coming here—

If it's coming here, I won't be able to escape it.

Chapter Forty-Two

SEREN

I AM UNEASY IN THE SOUL EATER'S PALACE. I HAVE BEEN HERE SOME weeks now, and he has yet to discover my presence, but I can feel him. His fading soul, his brittle power.

What would he do, if he found me here? If he discovered what I am?

I am not sure. But every time I pass the rows of potted birch trees, I fear to be frozen there with them: my feet caught in soil, bound in clay. My body stiff. My heart still.

I try not to look at them.

My human body grows strong, day by day. I am busy from morning till night. I ache when I sleep in my narrow bed in the servants' dormitory. I dream of my mother, breaking me into pieces and throwing me on the fire. I dream of the Soul Eater, binding me with iron. I dream of Owen, plunging a knife into my heart.

In this form, I do not like to dream.

The days are filled with work and walls, shut inside away from the sky. The evenings are mine. I spend them in the kitchen court-yard, soaking in the wind and the stars, remembering a time when I did not need food and rest. When I did not crave company. But for all that, I do not miss my siren form.

Because Owen is here. Alive and safe and well and *with me*. And the Soul Eater has not yet harmed him.

The evening after I brought Owen to see his sister, he appeared in the kitchen courtyard to thank me. He's come nearly every evening after, too, and I have learned to busy myself with outdoor tasks as the sun sets, so I'll be in the courtyard when he arrives.

Tonight, he comes through the gate with his hands plunged deep into his pockets. I am supposed to be shelling peas for Heledd, but the bowls lie abandoned on the bench by the door. I am crouched in the rose beds instead, complimenting the plants on their blossoms. They are white and blush-pink, as different as can be from the blood-red roses in my sister's hair.

"Bedwyn?"

I jerk upright, my skin warming in that way human skin does when I realize I have done something foolish. Ordinary humans do not talk to plants.

He smiles at me, tilting his head sideways. "How's Awela today?"

I brush dirt from my fingers and smile back. I have been checking on his sister for him, as often as I can—I am afraid Owen will get caught if he goes to see her again. "She is doing quite well. I smuggled her up an extra biscuit."

"I'm glad." He steps to the courtyard wall and climbs up, perching on top of it, as is his habit.

I climb up beside him. I am still unused to this human form, to the cool touch of the evening air on my neck, to the quickening of my pulse at his nearness. "What's wrong?" I ask, for clearly some-thing is.

"I think the king means to face the Gwydden. Fight the wood."

Ice shivers through my veins. "When?"

He glances sideways at me—perhaps not what he expected me to say. "Perhaps soon. The army is drilling with fire."

I try to suppress my shudder.

"Have you ever seen the wood?" he asks.

I cannot answer this truly. I just nod.

"The king will need more than fire. More than blades and musket rounds." His jaw is tense as he stares out over the army encampment.

Owen is right. But I know enough of the Eater to fear that he has more than weapons and blades. Or that he will soon.

"Will you fight the wood?" I ask. "If the king truly marches against it?"

A hardness comes into his face. "I have no love for the wood."

I scrape my finger across the top of the stone wall. Every time I see him, I want to tell him the truth. But I cannot. If he knew what I was, he would not sit so close to me, would not speak with me as if I were his friend. It makes the whole of me ache. I try to be content with this. It is all I can ever have.

But it is not all that I want.

Stars appear, in the black expanse of the sky. I want to move closer to Owen, but I do not dare.

He relaxes, as he sits there. He points at one of the brightest stars. "That's the planet Bugail, Shepherd," he says. "The stories say it keeps watch over the stars."

I smile. This is the sort of thing he would say on our hill in the wood. I imagine that he knows I am me. That he doesn't mind. Or that I am human in truth and what I used to be no longer matters. That I have a soul, deep within my being, that it burns just as brightly as his. "Tell me more about the stars," I say.

He looks over at me with a smile.

He tells me.

Chapter Forty-Three

OWEN

E VERY EVENING AFTER DINNER, I CLIMB THE HILL TO THE IRON gate of the prison courtyard, and try to see my father. The prison is on the opposite side of the hill from the kitchen, but despite the imposing gate and the numerous guards, the courtyards are strikingly similar to each other. The first night I attempt to see him, the guard actually lets me into the courtyard, tells me to wait while he checks the prison records to see if my father is allowed visitors. He's not.

"Do you even have permission from your commanding officer to be up here, soldier?" he asks suspiciously.

"Of course," I lie. "He knows all about it."

But by the next evening, he's checked with Taliesin and found I do *not* have permission—that in fact I've been specifically forbidden to see my father—and orders me away with an oath. That doesn't keep me from coming back every night, hoping he'll change his mind, or that there will be a different guard in place of him who'll make an exception for me. It never happens. I strike up an odd sort of camaraderie with the guard—after a week or two, he jokes he could set his watch by me, and reprimands me if I'm late. But he doesn't let me past the gate again.

Every evening after my attempt to see my father, I hike around the hill to the kitchen courtyard. Bedwyn is almost always there, dumping out scraps or sweeping up the feathers left over from plucking chickens. Sometimes she's just leaning against the wall, not doing anything. She always smiles when she sees me. I always smile back. And then I ask her how Awela is.

Somehow we've reached an understanding that she would check on my sister, as often as she can, because sneaking me back into the palace is too risky.

"I have befriended the nurse," she tells me, some weeks after my reunion with Awela. "She isn't quite as awful as she appears."

I grimace. "I don't believe you."

"It's true." Bedwyn clambers up onto the courtyard wall and sits facing the army encampment. Her legs dangle in open air.

I join her, the stones still warm from the afternoon sun. "But is Awela being taken care of? Is she happy?"

"The nurse loves her," Bedwyn says. "She is doing the best she can for your sister."

I sigh, rubbing my fingers along the stone. It reminds me of the wall my father built too late to keep the wood from stealing my mother. I push away the image of her clawing out her own heart.

"What is it?"

I glance at her. Tendrils of pale gold hair have escaped from her maid's cap, and the wind teases them about her face. Her freckles stand out starkly against her pale skin, and her eyes are the green of deep summer. The sunset traces her with yellow light. Suddenly I'm staring at her lips, wanting very badly to kiss her.

"Owen?"

I flush and look away again, out over the plains. I will my heart to stop its mad pounding. "I don't know how to help Awela or how to free my father—I can't even get in to see him."

"You will think of something," she says, with a quiet confidence I've grown to expect from her.

A few nights later, I tell her about my mother—not everything, just that she was lost to the witch in the wood.

Bedwyn grows quiet and pale. "I have no love for my own mother," she says. "I am sorry about yours." Her eyes lock onto mine. "Will you tell me about her?"

So I do—about her university days and her cello, about her infectious laughter and the sweet sound of her singing. Of the happiness we had when she was with us.

Tears drip down Bedwyn's cheeks. "You should not have had to lose her. Not like that. I am so sorry."

I take Bedwyn's hand. Her skin is rough with work, and there are freckles on her fingers. I try not to think of another hand, smooth and sharp at once. "It isn't your fault," I say.

A few nights after that, I ask her to tell me about herself, something I realize with embarrassment I should have asked a long time ago.

She's quiet for a while. We're up on the wall again, watching the twilight fade to black. It seems we're always up on the wall now.

"I am the youngest of eleven children," she says. "I never had a father and my mother is . . . unkind."

"Did you run away from home?"

She nods. "This is my first job. My first . . ." She spreads her hands out. "My first everything."

"Do you think you'll stay here, working in the palace?"

"No. I am only here until I understand what to do. Or until my time runs out."

"What do you mean?"

Her eyes peer into the growing darkness. "I am afraid that one day my mother will come looking for me. Take me home."

"Can't you just run away again?"

She shakes her head. "This is the only chance I will ever have."

Every evening I stay with Bedwyn on the wall a little longer than I should, and am always scrambling down to my bunk late into the night.

It's these meetings I look forward to every day, through the grueling hours of training and awful meals in the mess tent. It's because of her I haven't stormed the prison, or nabbed Awela from her nurse, and damn the consequences.

It's because of her I have a measure of contentment in this strange new life. That I almost don't want it to ever end.

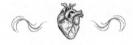

Our drills grow more and more taxing. There is no longer any question that they are meant to prepare us to face the wood. We fight with fire and swords. We're made to trudge through mud blindfolded with wax sealing our ears, to put axes into dummies, musket rounds into potted trees. It seemed almost like a game, at first. It doesn't now.

Baines and Rheinallt are grim and despairing in turns.

"I just wish Captain Taliesin or Commander Carys would *tell* us when we're meant to be sent against the wood," groans Rheinallt one evening, lounging in his chair in the mess hall. His pale skin is red and cracked with sunburn, his eyes bleary with smoke from our afternoon drills. Baines's eyes look just the same, and I suspect mine do too. They're certainly hot and itchy and give me a slightly blurred view of my dinner, which, as usual, is not necessarily a bad thing.

"Bad for morale," Baines grumbles. "Want your soldiers to think they've got a fighting chance, after all. None of us would train so hard if we were explicitly told we're being prepared for slaughter."

Rheinallt shrugs. He seems increasingly restless these days. I wonder if he'll ever get up the guts to tell Luned he admires her. I want to be there if he does—I'm sure she'd reject him, and then Baines and I would have further fuel for mockery. "Merrick's the only one who's ever been in the wood."

"That's right!" Baines wraps his huge hands around his beer tankard. "Tell us what we're up against, Merrick."

I don't know why, but I do tell them. About the attack on the train. The blood and the bodies. About a tree siren with violets in her hair. I tell them more than I should, more than I mean to: that she saved me, again and again, even though she was a monster. I even tell them, haltingly, of our meetings in the wood night after night. I don't tell them about the meteor shower or the shifting constellations. I don't tell them about my mother clawing out her own heart. Both feel too personal, though the former was spread across the world for all to see.

"It sounds to me," says Rheinallt, when I've lapsed into silence, "that your tree siren is something new. Not a monster anymore, not quite a woman."

Baines waggles his eyebrows and makes a rude gesture.

"Something new," Rheinallt repeats firmly, ignoring him. "But she clearly cares for you." His eyes go of their own accord to Luned, eating with the other officers a few tables away.

"She sounds human enough," says Baines. "No reason you can't bed her and be done with it."

"It isn't like that."

Baines laughs.

Rheinallt snorts. "Like hell it isn't."

Heat floods my body, and I kick at the table leg. The memory of kissing her in the wood overwhelms my senses—her chest against mine, her hands pressed over my ears, blocking out her sisters' music. I push it away with an effort. "It doesn't matter. I'm never going to see her again. And anyway my *point* is, the wood is dangerous. No one can step into the trees and live, unless the trees themselves will it. No one can stand against the Gwydden and her daughters. We can train all we want—it's useless."

Rheinallt has sobered again. His eyes fix on mine. "What will you do if the king's war leads us to your siren? Will you fight her?"

"My duty is to Tarian."

Baines shakes his head. "I'm not sure you know where your duties lie."

Thinking about Seren doesn't trouble me like it used to. I ponder that as I make another useless attempt to see my father, and as I climb around the hill to the kitchen courtyard.

The moment I see Bedwyn's face, the reason becomes clear. Bedwyn is so much more than Seren ever could be. There is a kinship with her I could never have had with Seren.

She is human. She is kind.

She is not a monster.

I forget all about the tree siren as I perch on the wall with Bedwyn, imagining what it might be like to kiss her as we laugh and talk under the stars.

Chapter Forty-Four

SEREN

THE SOUL EATER IS HAVING A PARTY. MUSIC DRIFTS DOWN from open balcony windows, swelling as the sun sets, not limited to only four minutes at a time. I wait for Owen to come, sweeping at nothing with my broom so I will look busy if Heledd peeks her head out.

I have been two months in the Soul Eater's palace, two months in my human form. Still I have escaped the Eater's notice. Still I fear to find him around every corner. I take what precautions I may, but I know it is not enough. If the Eater wants to find me, he will find me.

For now I wait, and watch, and listen. For now I pretend that nothing will ever go amiss, that I am truly just a girl, waiting for a boy to come and find her in the twilight.

It grows hard to remember that this form will fade. I begin to wonder if my brothers were wrong. But sometimes, if I put my hands to the earth, I can feel the distant heartbeat of the forest. I can sense every soul in the palace now, even the dim ones. My power seeps back, bit by bit. I wonder how long it will take for my monstrous skin to swallow this frail human form. To bury it forever.

"Bedwyn?"

I jump at his voice, turn to find him just coming through the gate, his lips tugging up.

"Hi," he says.

I smile, his presence banishing the last of my dark thoughts. I lean the broom against the wall. "Good evening."

He glances up at the looming palace and seems to recognize the music. His face falls a little. "My mother loved that piece."

Guilt slices through me, as it does each time he mentions his mother. Every night I am on the brink of telling him who I am, and every night I remember that I as good as slaughtered her, as I slaughtered so many others. How can I wish, even for a moment, for Owen to look at me as anything but a monster? In this form, I can be his friend. But when it fades . . . When it fades, I will return to the wood and lose myself in the depths of it. I will build a life for myself there, as my brothers have. I will forget my mother and sisters. I will forget Owen. And when my body grows weary of living, I will go to the hill where we danced together. I will sink my roots deep into the earth, and reach my branches up to the stars, and I will die as I was born, and become once more a tree.

He paces up to me, takes both my hands in his. "Hey," he says gently. "What's wrong?"

I fight the press of tears, hot behind my eyes.

"Would you like to dance?" he asks.

Those words—uttered to me on the hill, said to me again, here, in this moment. I nod. I do not trust myself to speak without telling him everything.

He steps closer to me, slips one hand onto my waist. He's a breath away from me, the barest of heartbeats. I could count his eyelashes. I could kiss him. I was taller than him, in my tree form.

I am eye level with him now.

We dance in the courtyard to the music spilling out from above. We move easily together, as we did on the hill. I wonder if he remembers that night with anything other than revulsion.

The music comes to an end—the orchestra taking a break between pieces, perhaps—but we keep dancing over the stones, between the slop bin and the wall. The stars come out, dimmer here than on our hill in the wood.

He pulls me closer still, until his chest is pressed up against mine. His heart beats wild and quick. I look into his face and he looks into mine, and in the moment before he leans his head to kiss me, I break away from him.

If I ever see you again, I'll kill you.

I stare at him in the dark of the courtyard.

"I'm sorry," he stammers. "I thought—"

"Don't be sorry." There's a lump in my throat. A pressure between my ribs. At my feet, a seedling grows up between a crack in the stone, and I know it's because of me. This cannot be it. I cannot shed my human form in front of him when he was about to—

"Owen." I go and take his hand again. "Please don't be sorry."

He quirks a smile at me, raises his free hand to smooth his fingers across my cheek. I lean into him.

We start dancing again, without really meaning to. And as we spin about the little courtyard, more seedlings spring up between the cracks in the stone. I hope he does not notice. I hope he does.

He makes no further attempt to kiss me.

It is very late when Owen goes down to his bed. Music lingers on in the palace as I leave our courtyard and come inside.

In the corridor, a hand closes around my arm and tugs me through a doorway.

Light flares around us, illuminating a small sitting room, though no one is here to strike a match. Electricity buzzes through my skin.

The scent of decay chokes me.

I turn to face the Soul Eater. I cannot feel the beat of my heart.

He looms above me, tall, thin. His soul is fading, it's true, there's barely any spark to it. But his power is ancient and strong. Stronger than mine. Maybe even stronger than my mother's.

I forgot he was once human. But though we both of us now wear human forms, these bodies are not our own.

He lets go of my arm. I can feel every place his fingers touched me, like patches of rot on a fallen branch.

He frowns. "I don't understand. You're just a scrawny girl. Why did my instruments lead me to you?"

I stand frozen, terror flooding my veins. Every instinct urges me to turn, to run. But if I do, he will know what I am. If I do, he will destroy me.

"Answer me, girl!"

I jump at the sharpness in his voice. "I do not know."

He eyes me with distrust. With disdain. "Something of *hers* has crept into my palace. Past my defenses. Past my wards. It shouldn't be possible, and yet—"

He circles me, studying every piece of me with his muddy green eyes. "My instruments are never wrong." He taps the medallion hanging about his neck. Its components are incomprehensible to me: some dark magic of metal and gears. It hums against his breastbone. "You are of the wood," he says. "Aren't you?"

"I am a humble servant, Your Majesty." I bow.

He catches my wrist, jerks me up again. "You *stink* of her, you know that? Of the wood. Of her devilish magic. What *are* you?"

I force myself not to tremble before him. "I am my own being.

I am none of hers."

He shakes his head. He tugs the medallion from his neck with his free hand. For one brief, agonizing moment, he presses the medallion against my chest. There is a flash of white pain. A sear of heat.

He lets go of me and I fall back from him, landing in a tangle of limbs on a moss-green rug.

The Soul Eater consults his device. He shakes his head in amazement. Amusement? I do not know which. "You haven't any soul! How do you manage that? No soul at all. Not even a trace."

I push myself to my feet. I dart toward the door.

Once more, he seizes my wrist. He holds me back from my escape. I look down the corridor, where small ash trees grow in clay pots, prisoners to his will.

"Are you a spy? An assassin?"

My heart screams inside of me.

"Rather ineffective, if you are."

"Your Majesty?"

I turn my head. A servant bows in the corridor. He straightens again, his eyes traveling uneasily from the Soul Eater's hand on my wrist to the Soul Eater himself.

"What is it?" snaps the Eater.

"Your pardon, Majesty, but your guests await you to lead the evening's last dance."

I am aware, belatedly, of the Soul Eater's rich clothing: deep velvet embroidered in gold, studded with flashing jewels. He left his party to come find me. If he had come any sooner, if he had come into the courtyard looking for me, he would have found Owen, too.

The Soul Eater lets go of my wrist.

I don't wait for him to notice the tiny seedling that has pushed its way up through the carpet at my feet, and realize what I am.

I bolt down the hall like a deer with a wolf at my heels.

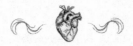

No soul at all. Not even a trace.

His words pierce me, thorns in my heart.

I had hoped.

Despite my brothers' words, I had hoped that this form was something more. Something deeper.

But I am what I always have been. What I will always be.

No soul at all.

I can feel him, now: the Eater, in the palace somewhere below me. I can sense his power, his soul. I wonder why he has waited so long to act, when my mother spelled out the truth of his death in the stars so many weeks ago.

He will not forget about me. I cannot dwell in the palace any longer in safety—I have to get out. But I will not go alone.

Not even a trace.

I climb to Awela's rooms. Her nurse greets me at the door, her face creased with worry.

"What is it?"

"I'm to be let go." Her voice cracks. "I was told to pack my things, that someone will come for the child tonight."

Dread sprouts inside of me. Whatever he was waiting for, the Eater is acting now. "Has the king been to see her?"

The nurse nods. "How did you know? He came last night, banished me out into the hall. When at last he left and I went back in, the poor child was inconsolable. There was no mark on her—the king did not hurt her, of course." She says this last bit in a rush, anxious that I not think her to be saying anything ill of the Soul Eater.

"Can I see her?"

"Of course. Come in."

I step into the nursery. Awela sits on her bed, looking blankly out into the room. She doesn't seem to have any interest in the books and toys spread about her. I kneel by the bed, take her little hands in mine, and reach, gently, for her soul. It's still there, bright and intact. The Soul Eater hasn't swallowed it yet. But he's prodded it and examined it to assess how he might best go about it. And if he's banishing the nurse, he's found it. I reach for his soul, making sure he is still far away from this room. Far away from Awela and the nurse and me.

A leaf falls from my hair onto the floor. The nurse doesn't notice.

"Do you love this child?" I ask her.

"Of course I do." Her eyes swim with tears.

"Enough to defy the king?"

"What do you mean?" She strokes Awela's hair, and the girl whimpers and leans into her.

"You saw the effect he had on her last night. He's planning something much, much worse. If you don't take her away right now, he'll kill her."

"Kill her?"

"He wants her soul," I say darkly. "Such a young thing cannot live without one."

The nurse shudders, her eyes flicking between Awela and me. "What are you?"

"Someone who understands monsters. Someone who means to defeat at least one. Will you take her?"

"Where will I go? How will I hide her?"

I reach underneath my collar and tug out the strand of rowan berries concealed there. Pren gave them to me, before he and my other brothers bid me farewell. I pull it off, and offer it to the nurse. "Take this into the southern woods. Call for my brothers: Pren and Criafol and Cangen. Show them the necklace and tell them my name. They will help you."

"Call Pren and Criafol and Cangen," she repeats. "Tell them Bedwyn sent us."

I shake my head. "My true name is Seren. That's the name you must give them. Can you do it?"

She nods, studying me with dark eyes as she scoops Awela into her arms. I wrap a blanket around the little girl.

"How am I to escape the palace without being seen?"

"I will clear a path for you," I promise.

She grasps my arm. "Thank you."

The thought of Owen discovering his sister is gone wrenches at me. "Take care of her. Please."

"I will, child." She slips out the door with Awela, and I sink to my knees and feel for all the souls in the palace. Quietly, I tug them away from the nurse and Awela. She walks unhindered through the servants' gate, and out over the plain.

I take a breath. I have done all I can for Awela and her nurse. I only hope they make it safely to my brothers.

Now to send Owen away. It is what I should have done when I first arrived. I did not want Owen to go. I wanted him near me. I still do. But my monstrous form pushes against my human skin. Leaves drip from my hair. Seedlings sprout beneath my feet.

I cannot hide my true self from him much longer.

Chapter Forty-Five

OWEN

THE PRISON GUARD PEERS AT ME THROUGH THE IRON GATE.
"You're late," he says. "Thought you weren't coming
tonight."

I try to swallow my guilt. I'd heard the music spilling out of the
palace and gone to Bedwyn first. "I'm here now."

His face is grim in the torchlight. "Your father isn't doing well."

Terror grips me. "What do you mean?"

He avoids my gaze. All the nights we've bantered through the
gate, he's never told me his name. "I mean he won't last till morning."

I grip the bars. Something sour twists in my gut. I know what
the guard is saying without actually saying it: That bastard of a
king has been torturing him, and my father can't take any more. I
swallow past the acrid taste of bile. "Let me see him."

"The king would have my head."

"*Please.*"

He shifts his weight with a jingle of armor. The planes of his face are hard in the torchlight. "Come back in an hour," he says in an undertone. "I'm alone on duty then. I'll take you to him."

I know what he's risking: a flogging, dismissal from the army, maybe execution. It humbles me. "Thank you."

He gives me a brisk nod, then says in a louder, overexaggerated voice: "I tell you every night, Merrick, you're not getting through the gate no matter how much you beg!"

I touch my hand to my heart, a gesture of respect, and turn away without another word.

For a while I huddle against the side of the hill, shaking uncontrollably. I'm out of time, and there's no one to blame but myself.

Even if I could break my father out of prison, it's too late now. I don't know the extent of his . . . injuries. I don't know if a physician could help him. The king has been torturing my father *to death* all this time I've been playing at being a soldier and flirting with a pretty kitchen maid.

Now there's not a single thing I can do about it.

I'll go and see my father. Maybe I'm wrong. Maybe I *can* help him. Maybe the guard will let us go free, find us a physician. Then Father, Awela, and I can leave this place.

Tonight.

It's a flimsy, stupid hope. But it's a hope nonetheless. And if it's to come to fruition, I'll need help getting Awela out of the palace.

There's a hint of coolness in the air as I hike back around the hill to the kitchen courtyard, a sign that summer is waning. I'm so deep in my thoughts that I jump when Bedwyn steps into the courtyard, her pale hair blowing about her face in the light wind. She's lost her maid's cap somewhere.

"Owen," she breathes, grasping my arm and pulling me back toward the gate I just came through. "You have to leave. Tonight. The Soul Ea—the king is coming for you."

I gently shrug her off. "I *am* leaving—just as soon as I get my father and Awela out of here. Can you help me?"

"You don't understand." The wind picks up, blows a scattering of leaves through her hair. They must be from the potted trees indoors—there's none outside, not for miles. "You have to *leave*, Owen. While there's still time. Please."

Her eyes lock onto mine, green flecked with gold, and there's something in them that tugs at me, some bit of recognition from another time, another place.

"I'm not leaving without my sister and my father. You have to understand that."

"He's going to kill you. He's going to *worse*-than-kill you."

"What's worse than death?" But I know: It's being a slave to the Gwydden with your soul swallowed up; it's clawing your own heart out and turning to ash in the rainy wood. "Will you help me?"

She worries at her lip, and puts one hand on my chest, her fingers splayed out.

For an instant, there's a sharp, tugging sensation from somewhere deep inside of me, but the next instant it's gone and her hand is still there, pressed against my heart. I put my left hand on her head. I tug her gently toward me.

She's the one who closes the gap between us, who presses her mouth to mine with a wildness that robs me of breath. I tangle my fingers in her hair and kiss her back. The heat of her rages through my veins, and I can't think past her lips and her breath and her body, crushed against mine.

The wind shrieks around us, chickens squawk from their coop. Bells sound from down in the city, tolling the hour. Awareness slams through me, and I jerk away from her, devoured by the mad pace of my heart. I let myself forget that my father is dying, somewhere beneath me. That I have to get my sister out. Tonight.

Bedwyn is breathing hard. She stares at me as she shivers in the wind. More leaves swirl around her.

My body is a traitor—I don't want to think about my father or what the king has done to him. I want to draw her to me again, to kiss her until neither one of us can breathe, to take her hand and run far away, to never let her go.

"You have to trust me, Owen. You have to get out of here." Her voice is hollow and strange, like she's fighting for every word.

"I *do* trust you. But please, Bedwyn. Can you get Awela? Can you wait with her outside the city walls? I'll come as soon as I can. Before dawn, if I can manage it."

She looks beautiful in the light of the rising moon, her tall form and her halo of gold hair. But every line of her face screams sorrow. "I will get Awela out," she promises.

I exhale in relief. I grab her hand. Squeeze it. "Thank you. *Thank you!*"

She smiles, sharp and sad.

"I have to go," I tell her. "I'll see you before dawn."

"Before dawn," she echoes.

I step through the gate, and steal one backward glance at her. For a moment, I think there are leaves dripping from her hair, seedlings struggling to grow up in the cracks between stones at her feet. For a moment, I think I catch the faint scent of violets.

But then I blink and it is only Bedwyn, staring at me with a haunted look in her eyes.

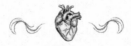

The gate doesn't make a sound as the guard swings it open.

The prison courtyard is eerily quiet. There are a few potted trees here, which surprises me, although when I look closely at them I see why. They're birch trees, but their trunks are twisted, their branches growing out at awkward angles. They aren't pristine enough for the king's palace. Wind stirs through their dappled leaves, and an uneasy chill curls down my spine.

Then the guard is unlocking a heavy iron door, and ushering me into the prison proper.

We descend a long flight of stone stairs, and with every step, cold and damp and rot seep deeper into my skin. The guard doesn't speak. He's a hulking shadow in the light of the torch he carries, and I can't help thinking I'm a dead soul that he's ushering into the underworld.

At the bottom of the stairs is another door, another guard. He eyes my guard. "Highly irregular, Drystan."

My guard—Drystan—shrugs. "I don't want to bash your head in, Aled, but I'm in enough trouble already, so I might as well."

Aled rolls his eyes and unlocks the door, waving us through.

I recognize the utter futility of ever imagining I could break my father out of this place.

Drystan takes me to the cell at the very end of a long, dim corridor. There's a dead torch in a bracket on the wall—Drystan touches it with his, and it flares to life.

I am hot and cold all over, dizzy with horror and pain and fear.

I hardly recognize my father.

He's curled up on the floor of the cell, his skin dirty and bruised and scabbed, his clothes scraps of rags that hardly cover him. There are threads of silver in his hair that weren't there two months ago, and he's alarmingly thin, his shoulder blades bony knobs in his back.

Drystan unlocks the door and pushes it open. It doesn't make a noise either, the hinges well oiled. He squeezes my arm. "I can only give you ten minutes. I'm sorry."

He retreats down the corridor, and I step into the cell, sinking to my knees. "Father?" I whisper.

He lifts his head, and pushes himself up on his hands, offering me a full view of his chest: It's riddled with holes that leak dark blood onto the floor. "Owen." The word is raspy-rough, as if he hasn't spoken in days. Or as if his throat is raw from screaming.

I wrap my arm around him, trying not to shudder at the slick warmth that seeps through my shirt.

He leans against me, little more than skin and bones.

A sob pulls out of me. "Father. Father, I'm so sorry."

Tears dribble from his eyes. "Forgive me, Owen."

"I should have been at the house when the soldiers came for you," I babble. "I should have told you not to send the telegram. I should have—"

"That doesn't matter," he says. "You have to listen to me, Owen. There is a way to save her. There is a way to stop all of this."

"I'll look after Awela," I promise, thinking of Bedwyn waiting for me outside the city gates until dawn. "We'll be safe."

"Not Awela." Father tightens his grip on my hands. "The Gwydden."

Anger sparks hot. "The wood witch doesn't need saving."

"You must only give back what he stole," he says, "and what she sacrificed. Then her curse will be broken, and all will be as it was."

Fear closes up my throat. "What curse? I don't know what you mean, Father."

"It's what the stars have been telling us, all this time." Father lifts one hand to touch my face. "What he stole, and what she sacrificed. You must remember. Promise me."

"I love you, Father." Tears choke me, but I push through them. "I'm going to get you out of here."

He smooths his thumb across my cheek. "I love you too, my boy. But you must promise me you'll remember. What he stole. What she sacrificed."

I squeeze Father's free hand as my heart breaks. "I promise."

He sags against me, his eyes drifting shut. "I'm glad you're here with me, Owen. To say goodbye."

"I'm getting you out of here."

"My body is broken. The king has carved every ounce of my supposed treason out of me. But that doesn't matter now."

"Of course it does! I'll get you to a physician—"

"A physician can't help me. It's enough that God sent you to me. At the end. I only wish Awela were here, too. And that I could have seen Eira, one last time."

Grief chokes me. "There's something else I have to tell you. I saw—I saw Mother, in the wood. She wasn't dead. All this time she wasn't dead. The Gwydden bound her to a strange tree in the heart of the forest. The Gwydden took her soul. But Mother was so strong. She used the magic of the tree to look out for us. To protect you and me and Awela. It's why the wood shut you out when Awela and I went missing. That was *her*. Protecting you."

Father shakes. Blood pours thicker from his wounds. "But she's gone now, isn't she? For good?"

I can't tell him. I can't bear it. "She said she loved you, in the end."

"I will see her soon," he rasps.

"Father."

"Don't despair, my boy. There is much for you to do yet, I think. I saw her, you know, when I went into the wood the day she was lost. The wind blew through her hair and there was blood on her face. She was still so beautiful. She sent me away. It was too late for her. But you needed me. You and Awela. So I came back. I am glad to have had all these extra days with you. But I have never truly lived since I lost her. Do not mourn me, Owen. I am happy. I am with her."

"Father—"

Between one heartbeat and the next, he goes limp in my arms. His soul winks out of him. He dies with a smile on his lips.

"Merrick?"

I can barely see Drystan through the haze of tears. The world seems to waver and bob in the torchlight.

"Another guard joins me on duty in five minutes."

Meaning if Drystan's trespass is to go unnoticed, the only chance of it is now.

I drag myself to my feet. I sway. Drystan catches my arm.

He helps me back down the corridor, up the stairs, out into the blinding moonlight, through the courtyard. Leaves swirl in the wind. Inside, I'm screaming. Outside, I'm horribly, deathly calm.

I walk numbly through the gate and out onto the hill. Drystan locks it behind me. He peers at me between the bars. "I'm sorry, Merrick."

There's a buzzing in my head. "Thank you for taking me to him."

"He'll have a proper burial."

I want to scream. I want to burn the world down. I want to drive a knife into the king's heart and watch the bastard bleed.

I focus my eyes on Drystan. "Where can I find the king?"

He frowns. "The king?"

"You've been on duty in the palace before, haven't you?"

"Yes." He looks wary.

"Then you know the layout better than me. Do you know where the king's private chambers are? His office?"

"Merrick, taking you to see your dying father is a trifle different than helping you commit regicide. I'm not a fool."

"Then you know that what he did to my father isn't right. You know he's not the hero all of Tarian believes him to be."

Drystan's lips press hard together. The wind rattles leaves over the courtyard stones. "There's a stair on the fifth floor that will take you up to his private tower. But you shouldn't go. He's stronger than you think. He'll destroy you."

My hand goes to the knife at my hip. "He murdered my father—I'd like to see him try."

Chapter Forty-Six

SEREN

I STAND ALONE IN THE COURTYARD, IN THE MOONLIGHT AND THE wind. Leaves skitter around me, new plants push up between the cracks in the stone. I shut my eyes and reach through the palace, feeling gently for all the souls inside. There is the Eater's soul: thin and tremulous, surrounded by scores of others. He is still dancing, then. Owen's soul is farther away, down in the earth, but it is so much brighter than the Eater's. So much stronger. There is another soul beside Owen's. I feel it flicker. I feel it die. I feel Owen's anguish and rage. Enough to swallow my mother and the Eater, too. I ache for him—it was his father's soul. Now it is gone.

I promised Owen something I cannot give. I have already gotten Awela out, but she is safe with my brothers now. When he comes to me outside the palace walls, I will explain it to him. I will tell him how to find her.

If my true form has not wholly consumed me by then.

I should go now, while the Eater is dancing. While I am still free.

But something keeps me standing here, staring up at the stars.

The wind is blowing so wild I do not hear him come. I do not know he is here until his blade is pressed sharp against my throat and the stink of him is choking me.

"I'm still not sure what you are," the Eater hisses. "But I'm going to find out. Did you think I'd forget you so easily?"

Leaves blow into his face, and he spits them out. "You're hers. Somehow, you're hers, and if you're what I *think* you are—" He laughs as he traces one cold finger down the curve of my cheek.

If I had my true form, he would already be dead.

But in this form, I am weak. Fragile.

I writhe in his grasp as he drags me through the courtyard and into the kitchens. I cannot get free. His fingers bite deep into my arm. His blade presses harder into my neck. Something warm and wet trickles down into my collar. I think of cutting myself peeling potatoes and nearly fainting in Owen's arms.

Owen! Where is he? I reach for him as the Eater hauls me through the palace corridor, past a rigid row of captive elms, into an antechamber with one tiny window looking into the north sky. He flings me to the ground. I land hard on one arm. It twists wrong beneath me. Pain flares, swift and sharp.

"I've something to attend to," says the Eater. "I'll be back soon." There is sincerity in his words. Danger. The promise of pain.

I catch the thread of Owen's soul. He is far from the Eater. He is safe.

The Eater steps into the hall, barring the door behind him. Sealing me inside.

"Wait!"

I leap at the door, pound against it with my useless human hands.

But the Eater has trapped me.

I am a girl in a cage.

A tree in a pot.

No way out.

I reach again for Owen's soul. He is no longer safe inside the earth. He burns with rage. And I know where he is going.

To face the Eater.

Chapter Forty-Seven

OWEN

THE PALACE IS QUIET, TOO QUIET. THE CORRIDORS ARE EMPTY, the long rows of potted trees casting eerie shadows in the light of the oil lamps. I hide around every corner, listen cautiously before ascending every stair, but I needn't have. I meet no one. Maybe all the courtiers are still in the ballroom. Maybe the king is, too.

Rage burns me from the inside. I can't think about my grief right now. If I do, it will break me. All that's left is anger.

The winding stair to the king's private tower is narrow and dim—no one has come to light the lamps here, which means it may very well be unoccupied. That's fine with me. I'll wait for him. I tighten my grip on my knife hilt. I wonder what it will feel like to drive it into his heart.

The spiral stair seems to go on forever, then ends all at once at a tall iron door that creaks open when I push it.

I'm not prepared for what is waiting on the other side: a large, domed room, the ceiling made all of glass. It's an observatory, of a sort. It lacks only a telescope. The walls are plastered with my and my father's star charts. A desk on one end of the chamber over-flows with books and pages upon pages of handwritten notes. The whole place reeks of rot and earth and leaves, and sizzles with eerie electricity, though there are no electric lamps that I can see. In the center of the room stands an iron table, empty except for a scattering of glass vials and a knife. It looks out of place with everything else.

I pace around the room, my bewildered curiosity momentarily dulling my rage. I peer at the charts as I go; there are hundreds upon hundreds of them, dating back to when the king first hired my father as an astronomer and gifted him the house on the edge of the wood. Someone—I can only assume the king—has scrawled indecipherable notes on nearly every chart in a shimmery silver ink.

I'm halfway round the room before I pick up the pattern. Almost all of the notes seem to center around the constellations that shifted in the impossible meteor shower: the Twysog Mileinig, the Spiteful Prince, and the Morwyn, the Maiden. He stole her crown, the stories go, and she's been chasing him to get it back, grasping for his heel but never quite catching hold of him.

I watch the progression of those two constellations from chart to chart and year to year. They slide off of the visible half of the ecliptic during the autumn and winter months, and come back into view in the spring. They hardly change at all, even after a decade of charting, which of course they wouldn't. I finish my circuit of the room on the opposite side of the door from where I started, and find the final charts, the ones marking the new positions of the constellations after the meteor shower. Here the Morwyn has all but swallowed the Spiteful Prince, the bright star that represented her crown burning now in the midst of her. Eight other bright stars are grouped at her right shoulder, with countless others on her left side and even more scattered at her feet. I remember how there were too many to mark them all down.

Understanding begins to take root inside of me. I pace around the room again, studying the charts until they lead me once more to the final ones.

I walk over to the desk, rifle through the pages of notes—more of that silver writing I can't read. The books are ancient, their spines cracked and their pages brittle. I open a few. They're written in the same language as the silver notes, but it's the pictures that startle me. They're faded now from their once-bright colors, but they seem to be illustrations of children's fairy tales. There's a picture of mermaids, bathing on rocks with a waterfall behind them, their long hair barely covering their breasts. I flush and turn the page. A dragon breathes fire across an ocean, transforming it into a barren desert. There's pictures of men who appear to be made of rocks, of a royal family riding out on a hunt. There's a picture of a beautiful wood nymph, her green hair tangled with bluebells, her body clothed in a garment of bark and leaves. I open another of the books, and find similar illustrations.

Underneath all the pages and books is a sheet of crackly parchment, so brittle the edges crumble away when I touch it. It's hard to make out in the dim light, but I finally realize it's an ancient star chart. It seems to be of the same patch of sky where the Morwyn chases after the Spiteful Prince, but their constellations are missing.

What if, I think, peering at the ancient chart. *What if.*

I tell myself a story.

Once, long ago, a spiteful prince stole the crown of a maiden. But not just any maiden. A wood nymph powerful enough to make children from trees. Powerful enough to write the threat of her revenge in the heavens. The spiteful prince became a king. He built his fortress up around him, and he hired centuries of astronomers to watch the sky, to read the stars, so he would know when the wood nymph was about to take her revenge. So he could prepare himself to face her.

And then one day he receives a telegram: The impossible has happened. The stars have *changed*. There is no longer a spiteful prince hanging in the heavens, because the maiden has devoured him, and taken back her crown.

But what if it wasn't a crown at all?

What if it was her soul?

I go back to the final star chart my father filled in. The truth is spelled out before me, a truth my father knew, or guessed.

A truth that cost him his life.

Rage takes hold of me, stronger than before. The king is a liar. He's centuries old, steeped in the magic he claims to abhor. If the people of Tarian knew that not only is he no better than the Gwydden, *he created her*, they would riot.

That is my father's treason. *That* is what the king didn't want me to know.

The sudden creak of the door makes me jump, and I have only a heartbeat to reach for my knife before the king's hands close around my throat.

Chapter Forty-Eight

SEREN

I TUG GENTLY AT THE SOULS IN THE PALACE, CLEARING OWEN A path. He does not need anyone barring his way. He will not find the Soul Eater. Not yet. The Eater is on his way to the nursery. He will find Awela gone. He will want Owen instead.

And I am trapped here.

Powerless.

I step up to the window in the antechamber, peer out at a circle of stars. They seem so unreachable here, so far from their nearness on the hill where we danced.

It was my mother who taught me the stories in the sky. I was hardly two winters old when she pointed into the heavens, and told me the name of every star. There was a star for her, and a star for me, and a star for each of my brothers and sisters.

Once, she said, *there lived a foolish wood nymph in a wide green forest. Her sisters married mermen and went away to sea. Her brothers married rock maidens and went to live in the mountains. She was the only one left. She did not care for rocks, nor the sea. She loved only a boy, with dark hair and eyes that gleamed like stars. He was a prince of his people, and he would make her his queen.*

But in the dead of night, when first they lay together in the darkness, he carved her soul from her body, and left her with only her heart. He swallowed her soul and gained immortality and power beyond reckoning.

She bled into the earth. She wanted to die, but the wood did not let her. It fed into her, and she drank it in, and from the trees she gathered power equal to the boy's, but hers was a power of growing. She grew the heartless tree. She grew her sons and daughters. And she grew her wood, more and more, up around her like the boy's castle. There she waited, banishing all the boy's kind from her fortress, waiting for the day when her power reached its height, when the stars and the trees obeyed her, when she could wield them like soldiers. When that happened, she would at last go to the boy again, and slaughter him for what he had done.

Once, she'd wanted her soul back, but she realized she had no need of it. She had her heart, and she had her power, and she had the souls of countless others to drink and drink and drink. That was enough.

My mother taught me my killing song. Taught me how to break the bodies of the men who came into the wood. They were the children of the Soul Eater, and they must die and die and die.

I know the truth now, as I did not then. The king may have swallowed my mother's soul, but she has swallowed far more. If anyone is a Soul Eater, it is her.

My heart beats hot within me. Leaves rattle down from my hair.

My time in this form grows very short.

I should have made Owen understand. I should have pulled him with me, away from the palace and the Eater, while I had the chance. I should have told him that I am no longer the monster I used to be. That I regret with every ounce of my being what happened to his mother in the forest.

I want him here with me, looking at the stars.

I want to tell him that I will save him, if I can.

That I love him, even though I do not have a soul.

I love him.

The words beat fragile and strong inside of me, butterflies with glass wings.

Awareness sears through me with the heat of a wildfire, and I grab for the tendrils of Owen's soul.

He is no longer alone.

The Eater has found him.

Chapter Forty-Nine

OWEN

T HE KING DRAGS ME FARTHER INTO THE ROOM, HIS HANDS
clamped around my throat, choking me. I thrash and gulp
for air. There's a humming in my ears, spots dancing black
in front of my eyes.

He hurls me to the floor and I crumple like paper. I lie there
gasping for breath, fighting to come back to myself.

It's almost laughable, that I thought I could kill him.

He crouches beside me, relieves me of my knife. "Do you have
any idea," he says, his voice low and cold, "what has happened to
your sister?"

I blink up at him. "You *murdered* my *father.*"

Without warning, he slams his fist into the side of my face,
sending me skidding along the floor. I scramble to a sitting position
and press my back against the wall by the desk. My heart skitters
and jumps. A slick red warmth drips down my jaw.

"Your *sister*," he spits at me. He comes over to me, crouches back down, his piercing green eyes on level with mine. He reeks of earth and rot and molding leaves. His beard is still neatly trimmed, but bits of his skin seem to be peeling away from his face, exposing patches of pulpy muscle I don't want to look at very closely. He hisses at me through his teeth and grabs my shoulder, hauling me to my feet. "The nursery is empty. Your sister has vanished, and now *you* are here. I know you had something to do with it. WHERE IS SHE?"

"I don't know." Somewhere inside my terror, relief throbs. Awela is safe from him. Bedwyn got her out and she's *safe*. Safer than I am, at the moment. I glance around the room. There's no way out but the iron door, and the king is barring my way. "I know your secret," I tell him. "I know you're not what you claim to be."

"Are you trying to blackmail me, boy?" He laughs as he drags me to the center of the room where the iron table waits.

I fight him, trying to jerk out of his grasp, but he's strong, unnaturally so. His fingers dig into my arms, down to bone. He throws me onto the table, and my leg smashes one of the vials. Broken glass slices through my trousers, embedding into my thigh.

He binds me to the table with leather straps cinched tight at my wrists and my ankles, and locks a collar around my neck. I twist and heave against the straps. They hold.

The king paces round me, stopping every few seconds to peer up through the glass ceiling at the dim stars. There's a medallion around his neck that whirs with gears and buzzes with electricity. It stinks of rot—or is that the king?

"I wanted your sister. I *needed* her. Her soul is strong—there's magic in it. She was born on the edge of the witch's wood, you know. The power wound itself into her soul. She burns with it. But you—" He prods my arms and legs, wipes a smear of blood off my cheek, and presses his medallion against my chest. A sharp pain sears through me for a fraction of an instant as the medallion flashes with a white light, then grows dark again. The king looks on with interest. He nods in satisfaction. "As I suspected, you are strong, too. You weren't born there, but you've lived there nearly all your life. I wanted you close, in case I was unsuccessful taking your sister's soul. So I would have another chance at yours."

I shudder where I'm bound, forced to stare up into the sky, the king a leering silhouette in my peripheral. "My *soul*? What do you mean? What *are* you?"

"What am I?" He stops above my head and looks down at me with a smile, as if he's humoring a child. "I'm as human as you are, or I was, once. But the witch is coming for me, and when she does, I mean to have the power to drive her deep into Hell where she belongs." He resumes his pacing, then drags something out from underneath the table.

From my sideways view, I watch him assemble some kind of metal device. He attaches it to the table, and shifts it over me: a long metal arm, a glass lens, a sort of gear-claw thing that makes my insides roil. He takes the medallion from around his neck and clicks it into the device.

"Why did you torture my father?" I screw my eyes shut. I can't look at the device, which is clearly about to inflict some excruciating pain. "Why did you murder him? No one would have had any idea what he was talking about, even if he *did* ever tell them about the stars. About what he guessed. You are Tarian's beloved king. You're *fighting* the Gwydden. That's all anyone would have believed."

"I needed to test my machine on someone," the king says dismissively. "Unlucky for him, there was nothing in his soul of any use to me. No power there. I checked. Repeatedly. But all that practice makes it more or less certain I'll be successful extracting *your* soul. I had to be sure I could do it, before I risked your sister. Or you, as it turns out."

Tears leak from my eyes without my consent. The wounds in

my father's chest—the king wasn't torturing him. He was *experimenting* on him. "You're a monster," I spit.

"It isn't my fault your father happened to be the astronomer in my employ when the witch put her signs in the sky. I've had quite a lot of them, you know."

My jaw is swelling and the glass in my leg *hurts*. If I don't dig it out soon, I might never walk properly again. But that doesn't matter when I'm about to die. When my mother ripped her heart out and my father died in my arms. At least Awela is safe. Bedwyn got her out.

Bedwyn.

I feel again the hot press of her mouth against mine, the pounding of her heart. Her hair, whipping cool about my neck.

There's a clank of metal, the sudden sear of pain in my chest.

My eyes fly open. The king is twisting the metal claw under my skin. He stops before he hits my ribs.

I gulp shallow breaths.

"I'll be so glad when this is all over," the king says conversationally. He adjusts the lens. "Do you know how tiresome it is to reinvent oneself every sixty years or so? Paying off servants, staging my own death again and again to pass the crown onto my 'son' or my 'nephew.' I even tried to conquer Gwaed a few centuries back, just for some variety, but that ended in disaster. I'm thoroughly sick of this wretched palace and this wretched kingdom. When the witch is dead, I can go where I please. I won't be bound here any longer, waiting for her to try and kill me." He frowns at the lens and makes another adjustment. "But I haven't been idle. I can wield as much magic as she does now. There's just one thing holding me back—I need a new soul. Mine is wasting away."

"Do you mean her soul?" I whisper. "Do you mean the Gwydden's soul?"

He laughs. "It hasn't belonged to her in centuries. She's stronger without it. Don't you think?"

"You made her what she is."

"And I will unmake her, too."

He flicks a switch on the side of his device.

Blinding, earth-shattering pain tears through me.

Then there's nothing but light and heat and the sound of my own screaming.

Chapter Fifty

SEREN

I POUND ON THE DOOR OF THE ANTECHAMBER. I POUND AND I scream. I do not stop when my throat is hoarse and my hands are bloody. I pound and pound.

Until footsteps sound on the other side. Until the door creaks open and Heledd is there, her face creased in alarm, in confusion. "Bedwyn! What—"

But there is no time.

I push past her.

I run.

Toward the feel of his soul.

Toward the reek of the Eater's power.

I run and I run, but this human body is not fast enough. I wish I were a bird, so I could wing up to the tower, so I could reach him faster, faster.

But I am slow. These lungs burn and this heart beats and all the while I run up the winding stair I hear him screaming. It tears at me like my mother's claws, until all of me is raw and bleeding.

With every step, I'm shedding leaves.

There is a door at the top of the tower, an iron door. It's locked. I beat against it with my human fists. I rage and rail, but it isn't enough, isn't enough.

And on the other side of the door, he's screaming.

I feel the change inside of me; I call it from within the core of my being: the power of the wood. *My* power.

The living branches burst from my fingers, grasp hold of the door, and rip it from its hinges with a horrific *screeeeech.*

Then all is stars and pain and blood and there is an iron branch in Owen and he's screaming.

The Soul Eater leans over him, and he does not frighten me anymore.

He is intent on stealing Owen's soul. He does not look up when I tear through the door. I do not think he even sees me.

The glass ceiling is alive with stars, blazing and flashing, fearful of the dark magic the Soul Eater has called on.

But it does not work. Owen's soul does not come.

His body shakes and flops on the table. His blood seeps red. He sweats and strains against the bonds that hold him.

"Stop this."

The Soul Eater jerks his head up. "*Witch!*" he seethes. "You cannot be here! I've woven protections, grown trees of my own to guard my palace. You cannot be here."

I grab the iron embedded in Owen's chest and pull it out in one swift movement. "I am not her."

Owen screams again. All the breath goes out of him.

His eyes are wandering, wild. He convulses. I rip the collar off of him, then the wrist straps, the ankle straps. He shakes and moans. His leg is bleeding, his face is too. But the wound in his chest is the deepest, the worst. It leaks red onto the iron table.

The Soul Eater grabs my arm, jerks me away from Owen. I wrench free and turn to face him.

"*You!*" he cries. "How did you get free? Who *are* you?"

"I am the Gwydden's youngest daughter. And you cannot have his soul."

Lightning flashes above our heads, an impossibility in a sky full of stars.

The last of my human form falls away from me.

Twiggy growth pushes up from my knuckles.

Bark unfolds on my face.

Leaves and violets whisper in my hair.

My heart does not change, from one moment to the next, but suddenly,

I

am

different.

No.

Suddenly

I

am

the

same

as I ever was.

Owen has pushed himself up on one elbow on the table. He stares at me.

"I am sorry." I have wanted to tell him this every day since his mother ripped out her heart. "Forgive me, if you can."

But I do not say the words that burn deep inside of me.

I cannot speak to him of love.

Because I am

a monster

and he

is not.

"Seren." His voice is a whisper. A plea. "I—"

There's a raging whirl of wind,

the scent of trees.

Branches reach

from nowhere,

writhing and twisting and studded with thorns.

They grow up around me. They block Owen from sight. They pin my arms to my sides.

Vines crawl down my throat and cinch tight around my ears.

There's a rushing darkness.

A roaring sense of cold and rot.

Then the vines retreat and the branches fall away.

I lie on the grass

under a sky strewn with stars.

I stare up

into the wrathful eyes

of

my

mother.

Chapter Fifty-One

OWEN

*L*EAVES IN HER HAIR. SAPLINGS AT HER FEET. THE SCENT OF VIOLETS. It can't be.

And yet it is. She found me in another form, to betray me all over again.

But I cannot see her betrayal in anything other than her shape. Because she told me the truth, didn't she? I should have known from the beginning, from the moment she told me her name.

Bedwyn.

Birch tree.

I stare at her. "Seren. I—"

A cold wind blows through the tower, raging and wild. It smells of the wood. Brambles twist out of nothing, coiling around her, pulling tight.

"Seren!"

I blink, and the wind and brambles are gone, and she's gone with them.

My life leaks red from my chest. I'm not strong enough to haul myself from the iron table without crumpling to the floor. So I lie here, propped up on my elbow, gasping for air like a fish.

She saved me. I don't know how or why. But she saved me.

And now she's gone.

The king radiates anger like pulsing heat. He paces between the iron table and the place the branches wrapped around her and spirited her away. Leaves swirl on some invisible wind. Leaves and violets.

She is all I can think about.

Peeling potatoes in the kitchen. A tray of food in the stables when I could barely move. Hiding under the couch waiting for the nobleman to leave, the feel of her hand caught fast in mine. Dancing in the courtyard to the distant strain of the orchestra.

Kissing her like the world was ending, like there would never be another moment to truly live.

I didn't know there really wouldn't be.

I press my hands against the gaping wound in my chest, trying to staunch the blood. It leaks through my fingers, slippery and hot.

Too much, too much.

My head wheels.

This is what it is, to die.

Oh God.

My father's words whisper through my mind. *Do not mourn me, Owen. I am happy. I am with her.*

I will go to them. Father. Mother. But I'll leave Awela behind. I'll leave Seren behind.

I can't bear it.

The king crouches in the place where she stood just a moment before, leaves still whirling in the air. Leaves and violets. They settle, slowly, to the floor, and he grabs a fistful, crushing them in his palm. I catch the scent of her: wild, intoxicating power. "I only needed a piece of one," he says, laughing as he opens his hand. "I should have known what she was. A gift. A sign." He pours the crushed leaves into an empty glass vial, and corks it.

He wheels on me, any hint of laughter gone. "What deal did you make with her? What has she done to you?"

"Nothing," I rasp. "Nothing." The world is going hazy at the edges.

He grabs my shoulders, shakes me hard. "There is wood magic in you. Your soul is protected. WHAT DEAL DID YOU MAKE WITH HER?"

He shoves me off the table, and I land with a jolt on the floor. Pain rushes up to swallow me. Blood slides between my fingers.

He kicks me in the side and I scream as a rib snaps.

"Worthless," he snarls. "You are *worthless* to me!" He paces over to the desk, grabs one of the ancient star charts, drags his fingers over the crumbly parchment. "I can wait for a new soul. I'll find a way to undo whatever it is she did to you. Wood magic, that's all I need. But until then, I'll make do without one. I will defeat her with a power older than souls. I will devour her, and burn her wood, and see all that she ever loved turn to *ash*."

I convulse on the floor. Darkness presses in.

The king stalks to the table where he bound me, climbs up onto it himself.

I try to breathe. I try to cling to consciousness. I don't want to bleed out on the floor. Not when she was here. Not when she *saved* me. Again.

Dancing in the courtyard, the wind in her hair.

Kissing her under the stars, her heat wending through me.

Now she's gone and gone and gone.

I struggle for my last breaths. They fill my ragged lungs, sharp as knives.

The king cries out, and I glance up to see him driving the metal claw into his own chest. He shouts a word to the sky, and the ceiling *explodes*.

Glass and light rain down. Heat sizzles and sears.

Somehow, through the blur of pain and confusion, I understand.

King Elynion has given up the remains of the Gwydden's soul for the power she wielded when she changed the stars.

Now the stars rush into him, light blazing into his chest and under his skin. He burns with it. I think he cannot possibly contain it all.

The light comes and comes. It will consume him. It will be the last thing I ever see.

But it stops, as suddenly as it started. The floor is a desert of broken glass.

The king lives.

He rips the iron from his chest, and laughs with pleasure as the wound heals itself, pulsing with light. He teems with impossible power.

He climbs from the table, hauls me to my feet. I can't stand on my own and I sag in his grip.

His hand is hot enough to burn through the ragged remains of my sleeves. But I can't jerk away. He smiles, and there are stars inside of him, light slipping through the cracks in his teeth. The rough patches of his flesh are smoothed over now. He seems to grow younger before my eyes.

"I have been a fool for far too long," he says. "I should not have held so tight to the witch's soul."

"I thought that was what gave you your power. Your long life."

"At first," he agrees. His voice sounds as if it's coming from a great distance away. "But I have long since learned my own useful bits of sorcery."

My vision blurs. My heart slows. I'm slipping away, and I'll never see her again.

Heat sears through my chest, tearing a scream from my throat. I open my eyes to see the king has touched my wound, commanded my flesh to knit itself back together.

"My dear Owen," he says. "I can't let you die here. I still mean to have your soul, you know. And now I have everything I need."

I shudder as I come back to myself. He didn't heal my broken rib or the wounds in my leg and my face. My whole body is embedded with shards of glass from the exploded ceiling. The pain seems almost more acute, now that the mortal wound is gone.

"Everything you need to take my soul?" I ask.

He smiles. "Everything I need to catch a tree siren. A piece of one—" He taps the vial of crushed leaves. "And something to use as bait." He smiles at me with everything but his horrible, horrible eyes. "I have both."

The king drags me to the prison himself—for all his healing of me, I can barely walk. Every breath sends pain stabbing through my broken rib, and if I don't dig the glass out of my leg soon—

I stumble along the same path I took barely a few hours ago to see my father. Through the prison courtyard, where Drystan regards me with shock and horror, down the long flight of stairs. All the while the king doesn't let go of my arm. The heat of him has lessened now, but I can sense it lurking, a beast ready to rear its head at his word.

He hauls me down the row of cells, to the place where my father drew his last breaths. His body is gone. No trace of him left.

The king opens the door to the cell across from my father's. He throws me in, and I collapse with a grunt. Tears leak from my eyes. I don't attempt to lift my head. "How long?" I ask, and hate myself for it. I don't even know what I'm asking, exactly. How long will he keep me here? How long do I have to live?

He smiles at me in the flickering torchlight. "Until I have need of you, Owen Merrick."

I shut my eyes. I turn away.

The cell rattles as he shuts the door. The key grates in the lock.

His footsteps fade down the corridor.

I am alone in the dark.

Chapter Fifty-Two

SEREN

BLOOD DRIPS
from my mother's horns.
Her face is peeling, caught in the midst of
shedding her skin.
She is clothed in briars,
wrapped about her like shiny, lethal snakes.
She used her power to pull me down from the tower,
away from Owen and the Soul Eater.
Now,
she
will
kill
me.
She grabs my shoulder, her claws digging deep.
She hauls me upright,
holds me so my feet dangle helplessly

while my shoulder tears and

blood

pours

down

my

arm.

She shrieks at me: "WHAT HAVE YOU DONE?" She drags her
other hand across my face, gouging deep cuts on both cheeks.

She slams me to the ground

and I cannot breathe.

Stars wheel

before my eyes.

I am afraid.

I

have

never

been

so

afraid.

"You've been to see *them*." She tugs a briar from her dress and
uses it to roughly bind my wrists. "Your *brothers*."

The thorns pierce my flesh.

My blood pours

amber and red into the grass:

the last drops

of my humanity.

"I can smell the stink of them on you, smell the monstrous,
blasphemous form you wore, the form that still clings to you like
moss. And why? *Why?* Because you were *protecting* a *human boy*!"

Dew leaks

from my eyes.

I gulp

and gulp for air.

My mother says: "I know. I KNOW! The trees have been watching you, and they told me when I asked. They told me that not only did you spare his life once, but you spared it again and again and again. That you hid him from your sisters, that you invited him into your bed."

I say: "I kissed him. I kissed him twice, and that is all."

I can still feel

the press

of his lips.

Their warmth.

Their softness.

The scratch of the stubble on his chin.

My mother yanks another briar from her dress. She lashes me across the stomach. Thorns tear through the maid's uniform and into the tender bark of my belly.

A scream tears out of me.

Amber and red.

Sap and blood.

Screaming.

All mine.

She hisses at me. "You DARE, you DARE to love a HUMAN, and then become LIKE him? You DARE?"

She binds my ankles with yet another briar.

She slings me across her shoulder

like the flour sacks the kitchen boys

haul in every morning.

My face and body fall

against her thorny dress,

and I cannot tell the night air apart

from the raging, fiery pain.

Each step she takes

is another brittle agony.

I whisper to the briars: "Where are you taking me?"

"To the wood, daughter."

"That is where you will kill me?"

Dew mingles

with the blood on my face.

The fear

is eating

me.

She carries me on through the darkness. "That is where you will feel every ounce of your betrayal. That is where you will die."

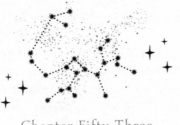

Chapter Fifty-Three

OWEN

I AM CONTENT TO DIE DOWN HERE. I WANT TO. I WELCOME IT. My body grows stiff on the hard floor. A chill seeps into my bones. I let my mind drift away. I think of the wind through the trees, of Awela cuddling close under my chin. I think of violets and fireflies. Of stars and cinnamon tea. It hurts to breathe, to move, to think of anything beyond these brief images.

But there's a scrape of boots on stone. A jingle of keys. The cell door swinging smoothly open.

Someone kneels beside me. Puts an arm under my head.

"Merrick, I need you to sit up."

"Go away." The words rasp out of me.

"Merrick." Arms pull me upright, prop me against the cell wall.

I open my eyes. Drystan is here, torchlight glancing off the brass buttons on his coat. To my shock, Rheinallt is with him. I stare at my pale-haired friend.

"His Majesty didn't leave any instructions against a physician," explains Drystan.

"Didn't order one either," Rheinallt adds dryly. "But here I am all the same. Where are you hurt?"

"My leg," I breathe. "And I think a broken rib."

Rheinallt frowns at the bloody hole in the front of my shirt. "What happened there?"

I start to shake my head and think better of it. "Too hard to explain."

"Be quick," says Drystan. "I'll come to let you out when you're done." He retreats into the corridor, locking the cell behind him. I wonder how many times tonight he's directly or indirectly disobeyed orders.

Rheinallt pulls a flask from the physician's bag he brought with him, and presses it into my hands. "Drink up. This won't feel great."

He digs the glass out of my leg, piece by piece. Every shard is another small agony. But one drink from the flask is enough for me—it burns all the way down into my gut and makes me cough.

Rheinallt spreads salve on the cuts when he's finished, and wraps a clean bandage around my leg. He presses gently on my rib cage, and I swallow a scream when his fingers find the broken bones.

"Not much I can do for the rib, I'm afraid, besides bandage it. Sorry, Merrick."

He does that, too, and the bandage at least makes me feel less like I'm going to fall apart at any moment.

He crouches back on his heels. "What happened?"

I can't tell him about the king. No one else needs to die because of what my father saw in the stars. "My father's dead. I . . . confronted the king."

Rheinallt lets out a colorful oath, clearly impressed. "Bold, Merrick."

Drystan appears at the cell door, and unlocks it. "Time to go."

Rheinallt gives me an apologetic look, and steps out into the corridor. For a moment, neither man moves.

"Rumor has it the army is marching soon," Rheinallt tells me. "The king means to face the Gwydden. Defeat her, once and for all."

I shudder at the memory of stars and glass raining down on Elynion.

"Baines thinks we'll march to our deaths. No one can stand against the wood. Against the sirens."

I see a flash of yellow eyes. Of bodies snapped in two with silver hands.

"The king wouldn't march without a plan," I say. "He wouldn't march unless he thought he could win."

Stars and souls. My fingers go to my chest, where the king healed a mortal wound with a simple touch.

"I hope you're right, Merrick," says Rheinallt. "And I hope you'll get out of there in time to march with us."

I give him a grimace that's meant to be a smile, and then Drystan escorts Rheinallt out of the prison, up into the freedom of night air.

I lean against the cell wall and shut my eyes, but I can't find the haze of pain anymore. I can't feel the insistent pull of death.

I can't shut out the memory of my father's last breath, of the life winking out of him, of his body going limp in my arms.

I bow my head into my knees, and sob.

Chapter Fifty-Four

SEREN

MY MOTHER BINDS ME WITH BRIARS TO THE HEARTLESS
tree.
I am pierced, every part of me,
a thousand small agonies.
I bleed and I bleed,
until all the human blood has run out
and only sap pours from my veins.
Even then, she does not let me go.
Even then, she does not kill me.
Around me
the world darkens and lightens
again and again.
I do not know how many times.
I cannot think clearly.
All is pain
and sticky sap.

Once, it rains.

For a few precious moments

I am washed clean

and the pain ebbs away.

But my mother comes hissing with displeasure.

She commands the tree to grow a wide branch over me

so I cannot feel the rain.

She commands the briars to pull tighter and tighter until I scream.

She pulls them tighter still.

The rain stops. Night comes.

Then dawn, blurred and silver.

My mother returns, singing a command to the briars.

They loosen enough to let me breathe a little easier.

She smiles. Her teeth spark

with the power

of a newly consumed soul.

She commands: "Sing, daughter. There is a village a league off, brimming with souls. Draw them to me. Sing."

I say: "No," and even this simple word

scrapes against my throat

like broken ice.

She squeezes her hand into a fist. She laughs. "It was not a request, little fool. Now *sing*."

My heart does not belong to her any longer,

but my will is still wholly hers.

She drags my song from me with her power.

It rips my mouth open,

tears the music from deep inside of me.

I can do nothing to stop it.

I cannot twist my head, cannot press my bound hands over my mouth.

I fight against her
with every heartbeat,
but it is not enough.
I sing
and sing
and sing.
After a time, the villagers come. They have walked very far.
They are young and old and in between.
My mother slaughters them
one
by
one.
She forces my eyes to stay open,
forces me to watch
as she feeds their souls
into the heartless tree.
I cannot stop her.
I cannot do anything.
The earth swallows the bodies,
choked
with
bones.
At last my mother opens her fist,
and my song is cut off.
She leaves me pinned to the heartless tree.
Dew pours down my cheeks.
If Owen were here,
he would be ashamed of me.
If he were here,
I would ask him
to drive a knife
into

my

heart.

My sisters come to laugh at me.

I have rarely seen them all together.

They are a copse of monsters,

a strange garden blooming in their hair:

foxglove and aster and thistle,

nettles and celandine and daisies.

Last of all, my sister with roses in her hair.

She waits. She watches.

My other sisters spit in my face.

They order the briars to squeeze tighter.

They shove berries down my throat that are poisonous to humans.

They make me drink brackish water.

They laugh and laugh.

Because none of these things can kill me in this monstrous form.

And our mother will not let me die.

Not yet.

The sister with thistles in her hair says: "You are weak, little sister. You are foolish and reckless and *weak*."

The sister with celandine adds: "A *human boy*! All this, for a *human boy*!"

They run out of ways to torment me. They grow tired of their fun. They fade back into the wood.

All but the sister with roses in her hair. She says: "I told you to run. I told you to run far and fast away, but you lingered. For a worthless boy."

Dust motes dance

in a shaft of sunlight.

Bees drink nectar from her roses.

I say: "He is not worthless."

She sneers: "Do you think he will come and *save* you?"

My heart beats

sluggish,

slow,

heavy with emptiness,

glutted with pain. "No. But you could."

She blinks at me. "I helped you once before. I will not degrade myself that way again."

"Then why are you still standing here?"

The wood shivers around us, every leaf listening.

I say: "Let me loose. Come away with me. Help me find a way to defeat our mother."

"There is no defeating her."

"You know she is evil. You know she is cruel. We can stop her together. We can become something more."

"Human?" she mocks me.

"Perhaps." It is hard to breathe and hard to speak; my sisters bound the briars too tight.

There is pity in her face.

I say: "Please. Please help me."

For a moment I think she will.

I feel her heart,

reaching out to mine.

But she shakes her head, and a cold wind rattles the leaves in her hair. "You brought this upon yourself, little sister. If you cannot bear it, that is not my fault."

She slips back into the wood.

I am once more

alone.

But the briars loosen, more than they have since my mother bound me.

I sag to the ground, dig my hands into the earth.

I reach out for the wood; I call to the trees. *Help me*, I plead. *Rise against her.*

But the trees

do not listen.

They belong wholly,

irrevocably,

to her.

I reach out for my brothers, in their wild dwelling place far away. *Cangen, Criafol, Pren. Help me stop her. Please.*

But my brothers do not come.

I reach out for Owen, but I cannot find him. He is far from the wood.

The sun rises and sets

again and again.

My mother and sisters do not come to me,

but I do not dare to think

I have been forgotten.

The briars yet bind me to the heartless tree,

choking away my power.

I cannot get free of them.

The wood grows day by day.

I can sense it

in the spaces

where the pain

does not reach,

the glimmerings of light

between shadows.

Growing and growing.

Blazing with souls.

It creeps toward the king and his palace.

It devours everything in its path.

I live,

I bleed,
I wait.
Then one morning, my mother comes to me.
She strips the briars from my body.
She tells me
we are going
to war.

Chapter Fifty-Five

OWEN

DAYS PASS IN THE DARK OF THE KING'S PRISON. I'M NOT SURE how many. Drystan brings me food sometimes. Rheinallt comes once to change the bandage on my leg.

I grow stronger. I grow restless.

There is far, far too much time.

To think. To fear. To rage.

I pace the cell, over and over until my legs ache. I try to sleep. But nightmares chase sleep away. It's better to be awake.

I pray that Awela is safe, and far from here.

I try not to think about Bedwyn. About *Seren*.

I can't reconcile what she did. What she is. What, somehow, she still means to me.

Bedwyn wasn't real, and yet—

And yet you kissed a monster, says a voice inside my head. *You kissed a monster, and you don't want to let her go.*

Not a monster, I tell myself stubbornly. *Not anymore. She saved me. She defied her mother and saved me so many times.*

But now—

What?

My mother is dead, ash in the wood.

My father is gone, buried somewhere in the cold earth.

Awela is out of my reach.

And Seren isn't here.

She isn't *here*.

I wish she were.

I wish she would have told me, when there was still time, that she was Seren. That she'd come back to me.

But would I have listened?

I pace the cell. I count the stones in the walls. I trace constellations in the spots of rust on the bars.

I'm afraid for her. I think the Gwydden pulled her back into the wood. I think she's in danger. But I'm powerless to save her—we are, both of us, on our own.

I dream one night of the king, sailing through the stars, the Gwydden lashed to the prow of his ship as a living figurehead. Below the stars the wood is burning. *Seren* is burning. The flames eat the silver-white form of her; her skin and hair pop and crack like peat in a fire. Violets shriek and shrivel. She turns all to ash, and the wind blows her away.

I wake with a start to the distant pulse of drums. The brassy call of a trumpet.

And, a little while later, boots on stone, coming toward me.

I jerk upright, pulse raging.

But it isn't the king.

It's Baines and Rheinallt, a torch held between them.

I *stare*. "What the hell are you two doing here?"

Baines takes the torch while Rheinallt fumbles with a ring of keys.

"Came to rescue you, idiot," says Baines.

Rheinallt fits a key into the lock, but it's clearly the wrong one. He curses and tries another one.

"Where's the guard?" I ask.

Rheinallt finds the right key. He unlocks the door. "Drugged him. Come on."

I feel a pang of regret for Drystan, if he's the one on duty. I don't move. "I'm not getting you in trouble."

"It won't matter," says Baines grimly. "We're going to war against the wood. Didn't you hear the drums? No one will notice if you're not here."

"The *king* will notice. And if he finds out who let me go—he'll tear you apart."

Rheinallt utters a string of increasingly colorful words until Baines claps a hand on his arm to stop him.

"You really want to stay there?" Baines says.

"I don't *want* to."

"Then don't," says Rheinallt. "Come fight with us. Help us send the witch and her wood back to Hell where she belongs." There's an intensity in his pale eyes that startles me.

Baines is still, solemn, his dark skin melding into the shadows. "Die with us, he means. No one can fight against the wood and live."

I sag against the wall. "Thank you for coming to save me. But you have to go now. Before you get caught. Please."

For a moment, I think my friends are going to drag me from the cell. But they don't. They salute me, first Baines, then Rheinallt, right fists to left shoulders.

"Don't die," I tell them.

Baines grimaces, but Rheinallt smiles. "You either."

And then they're gone, back down the corridor, back up the stairs.

I slump to the floor. I'm a fool. But I know the king isn't done with me yet. If I'd gone with them, he would have found us. He would have ripped their souls from their bodies, cast their husks to the ground. I couldn't do that to them.

Somehow I'm expecting the footsteps that approach my cell barely half an hour later.

I'm not surprised to lift my head and see the king through the bars, dressed for war in old-fashioned gold plate armor that's maybe as ancient as he is. He wrenches the cell door from its hinges, not bothering with a key. He hauls me up by one arm, pulls me into the corridor. "It's time," he says.

I try not to feel the awful heat of him. I try to tamp down my fear. "For what?"

"To catch a siren. To raze a wood. To kill a witch." He grins at me, a flash of white teeth. "To unbind your soul, so I can swallow it."

He drags me up the stairs, out into blinding starlight.

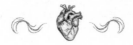

It isn't yet dawn.

Torches burn in the darkness, spilling out beyond my sightline, an army of raging stars: Tarian's army—ready to march.

King Elynion stands on the hill before them. His armor makes the torchlight writhe and shiver, or perhaps the fire cannot stand the heat of him, and strains to get away. He has not bound me— he doesn't need to. He crackles with power. With stars. If he snapped his fingers, I think I might burst into flame.

Four of his own personal guards stand with us, their eyes glittering under their helmets.

"Soldiers of Tarian!" Elynion shouts down the hill to the waiting army. "This is the day of our triumph! The day we take back what is ours, the day we grind the witch into the dirt under our heels and burn her wicked trees to ashes. She will no longer shadow our land! No longer fill us with fear! She will be a blight upon Tarian no more!"

The answering shout rolls up the hill like thunder, the whole of the army speaking as one: "NO MORE!"

"Death to the witch!" cries the king. "Death to her trees!" He thrusts his sword high into the air.

The army screams back, "DEATH!"

Then Elynion sheathes his sword, grabs my arm, and drags me down the hill. A huge black horse waits for him there, with other mounts for his guards. There is no horse for me. The king and his guards swing into their saddles, and the king fixes me with his horrible eyes. "Keep up, Merrick." He kicks his horse into motion; the guards follow suit.

"Better do as he says."

I look back to see the guard Luned on a horse of her own, a pair of unlit torches strapped to her saddle. Commander Carys is with her, and the whole of the army marches at their heels.

Luned hefts me up behind her, and then we're hurtling after the king, wind and darkness rushing by.

All is pain and fear, an eerie bend to the world, like I'm caught in a nightmare I can't escape from. I don't have my musket or my sword, not even a knife. I can't shut out the king's words, whispering eternally through my mind: *To unbind your soul, so I can swallow it.* Will I die like my mother, an empty shell? Will I turn to ash for the wind to blow away?

We've been riding less than an hour when the wood looms suddenly ahead of us—the wood I know is supposed to be miles and miles from here. A chill crawls down my spine.

Luned reins in her horse just behind Elynion and his guards, who have stopped on the very edge of the trees. Wind shudders through the branches, making the leaves scrape and chatter. The king swings to the ground. He glances back. His eyes meet mine. "Come," he says.

I climb from the saddle in a daze, my feet drawing me to the king, though my mind is screaming for me to turn, to run.

He steps past the border of the trees. I follow like a dog on a lead. The guards stay behind.

The wood is silent. Eerily so. Stars wink through chinks in the tree canopy. King Elynion carries no torch; he doesn't need one—light sparks between his fingers.

We stop at the base of an ash tree, tall and dark and strong. The king lifts his hands, slashes them in a sideways motion, and a shaft of impossibly bright light cleaves the tree in two. For a moment the trunk shudders, unsure, before toppling backward. It lands with a resounding *thud* that shakes the earth.

Elynion regards his handiwork with a smile. "Let's see what kind of fish will bite." He draws a glass vial from his breast pocket. A vial filled with crushed leaves.

Suddenly I'm more afraid even than I was in the observatory, with Elynion's machine boring into my chest and stars and glass raining down.

Now I have everything I need to catch a tree siren, the king said. *A piece of one. And something to use as bait.*

I stare at the newly hewn stump, a yawning pit of horror engulfing me.

I am numb as the king drags me to the stump, as he binds me with rough cords that cut into my chest and press against my broken rib. I am too afraid to feel the pain. "What are you going to do?" I choke out. "What are you going to do when—"

"When I catch one?" Elynion laughs. "Don't tell me you're sentimental about the witch's bloodthirsty monsters! I couldn't very well lead my army against the wood without some means of protecting them, you know. And to do that, I need a siren. What does it matter what happens to it?"

There's a fire in my chest and I can't breathe, can't breathe.

I flinch when he draws a knife against my arm, as the skin breaks, as blood drips hot.

Beyond the wood, the sun is rising. In its first rays of light, I notice from somewhere outside of myself that the leaves are just beginning to turn. Summer is gone. Autumn has crept in without me realizing.

The trees shiver in a wind I do not feel. Blood runs down my arm and I am numb, so numb. The world goes black around the edges.

A thread of song cuts through the haze, and I am suddenly, horribly, aware.

Now I have everything I need to catch a tree siren.

King Elynion stands just past my peripheral, watchful, waiting.

I heave against my bonds, jostling my broken rib; I hiss in agony.

The tree siren's song grows louder.

It's her.

I know it's her.

The king will harm her and *I can't bear it.*

I thrash in the ropes, heedless of the pain, and the music twists into me, deeper and deeper until I grow still again, until I lift my eyes toward the wood and see her coming, silver and white through the trees.

For a moment my will breaks through even the power of her song, and I shout "SEREN!" into the heedless air.

She laughs as she lunges toward me, as her claws graze against my cheek.

It's only then I realize that her eyes are all wrong, that there are roses in her hair instead of violets.

That she isn't Seren.

The king shouts a harsh word. There's a crackle of electricity, a smell of stars and crushed leaves. He flings the contents of the vial onto the siren, infusing them somehow with his power. Vines wind up out of thin air, coiling around the siren's wrists and ankles, weaving over her mouth until her song is cut suddenly and irrevocably off.

I blink, and I see the vines are twisted with strands of iron.

The king's magic has paralyzed her, but her eyes are vicious, wild.

Elynion strides into view, cutting my bonds with one efficient swipe of his knife. I fall to my knees on the forest floor, trembling all over.

The siren wears a necklace, similar to one Seren wore sometimes: an orb of pulsing light hanging on a piece of braided grass. The king yanks it from her throat and puts it on over his own head. It clinks against his plate armor. He looks at me impassively. "Get up, Merrick."

I just stare at him, the blood loss making my head wheel.

He frowns at the cut in my arm, as if forgetting he was the one who made it. He touches me with one searing finger. Heat blazes agonizingly through my skin, sealing the wound.

"I said get up."

I obey. The tree siren stands there, silent and seething. But there is an awful fear in her eyes. She is so like Seren—and yet so unlike her, too. Needles of iron pierce her skin, and I read something else in her glance: pain.

"Come," says Elynion.

Her body goes rigid. She steps up behind him.

Both of us follow him from the wood, back to where his guards and Luned are waiting.

The army is coming over the plain. They swell against the rising sun. I don't know what the king plans on doing with the tree siren, or with me. But in this moment I fear him more than the Gwydden herself.

I hope to God Seren is far, far away from this place.

Chapter Fifty-Six

SEREN

T HE WOOD AROUND ME
teems,
breathes,
moves.

The trees are marching. They pluck their roots from the ground and sink them down again. They ooze across the earth. Slow. Steady. Sure.

They are not quite alive—my mother did not give them hearts.

But they are more than they were.

Their anger pulses through the earth.

It frightens me.

This is my mother's army,

the one she fed with blood and souls.

She rides in the midst of the trees, on a giant creature that is something like a tree and something like a lion, and yet is neither. No natural beast would bear her.

So she ripped the heartless tree from the earth, and made it into a creature that would.

It creaks as it walks, its wood-skin dark with silver veins.

Its claws are hand-length thorns. Its fur is thousands of prickling pine needles. Its mane is bright golden leaves.

If I had not watched my mother twist it into its monstrous form, I would not believe it.

But she did.

My mother's antlers are dipped in fresh blood. Her green hair is woven with the same briars that bound me. They bloom with roses.

She wears a gown of bones. Human bones. They rattle and clack.

Somehow

she is as

beautiful

as she is

terrible.

But I could not revile her more.

She has put me in a cage made of bones, so small I must crouch and fold to fit.

Two of her trees bear the cage between them; I am hoisted high on barky shoulders.

With every step, I sway.

With every root

that plunges into the earth

and tears free again,

I am more afraid.

The cage reeks of death.

I wish

that mine

had already found me.

The wood moves and grows, moves and grows.

Six of my sisters flank my mother and the heartless lion,
three on one side,
three on the other.
They wear wooden armor, strapped to arms and chest and legs
with vines.
I am horrified they stripped tree bark to clothe themselves.
But they have never *cared* for the wood where we were born.
They begin to sing,
a war song that shrieks through the air.
The wood roars in answer.
The trees bearing my cage move faster, faster.
I look for my sister with roses in her hair,
but I do not see her.
She is the only one missing.
Clouds knot overhead,
heavy with lightning,
with rain.
I whisper yet another plea to my brothers,
though I know even if they were here,
they could not stop our mother.
She commands every tree in the forest.
She burns with the old anger.
At last, at last, she will have her revenge on the human king
and she will take
the whole world
with him.
I shudder in my cage.
I hope Owen is far from here.
I hope he will not come to face the fury of my mother's wood.
I want him to live.
To forget me.
To be happy.

I never should have left
violets
on his windowsill.
Tears
run
rivers
down
my
face.
They taste of salt,
the one bit of humanity
my monstrous body
still clings to.
The wood marches on and on.
We come to a village. The trees rip the buildings apart,
stone
by
stone.
The humans run from us, screaming.
My sisters lure them back with their song.
I am powerless to stop them.
They laugh as they kill, as bones break and blood drenches the
ground.
They fill their orbs with souls. The earth swallows the bodies.
And then there is nothing of the village left
save dust.
My mother watches all from atop the heartless lion.
When the slaughter is over, my sisters come and kneel before
her, offering their orbs.
My mother cracks them open one by one.
She drinks the souls.
Gorges herself.

She commands my sisters: "Go. The Eater and his army ride to meet us. He dares to think he can prevail against my wood. Show him he is wrong. Kill his soldiers. Kill them *all*, save the Eater alone."

My sisters bow. Then they are gone into the trees.

My mother laughs. She throws back her head and sings to the sky,

and her song
is even more beautiful
and terrible
than she is.
And then
she turns
to me.

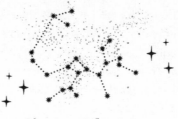

Chapter Fifty-Seven

OWEN

WE RIDE WEST, UNDER WRITHING CLOUDS, ALL THE KING'S army at our heels.

The siren is bound by a length of cord to the king's saddle, and she stumbles and trips as she tries to keep her feet and not be dragged.

I can't look at her. I can't keep my eyes off of her. In every line of her frame I see Seren. I'm sick and afraid.

And then we come, once more, to the wood.

It's a great, dark mass, branches snarled and stirring. It stretches out of sight to the north and the south, in a place that, even yesterday perhaps, was nothing but a grassy plain.

The king unhooks a torch from his saddle. He glances at it. It flares to life.

Luned reaches for her torch, and behind her, officers shout for all the soldiers to do the same.

Light flares all down the brow of the hill.

The siren shrinks from the heat of the king's torch, as if she fears he will burn her with it.

Instead, he kicks his horse into a run, and they plunge into the wood, jerking her behind.

Luned follows suit, and we lurch after the king, the Gwydden's Wood closing around us.

The king flings his torch into the undergrowth. Luned sets hers to the spindly branches of a dead tree.

The vanguard reaches the border of the wood, and then there are more torches than I can count.

A wall of heat and light flares up. With it comes the sound of high, inhuman keening.

The trees are screaming.

The king leads us through the forest, racing into the flames, fanning them hotter, brighter.

The siren trips, choking after him, a helpless creature in the smoke.

The trees leer over us, grabbing at us with hanging branches, tripping horses with rapidly growing vines, dragging soldiers to the ground and strangling them with roots.

But they cannot fight against the flames.

"TAKE MY SWORD!" screams Luned.

I fumble to pull it from her saddle, but I cannot bring myself to attack the trees.

She curses, shoving the torch into my hand and claiming the sword for herself. She hacks off tree limbs and they crash to the ground.

The wood burns and the wood screams, and all is a rush of speed and heat.

The trees reach for me. Branches graze my shoulders, snag in my hair.

I fight them off and duck low, struggling to keep my seat.

Smoke burns my eyes. Soldiers scream and the wood howls. I can't keep my eyes off the tree siren. I can't help but think that Seren would mourn the death of the trees, if she were here. So part of me mourns, too.

Luned shouts as a branch grabs her, nearly shaking her from the horse. I fling her torch at the tree. It hisses and shrinks back, and Luned and I ride onward.

I hear their music before I see them, sudden and silver in the air. Their song twists through the noise of the screeching trees, creating a mad and horrible counterpoint.

The bound siren turns toward the music, and in her there is suddenly a hard, wild joy.

They come through the smoke and the fire: six of them, silver and shining among the dark trees. My heart seizes and my breath chokes off.

But none of them have violets in their hair.

They are so like her, but they are not her. They are monstrous. She is not.

Oh God.

Oh God. She is not.

The king howls in some awful, mad delight, and swings off his horse. He seizes the captured siren by the throat. "Now to earn your keep, little witch!"

He rips the vines from her mouth with one hand, while he snaps the fingers of his other. A miniature star dances white-hot in his palm.

The clamor of the sirens' music shrieks around us, tangled with the wind and the howling trees.

The captured siren grins. Opens her mouth.

But before a single note can drop from her lips, the king shoves the star down her throat.

He shouts a word into the air, a word that crackles with heat and magic.

One moment the siren is screaming in agony and her sisters are shrieking their awful music.

The next moment all is silent but for the crackling trees.

The six sirens still stand in the midst of the wood.

But they have stopped singing.

They open their mouths. No sound escapes.

I have only a moment to stare before the king is yanking me down from Luned's horse.

"A silence spell," the king says, as if we're conversing at a dinner party. "To level the playing field. Give my soldiers a fighting chance."

The siren with roses in her hair collapses to the ground, hands gripping her throat. Her eyes roll wild. She gasps for breath.

"What did you do?" I choke out.

The king shrugs. "Burned her vocal cords. Used magic to counteract the sirens' song. Silence spell. Now to give myself a little extra boost."

Suddenly he's gripping my shoulder so hard I hiss in pain, and yanking the siren's necklace from his throat. He shoves the orb into my chest.

A scream rips out of me. I'm back in the king's observatory, his clawed machine sunk into me, scrabbling for my soul.

Pain swallows me. The trees overhead thrash and howl. Dimly, I'm aware of the clash of battle, the snap of wood, of bone.

The king curses, flings me to the ground.

Suddenly I can breathe again.

The orb has shattered in his hands.

"Something stronger than wood magic has bound your soul," he hisses. "You're of no use to me. Either of you." He curses again, stomps on my arm with his boot.

I shriek as the bone snaps, as pain bursts white behind my eyes.

I try to heave myself up with my good arm, turning my head in time to see Elynion drive his knife into the wounded siren's heart.

For a moment, her eyes grow wide. Then she is still. Her lips are black and charred. Smoke curls off of her.

Elynion leaves me where I lie.

I blink and see my mother in the mud, pressing her hand against my chest. Her words echo in my mind. *One last spark of power. To guard you from her. So she can never take your soul, the way she took mine.*

It was my mother, protecting me all this time. Her love was stronger than wood magic, stronger than Elynion's machines, even stronger than a tree siren's orb.

Grief weighs on me, so heavy I want to lie here forever and let it turn me, bit by bit, to dust.

The battle rages past me. I lift my bleary eyes to see the sirens locked in combat with soldier after soldier. They no longer have their music, but they still have their strength. Their rage.

They twist bodies and break necks. They open their mouths in soundless screams as they kill and kill and kill.

The trees burn, but still the sirens fight. Still they lead the wood against Elynion's army.

And even without their music, they're *winning*.

I stare, numb, as they push the army back, past the body of their dead sister, past the flaming trees. I can't see Elynion anymore.

There is nothing but smoke and ash, raining down around me like snow.

I wish the king *had* taken my soul. I don't even want it anymore.

I let my eyes drift shut.

"Merrick. *Merrick.*"

I open my eyes. Baines kneels over me, his face streaked with blood and ash. "I've lost Rheinallt. I'm not losing you. Come on."

He helps me to a sitting position, makes an awkward sling for my arm out of his jacket.

He glances at the dead siren and shudders.

"Rheinallt?" I whisper as he tugs me to my feet.

There's a riderless horse rearing and thrashing, its reins tangled in a burning tree. Baines frees the creature, calms it. Hoists me into the saddle and climbs up behind me.

The horse lurches forward, and we ride through the burning wood, out onto the plain.

"Rheinallt is dead?" I say.

Behind me, Baines shakes his head. "He deserted. Disappeared after we tried to spring you from prison."

"Wouldn't have thought it of him," I gasp.

"Me neither."

Another force of trees have come down from the north. They join the tree sirens, push Elynion's soldiers back and back. They are the ocean, the king and his army a dwindling fleet before them.

But there are a handful more horsemen who have escaped the burning wood. We ride to join them. One by one, we salute each other.

"To the king," says Baines, unsheathing his sword.

There's a spare sword strapped to the saddle, and I draw it with my good arm.

"To the king," I echo.

"To the king!" the other soldiers shout.

We ride hard across the plain, to where the battle rages on. If there is the smallest chance that Elynion, in all his brutality, can stand against the Gwydden, can keep her wood from devouring the world, I must fight with him. When it's over, I'll kill him for what he did to my father.

We hurtle toward the sirens and the wood, and I wonder where Seren is, if she remembers our nights on the hill, if she will come and help to turn the tide against her mother.

Or if she has chosen to become, once more, a monster.

Chapter Fifty-Eight

SEREN

M Y MOTHER DISMOUNTS FROM THE HEARTLESS LION.
The bones of her dress clack and clatter,
a twisted music
for a soulless queen.

The trees carrying my cage set me on the ground. With a wave of her hand, my mother sends them on to fight with the rest. Her eyes do not leave mine. "As for you, my youngest." She flicks her wrist and the bone cage bursts outward.

My terror brings me to my knees.
This is the moment
of my death.
When my mother has slain me,
I will go into darkness
if I go into anything at all.
I
do

not

have

a

soul.

Beyond this world,

there is nothing for me.

I bow before her. My head presses into the grass. It reeks of blood and waste, the tangible scent of fear chased with the tang of the burgeoning storm.

She commands me: "Get up."

I do not. How can I?

"GET UP!"

I lift my head, drag myself to my feet.

"Death is too easy for you, little one. Do not think I will grant it to you. You will live to see my triumph. You will help to make it happen. When the boy comes, you will kill him. After he is dead, I will pluck your heart from your body, and tear you apart limb by limb, keeping you alive long enough to feel every possible ounce of pain. Then, and only then, will I let you die. Do you understand?"

I am ragged with terror, every fiber raw.

Her mouth twists. "Do not doubt I have the power to make certain one small *human boy* appears when I wish him to."

I reach out for his soul without meaning to.

She is right.

I can feel him, not far away.

I shake.

I weep.

She grabs my chin and forces her claws deep, deep, down to the wood of my bones.

Sap runs down my neck, sticky, warm. "You cannot make me kill him."

She flings me away, and I land

on a corpse the earth has not yet swallowed.

I cry and leap off of it.

I try not to look.

But still I see:

a soldier,

a boy.

His neck is twisted.

His eyes are vacant.

The wind rises.

My mother is still smiling. Her hand is amber with my blood. "Oh, daughter. When will you understand that your heart belongs to me? When will you understand that you will do whatever I command?"

"Never." It hurts to talk. I press one hand under my jaw. There is a feeling like fire in my throat, burning, burning. I choke.

My mother peers at me. She closes the distance between us in two long strides. The heartless lion growls at her heels.

She plunges her hand into my chest.

The pain is

sharp,

hot,

an all-consuming

agony.

She hisses in my ear: "I made you what you are. Whatever magic your wretched brothers worked on you has long since fallen away. They cannot save you now. You are *my* creature, and you will obey my every command."

I can't see through the haze of sap and tears. My mother holds my heart in her hand. She always has. The pulses of my life are spent, one by one. "Please." The word creeps past my lips. "Ple—" The word chokes off. I try again. I cannot speak.

My mother taps one finger against my neck. A hardness comes

into her eyes. "The Eater is working magic. But no matter."

She smiles again, that cruel twist of her mouth.

She laughs

as she sends her power searing into my heart.

She laughs

as she yanks her hand from my chest, and I collapse on the ground.

She laughs

as I writhe in pain and horror,

as I feel her power flowing through me

with every beat of my heart.

Pulse.

Pulse.

Pulse.

I am my mother's monster.

As I always have been.

She mounts the heartless lion, her bone skirt scraping against the needles of its body. "Come, daughter. We have work to do. The Soul Eater is near. Let us go hunting."

The heartless lion leaps into a run.

My mother's power jerks me after.

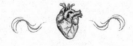

In the ruined wood

I see her.

Roses in her hair.

Ashes on her lips.

Agony in her eyes.

I kneel beside her.

My mother reins in the heartless lion.

She looks at what I have found:
my sister,
dead at the Eater's hand.
My mother snarls in rage.
There is something else.
A shattered orb.
It glimmers in the ashes,
in the rain that drips
through dead trees.
It is jagged and sharp.
It shines like he does.
It shines like Owen.
I am so afraid that he is gone.
That this is the place
where he died,
and I cannot bear it.

My mother spits: "He will pay. For the death of my daughter.
For stealing the song I gave the rest of them."

I understand. Somehow, the Eater slew my sister to silence our
song.

He has robbed me
of my voice,
as my mother has robbed me
of my will.
There is nothing left to me
that is my own.
There is no part of me
that does not belong to someone else.

My mother hisses. The heartless lion leaps once more into
motion.

We pass through the ashes of the wood, out onto a grassy plain.
Rain sluices off my face and my body as I run behind them.

Saplings sprout up every place my foot touches, the wood growing and growing. Unstoppable.

It is her power, flowing through me.

I can still feel

the prints of her fingers

like bands of iron

around my heart.

Her will compels me on and on.

The Soul Eater's army looms close.

He wars with my sisters and my mother's trees.

The ground is slick and muddy in the rain. There are bodies. Fire.

The trees are burning.

The heartless lion snarls as my mother jerks it to a stop. It is angry at being held back.

I, too, grow still,

the creature

she shaped

to take her form.

To bear her heart.

Lightning sears the sky.

My mother says: "The Eater will come to meet me. And then the one who eats will become the eaten. My soul has fed him well for four centuries, but he should have chosen better than a simple dryad. Even dryads die."

He is weak enough for her to kill him. I sensed it in the palace, in the light of his dimming soul. My mother's soul.

When he is dead,

she will grow her wood until it has swallowed the land.

Then she will begin upon the sea.

And when all the world is choked in her trees,

when she has slaughtered every last human

for the crime the Soul Eater committed against her—
What will she do?
Will she wander alone
through her fathomless wood?
Will she regret
the things
she has done?
I will not live to see that day.
My death will come
before the night.

I kneel in the muddy grass. I press my fingers into the earth. I reach out for my brothers. *Pren, Criafol, Cangen. You have to stop her before she destroys everything. You are the only ones who can. Please. Do not leave me here to die for nothing.*

Another wave of the Eater's army crashes into my mother's wood.

The trees snap their bodies
and cast them aside
like so many twigs.
My mother waits quietly, a hard set to her eyes.
The rain has washed the blood from her antlers.
She gleams
in the wet
and the wildness of the storm,
as strong and bright
as lightning.

Across the plain, my sisters and my mother's trees rip the Eater's soldiers apart.

Bodies are strewn on the rain-soaked ground.
Trees burn and burn.
Still my mother waits.
She turns her head and sees me still kneeling in the grass.

She frowns. One crook of her finger, and I am jerked upright again, as if on an invisible lead. "It is time for you to prove your worth, worthless one."

I am dimly aware

of the thud of hooves coming from the southwest.

Of shapes coming toward us, mud thick and flying.

I blink the rain from my eyes, and the shapes come into focus: six horsemen, ragged and wounded.

One of them is riding double with another soldier, his left arm pinned to his side in a sling.

I know his shape

as I know his soul.

My body flashes cold with pain.

My heart falls.

My mother smiles her vicious smile.

She clenches her hand, and my body jolts into motion.

She orders: "Kill the boy. Kill him slowly. And when you have done it, bring me his soul. Perhaps then I will have mercy on you, and make your death swift. Go. Now." She waves her hand.

Against my will, I move to meet the riders.

I raise my own hands,

feel the power trembling inside of them.

Tears pour down my face; they mingle with the rain.

Lightning crackles just above my head, illuminating the ground, the mud flying up from the horses' hooves.

More of my mother's wood has come behind us.

The trees plunge their roots into the ground and rip them up again.

Marching. To her.

This is what she was waiting for.

Reinforcements.

She makes it look as if I am commanding them.

As if I am the one
compelling them to drag the soldiers from their horses,
to skewer them with sharp fingers and cause
blood to bubble up out of their mouths.
That is what Owen must think.
He is dragged from his horse with the rest of them, but the trees do not kill him.
They drop him at my feet.
He raises his head,
looks
into
my
eyes.
His horror is visceral.
His sense of betrayal
acrid as blood.
For he sees
that I am
at the last
what he always knew I was:
a
soulless
monster.
I struggle against my mother's will.
I fail.
I haul him up by his collar.
I set him on his feet.
I cannot even tell him I am sorry.
I cannot even tell him goodbye.
The Eater has stolen my voice.
My mother, everything else.
He will die

thinking
it was always going to end this way.
He will die
thinking
the monster in the wood
never lost her heart
to the boy
who is lost in the stars.

Chapter Fifty-Nine

OWEN

S HE SHINES IN THE RAIN, SMEARED WITH BLOOD, WITH DIRT. FOR an instant, a crack of lightning illuminates her clearly. Her green and gold hair is knotted with burrs, the ragged remains of her maid's uniform still clinging to her body. The violets in her hair have been shredded, the pieces of them that are left plastered to her head. Her silver skin is scored with dark wounds.

She opens her mouth in a soundless scream and shoves me away from her. I fall backward into the dirt, landing on my broken arm. I yelp in pain. There's a rain-slicked body beside me. Her cap has fallen off, and the singed edges of her hair still smell of smoke: Luned, dead. My throat closes. Four other soldiers lie tumbled on the ground like discarded toys. One of them is Baines. He clings to life, but barely, his breaths coming too shallow, too quick. The trees yanked him down from the horse we were riding, twisted his body with a sickening snap of bones, and flung him aside in their haste to get to me. The others weren't so lucky; the trees killed them instantly. I am numb with shock, with horror. I don't understand. They were alive mere moments ago.

Now they're gone.

The trees didn't harm me.

The trees brought me to her. To Seren.

I shake as I stare at her, as I drag myself upright again. The remains of Elynion's army fight the wood mere yards away, but it might as well be a hundred miles. There is no rescue for me. I am at her mercy, and her mercy alone.

But what is she?

There is pain in her eyes. Rage. She trembles with it. But she doesn't lunge for me. Just stares back, dripping with rain.

"Seren?" I breathe.

Past her shoulder the Gwydden looms. I gasp. She is crowned with antlers and clothed in bones, mounted on a nightmare creature. Her eyes meet mine.

I thought I knew what fear was.

I was wrong.

I jerk backward, stumbling on Luned's dead arm. My head wheels with terror, and Seren stares at me and stares at me, and I am trapped forever in an evil dream.

The Gwydden's voice bores into my brain like a steel screw, twisting and twisting. "Did I not make myself clear, little monster? Kill him. KILL HIM!" She waves her hand.

Seren opens her mouth, but no song pours out. Elynion's spell has silenced her, too. The realization wrenches me, wrecks me. He had no right to steal her voice.

Yet somehow my senses are still assaulted with her magic, silvery, intoxicating, bright. It sinks into me with barbed fingers. I take a step toward her.

"Seren," I say. "You are not hers. You are not hers." It's a question, a plea.

The Gwydden snaps her fingers, and a sword unfolds itself in Seren's hand. It's made of bone and birchwood, twisted together and honed to a spear's edge.

I take another step, and another.

Seren waits for me. The point of her sword trembles.

Her face twists. I realize she's crying.

And I know—

She is not her mother's creature.

She does not want this.

The relief, the *joy*, makes me ache.

Her magic draws me to her, closer and closer. But the piece of my will that is still mine looses my own sword, readies it against her. Because I know, I know, I know—

If I let her kill me, if I don't even *try* to stop her, she will never forgive herself. She will never think she can be anything but a monster.

I can bear many things.

Not that.

She lunges at me and our swords clash, steel on wood and bone.

I think of the wonder in her eyes when she peered through the telescope. The pulse of her heart as we danced on the hill. Her rough hands, pressed tight over my ears, sheltering me from her sisters' song. Her mouth on mine. Her body on mine.

She strikes out again and I block her, the force of it reverberating through me. I am weak and wounded. I won't be able to stand against her very long.

Power pulses off of her, power that is not her own. Her movements are jerky and wild—she's fighting the Gwydden for control of her body. She slashes with her bone and wood blade. I stumble backward. "You are not hers," I say. "You belong only to yourself."

But Elynion's spell keeps her silent, as the Gwydden's magic keeps her fighting me.

Her blows come fiercer and faster with every passing moment. I struggle to block them. "Seren. You are not hers. *You are not hers.*"

Seren's mouth opens, her jaw works. A voice tears out of her— but it is not her voice. It is her mother's. "You are *wrong*, boy. She has never belonged to anyone but *me*."

The Gwydden flings out her arm and Seren hurls her sword into the mud. Her face twists. Vines sprout from her fingers, lash out at me. They coil tight around my body, drag me toward her.

Then I'm pressed up against her, close enough to see the tears trembling on her lashes, the helpless horror in her eyes as branches burst from her knuckles and skewer straight through my chest. Sudden, agonizing pain makes my vision go white.

Her mouth is at my ear. Her breath is warm. "She should have killed you the first time she saw you," hisses the Gwydden's voice.

Seren's heart beats quickly. Her body trembles against mine. Something drips into my mouth and I taste salt.

"I know she's making you do this," I rasp. "But you're stronger than her. Seren. You're stronger."

Her vines coil tighter, choking the breath out of me. Blood seeps from the wounds in my chest, too much, far too much.

But she doesn't strike the killing blow. Just holds me there. She fights the pull of her mother's magic; she trembles with it, as if the fighting is tearing her apart.

Another flash of lightning splits the sky, and a cold wind rips between us.

Seren sucks in a soundless breath, and the vines retract, leaving me to slump to the ground.

I barely have the strength to lift my head.

King Elynion rides through the ranks of his dying army, the rain rattling his gold plate armor. He pulls up short a pace or two from the Gwydden and her nightmare creature and dismounts. In one swift motion, he takes his helmet off. His dark hair whips in the wind and the rain, and he raises his hand to the sky. He snaps his fingers and light sears the ground, so close I feel the crackle, smell the sizzle of heat. He's calling down pieces of stars.

The Gwydden swings off her own mount, and strides up to meet him.

Chapter Sixty

SEREN

OWEN STARES AT ME.
His jaw moves, yet he does not speak.
His eyes pierce mine.
He implores me.
But he does not understand.
I can do nothing to help him.
He is *wrong*.
I do not belong to myself.
I only belong to *her*.
Were it not for the Eater, riding through the rain,
she would have made me kill him,
and he would lie even now
in pieces at my feet.
He might be dying anyway.
There is so much red pouring out of him.
My mother is distracted by the Eater.

I should run

far,

far

away.

But I just stand here.

Rooted.

I will not leave him

bleeding in the mud.

I cannot.

There is an undulation in the ground.

Past Owen and the slaughtered soldiers,

something new fights the wood.

Dark creatures, fierce and tall.

Their bellows fill the sky:

Cangen, Criafol, Pren, drenched in rain.

They wield stone swords that look as if they were hewn from their mountain. They drive the trees back. Drive our sisters back.

If my mother sees them, I cannot tell.

She faces the Soul Eater in the lashing rain. Wind rattles the bones of her dress.

He is gold, and she is silver,

and it seems

all the world

rages because of them.

They stare at each other.

For long heartbeats, they only stare.

My mother seems to tremble before him,

a leaf in a storm.

Surely she does not fear the Eater.

And yet—

her power in me weakens.

Owen gasps for breath in the grass. He lies near the body of a girl hardly older than he is. The trees killed her. Killed all of them.

I did not stop it.

On the hill, the Eater still stares at my mother. "I had forgotten what a hideous monster you are."

My mother bares her teeth. She pulses with rage, and something else I do not understand: sorrow. "You did not think so, once. There was a time when you were not ashamed to kiss a monster in the dark."

The Eater laughs at her. "You are wrong, witch. You have never been anything to me but a thorn in my heel. I have only been finding a sharp enough knife to cut you out."

My mother stands tall and cold in the rain.

I do not know

how the Eater

does not quake before her.

Her voice is deep with danger,

with the promise of his death.

"I wished for you to come with repentance in your eyes. Even after all this time, we could have mended what was torn. We could have been so powerful, together. No one could have stood against us."

The Eater sneers. "Do not think I come powerless to meet you."

He calls down a piece of star. It dances in his hand. It flashes white.

He hurls it to the ground, and

it bursts in a blaze of fire,

scorching the grass at my mother's feet.

"Do not think I fear your pathetic show of magic, fool. You say I am a thorn. So I will be a thorn." My mother waves her hand.

The heartless lion leaps at the Eater,

knocks him to the ground.

"And do not think I have forgotten you, *daughter*." My mother's attention fixes suddenly on me.

I cower under her gaze.

"I told you. To *kill* him." She snaps a word at the sky.

Her power sears through me, forces me to turn, to go back to Owen.

Beyond him, beyond the bodies and the burning trees, my brothers battle the wood. Everything screams.

The rain

falls

on

and

on.

My mother roars: "KILL HIM!"

I am hurled toward Owen. Branches shoot from my arms, my hands. They pierce him through. Wrap around his throat. Squeeze.

I fight her control with everything that is in me.

But I am helpless against her.

I cannot save him.

I am undone by his eyes.

They are clear, bright.

He looks at me as if he trusts me.

As if I am not choking the life out of him.

I weep

as

I

kill

him.

But I do not shut my eyes.

I will not look away

in the moment

of his death.

It is all I can give him.

Chapter Sixty-One

OWEN

I WANT TO TELL HER SO MANY THINGS, BUT I DON'T HAVE THE breath to say them. So I just look at her. I look at her, and will her to understand.

That I don't blame her.

That I'm glad we had all those nights together under the stars: in the wood, on the wall.

That I hope she will remember me, when I am gone.

Pain swallows me.

I can't breathe, can't—

Chapter Sixty-Two

SEREN

H IS SOUL DIMS.

His heart quiets.

Rain and tears blind me.

My mother's focus wanders from me

enough that I

retract the branches piercing him through.

He gasps and chokes.

Blood seeps from his wounds.

But he lives, he lives.

Behind us, the Soul Eater slides in the mud. The heartless lion lunges at him.

The Eater shouts a word to the sky and a slice of star jolts through the heartless lion, ripping it in half.

My mother screams

in anguish,

in rage.

She calls branches up from the earth, sharp as blades.

She hurls them at the Eater,

one

by

one.

He shrieks: "You cannot win! I will eat your heart like I ate your soul, and I will live, and you will die, and no one will remember you."

My mother spits: "You FOOL. When I have killed you, I will grind your bones to powder and drive them into the earth with my heel. You are nothing before me. You are a *worm*."

The Eater rages against my mother.

My mother rages back.

There comes the noise of thundering hoofbeats:

another army, coming across the plain to meet the ragged remnants of the Eater's forces.

They collide with the wood and my snarling sisters. They wield torches and swords.

The trees ignite.

Despite the rain, they burn.

All is smoke and fire and screaming.

All is blood and stars.

My mother's power still holds me.

Owen lives. But she will not let me release him.

He dangles before me.

His blood mingles with the rain. It runs a watery red into the grass.

Through storm and heat and trees I see Pren's face: his piercing eyes, his mossy beard.

His voice echoes in my mind: *To become wholly as you are, you must give up the thing you hold most dear.*

I stare at Owen,

alive

but

dying

in my arms.

My heart beats within my chest.

But it is too late.

My human form is gone.

I cannot get it back again.

You must give up the thing you hold most dear.

"Owen." His name chokes out of me. The Eater's spell is waning.

His eyes focus on mine.

Somehow he has the strength

to raise his hand

to cup my cheek,

to smooth his fingers along the ridges of my skin.

I tell him: "I am sorry about your mother. I am sorry about everything. I wanted to be more than a monster. I tried to choose. But I was not strong enough to fight her. I was not strong enough—"

"You have always been strong." His voice is thin and weak. His bright soul fades bit by bit.

He is dying and dying, and

it

is

all

my

fault.

My tears drown me.

I wonder if the roaring I hear is outside of me,

or if it merely

rages

inside my own head.

He smiles. Blood and rain run down his lips.

The flaming trees paint him in orange light.

He says: "You're not a monster."

Pain blooms through me as my mother forces another branch to push out from my hands, to pierce his shoulder.

He cries out in

agony.

I cannot bear

his eyes.

I cannot bear

his touch.

I cannot bear

him dying

in my arms

because

I

am

killing

him

even now.

You must carve out your heart, and bury it in the green earth.

I push through my tears,

through the yawning horror

that engulfs me.

"Owen."

He whispers: "Seren. I—I love you."

The light dims in his eyes.

It might already be

too late.

I say: "You have my heart."

I thrust him away from me

and plunge my hand

into my chest.

His voice is far away as

he screams

my name.

I hardly hear him.

My life is beating in my hands,

warm

soft

wet.

I count the pulses:

one

two

three

four.

And then I tear it out.

I crumple to the ground,

my heart

in

my

hand.

For one single moment more, I am aware.

There is the rain,

the grass,

the burning wood.

Then

there

is

nothing.

Chapter Sixty-Three

OWEN

A ROAR TEARS OUT OF ME AS SHE SLIDES TO THE GROUND, HER bloody heart in her hand. The rain falls on and on. For a heartbeat she stares up into the sky. Then a horrible stillness steals over her face, and her eyes grow dim.

Too late I am beside her, my knees digging into the mud. I take her hand, thread her fingers through mine. But already she is stiff and cold. Her skin peels up, more like tree bark than I have ever seen it. The violets and leaves in her hair are brittle, dead. Her heart is still cradled in her other hand, rain and blood stirring into the ground.

"Seren. Seren, *please*." Ragged sobs wrack my whole body as my own blood leaks from the places she pierced me. I've lost too much. I'm lightheaded, weak. She ripped out her heart to free herself from the Gwydden's will. She ripped out her heart to save me.

I loved her.

And now she's gone.

She's *gone.*

My head wheels. I can't think, can't feel.

How can she be gone?

She's just a body now. Dead in the mud.

I can't bear it.

I can't see through my tears.

"Please." I rub her cold hand, desperate for it to warm, for her to stir. "Seren, *please.*"

But she just lies there.

Dead

Dead

Dead.

Behind me, the wood burns. Another army has come to join the fight—an army wearing violet and white. Dimly, I know those colors belong to Gwaed, the country across the mountain. I don't know how or why they're here. But without them, Tarian would already be lost to the Gwydden's trees.

Before me, the Gwydden is locked in mortal combat with King Elynion.

I understand now, as I did not before, what it will mean if the king is triumphant, if he kills the Gwydden in the mud. There will be no more check upon his power. No need for him to hide behind his walls and pay a man like my father to read the stars to warn him of his impending death. He will burn the wood to the ground. He will conquer Gwaed, and Saeth too. He will cross the sea when he is done, and all the realms of the world will fall to him. He is no better than the Gwydden. He does not bear the form of a monster—only the heart of one.

I see my father, bloody and dead in his prison cell, his chest riddled with holes from Elynion's machine. His voice echoes through my mind: *There is a way to save her. There is a way to stop all of this. It's what the stars have been telling us, all this time.*

My heart constricts as I stare down at Seren. She deserved so much more than this. She *was* so much more. She tore out her heart to save me, and I refuse to let her die in vain.

You must only give back what he stole, and what she sacrificed.

I shake as I bend to kiss Seren's forehead, cold and rough against my lips. I weep as I bid her farewell.

But when I pick myself up off the ground and limp the muddy steps to where the Gwydden and the king battle with trees and stars, the tears have gone. My spine is straight. Not even my fingers tremble.

Then her curse will be broken, and all will be as it was.

The Gwydden has beaten the king back, her face and arms seared with angry welts. The stars do not come so easily at his call anymore. He stumbles, falls into the mud.

She hisses as she causes vines to curl up out of the earth, to wrap around his wrists, his waist, his ankles. His face is blanched of color, but he presses his thin lips hard together. He will not grovel before her when she kills him. He will not bend to her anger. He will not admit to his guilt.

"Gwydden."

The wood witch turns to look at me, and I'm nearly undone by her brutal stare.

It's Seren's sacrifice that gives me the strength to stand unshaken before her. That gives me the boldness to stare straight into her horrible eyes and not blanch, the courage or the stupidity to kneel in the mud and say what I say to her.

"You cannot take back what he stole from you." I nod at the king, who writhes on the ground, all the color gone from his face. "He's used up your soul, every piece of it."

"As I have used up my heart," the Gwydden sneers. "My worthless daughter wasted her life on you."

I am not deterred. "Take my soul instead. Take it freely. Let it burn inside of you in place of your own. Let it fill you up, make you whole again."

She turns all her focus on me, and the fear is back, crawling up my spine and tingling in my fingers. But I force myself not to quail.

"I have taken many souls. I will take many more, before my wood has grown over all the earth."

"Yes, but you have taken none for your own. You have fed them into the wood, given it the power to grow and grow and grow. You did not want those souls. You wanted yours. You wanted the one that was stolen from you—it was the only one that would suit you. But now you see not even that will satisfy you anymore."

Her glance shifts to the king, dying in agony on the ground as rain runs off his worthless plate armor.

"Take my soul," I say. "Take it freely." I know now why my mother protected my soul against the king. She was protecting it for this moment. For this reason.

I see the Gwydden consider it, the hardness on her strange face, the astuteness in her dark eyes. "Why would you give me your soul?"

"Because what he did to you was wrong. Because everyone deserves a chance to make it right. Because I suspect that a soul freely given will burn stronger inside you than one ripped away. And because Seren is gone, and I could not give my soul to her."

The Gwydden frowns. "Seren? Who is Seren?"

My shoulders stiffen. My heart constricts. "Your youngest daughter."

She looks past me to Seren's form, still and cold in the muddy grass, and if the Gwydden feels anything for her, it doesn't show. "My daughter has no name save Fool."

The king whimpers and gurgles, his eyes rolling back into his head. He was so mighty, and now he is nothing.

Impassively, the Gwydden watches Elynion die, one last sharpened branch thrust through his heart. When his body goes limp, her branches release him, and he crumples to the ground. She crosses the short distance between them, and crouches beside him. She smooths the hair on his brow, closes his eyes with gentle fingers.

I don't understand how the Gwydden can be gentle.

She puts his hands on his chest and begins to sing, a simple melody that twists into the air. A wisp rises out of him, a simple coil of smoke that is there and then gone in an instant, washed away by the rain.

The Gwydden turns back to me, and the sorrow on her face nearly unravels me. How can she feel sorrow for the man she killed? The man she's hated for centuries?

And yet clearly, she does.

"You are right," she says. "There is nothing left of his soul." She looks to the battle that rages on between the burning wood and the Gwaed army. Three strange tree-like creatures are fighting, too. Not with the wood—against it.

"Then will you take mine?" I ask her.

"It would kill you."

I shrug. "I would not want to live without a soul." I wince at my words—that is what the Gwydden has done. That is what Seren has done. What my mother did, for over a year. Grief wrenches me.

The Gwydden looks suddenly smaller, like all the fight and the anger has gone out of her with the death of the king. "I will take your soul," she says. "If you will give it to me."

I nod. My throat is dry, my body chilled through. I pace to where Seren lies, and kneel beside her in the blood that has spilled out from her heart. It is dark around her, almost indistinguishable from the mud. A single shredded violet trembles in her hair.

The Gwydden follows. She looks down at me with something like pity and something like sorrow. And yet there is hunger in her eyes. "Farewell, boy."

A thousand needle-like branches shoot up from the ground, and between one breath and the next, they pierce through me. For an instant, the shock of it numbs the pain, but then it's there, raging and roaring. I am skewered like an insect on a board. I cannot breathe or see or hear—there are thorns in my nose, my mouth, my eyes. Panic seizes me. There is blood in my mouth, blood pouring from my eyes and down my face. I choke on it.

Through the haze I sense the Gwydden. I hear her voice in my head: *You did not think when you offered your soul. You did not think how much it would hurt.*

I cannot hurt more. I know I cannot.

And yet I feel her pulling my soul from me, like an arrowhead from a wound. It snags and tears; I don't know if it's the protection my mother wove around it, or if my soul simply does not want to leave me. But I tell it to go. I let it go.

It listens.

I do not know what shape my soul is. I do not know its essence or its color.

But when she rips it out of me in one final burst of agonizing, devouring pain, I feel the lack of it. The place it should have been.

I am empty of everything but pain.

My heart echoes inside of me like a stone dropped in an empty room.

You have my heart, whispers the memory of Seren's voice.

And you have my soul, I answer her.

Blackness folds over me.

I step into the welcoming arms of death.

Chapter Sixty-Four

OWEN

A BURST OF PAIN.

The cold touch of rain on my skin.

The rushing of my soul back into my body, filling up the yawning void.

And I am not dead.

My eyes fly open.

The Gwydden is crouched on her heels, screaming and weeping, her hands pressed against her ears. She shimmers with silver light, but there is blood on her feet and her hands, blood on the bones of her horrible dress.

And I know with perfect certainty that it is Seren's blood. That somehow it has saved me.

That wisp of smoke that came out of the king materializes once again, shrinking to a single kernel of light. It slips into the Gwydden.

She shrieks, clawing at her hair and her face. The last bit of her soul, returned to her.

But how?

Elynion's corpse shrivels up and turns to dust before my eyes. The rain washes what's left of him away.

The Gwydden has grown silent again. She kneels in the mud, her arms wrapped tight around her chest. She rocks back and forth, back and forth. She whimpers like a small child, a frightened puppy.

Her antlers shrink away into her head until they're gone. Her skin shifts to a deeper green, mottled with gray. The bones of her dress turn to ash, and she's left wearing a garment made all of leaves. Flowers grow from the crown of her head. Violets.

My hand goes to my mouth as I choke back a sob.

The Gwydden raises her head. She looks young. Fragile. "What's wrong, boy?"

"I don't understand. I don't understand why I'm not dead. Why—"

"Why your soul came back to you?" says a voice behind me.

I turn to find one of the tree-like creatures gazing down at me. He has a beard that seems to be made of moss, and his eyes look very sad. "My mother touched my sister's heartblood, and when that heartblood was tangled up with the powerful protection woven around your soul—"

"It would not stay within me," says the Gwydden, with marked bitterness. "It could not. And so all I am left with is the seed of the soul that once belonged to me. A burnt-out, useless husk."

"Not altogether useless," the mossy-bearded creature says. "It has made you into what you once were. The thing you were born as, before the Soul Eater cursed you."

Once more, my father's words echo inside of me. *There is a way to save her. There is a way to stop all of this. It's what the stars have been telling us, all this time. You must only give back what he stole, and what she sacrificed.*

This is what he meant: a heart, a soul. It's all it took to free the

Gwydden. Seren's heart. My soul.

But it isn't right, and it isn't fair. We both of us sacrificed ourselves, but Seren died, and I lived. And here I am. Without her.

"I am powerless," whispers the Gwydden. "I am nothing."

"You are not nothing," says the tree creature.

She looks miserably at the wood, which stands still and silent now, wreathed with smoke in the falling rain. Lifeless, without her power to feed it. The remains of Gwaed's army stand in a daze, blinking and bewildered. Through the trees come Seren's six remaining sisters. They are weeping. Begging.

They turn, one by one, back into the trees they were made from. I blink, and six birches stand all in a line, the rain drenching their dappled leaves.

The other two tree creatures join the one with the mossy beard, solemn and sad. Slowly, their features freeze, bark creeping up their bodies, faces smoothing away, arms growing longer and splitting off into others. And then they are nothing but three stately pines, all indistinguishable.

Grief claws up my throat.

"So pass my daughters," says the Gwydden, "and so my sons."

She looks to me with clear eyes, and I see in her a glimpse of what she must have been, once, when she was young and lost her heart to a boy hardly older than myself.

"There is only me now, fixed into this life that I no longer desire."

"Gwydden——"

"That is not my name, you know."

My heart pulses painfully. "What is your name?"

"Enaid," she says.

It is a bitter name, but a true one. It means soul.

Enaid lifts her arms to the sky, tilts her head back so the rain washes over her. She has little power left, but enough, it seems, that she can will her own life away. One moment she is there, smiling into the sky.

The next she is smoke, dissolved on the wind.

Then I am alone in a field of corpses and wounded soldiers, the Gwaed army and the leaves of the smoldering forest my only company.

I kneel beside Seren's body, brushing my fingers across her cold face. It is cruel that I am here and she is not. She was not even afforded the honor of her brothers and sisters. She does not even get to become again the tree she once was. Her body shimmers. It turns to ash. The rain washes it away.

"NO!" I scramble to grasp the remains of her, but it is impossible to hold onto dust in a rainstorm.

She is gone and gone and gone.

I sob, broken, undone. I whisper the name she took for herself. "Seren, Seren, Seren."

It does not bring her back.

But when a pair of Gwaed soldiers take me by my good arm and help me to my feet, I see what she left me: her heart, washed clean by the rain.

For one breath, two, I think I hear it beating.

But by the time I scramble to cradle it in my hands, it has gone irrevocably still.

Chapter Sixty-Five

OWEN

I BURY SEREN'S HEART ON THE HILL IN THE MIDST OF THE WOOD, where we danced four minutes at a time to the music of my mother's phonograph. I dig the hole as the sun sets, awkward with my one good arm, and wait until the stars glimmer into being to lay this last piece of her to rest. I made a wooden box for her heart. I carved it with leaves and stars.

"I still don't believe you," I tell her conversationally as I smooth the dirt overtop of her. "I still think you have a soul."

I sit with her as the moon rises cold above the tree line. I play my mother's cello for her. I weep.

When dawn glimmers silver, I tell her that I have to go away for a little while, because I have to go and fetch my sister. "You remember Awela," I say. "You watched over her, that day in the woods, instead of killing her. And then when I came, you watched over me, too." I touch the patch of earth where her heart lies with gentle fingers. My throat constricts. "When I've brought her home again, I will come and visit you every single day. I won't miss even one." Fresh tears burn my eyes. "Not even in midwinter."

Light floods the hill, and my shadow skews stark against the grass. "The wood is quieter, you know." I swallow. "Without you."

I get reluctantly to my feet, and follow the path back through the wood to my parents' cottage, which is exactly how I left it, save for a layer of dust I'll attack with soap and rags when I get back with Awela.

It's painful to leave the house and the wood, to buy a ticket from Mairwen Griffith and board the train to Breindal City. If I didn't yearn for Awela, I couldn't have made myself leave at all.

The miles blur past the train window, but not as swiftly as I wish. I am still stiff and sore, bandages wound about every inch of my chest. My broken arm hangs useless in a sling. All of me is starting to itch, which the nurse who tended me—the same nurse who once bandaged my lash marks—said would be a good sign. It's a miracle I survived, she said. I'd lost far too much blood. By rights I should be dead.

But I'm not. I'm still here.

God knows there was more work for gravediggers than physicians after the battle with the wood.

When Rheinallt found me in the medical tent, I was in a bad way. Frantic about Seren's heart. Frantic about Awela. I explained to Rheinallt that my sister was missing, that I didn't know where she was, but I thought she must be hidden somewhere near the palace.

I was desperate to find her, desperate to know she was all right.

But Rheinallt didn't miss the way my eyes refused to stray from the box I held tight in my hands, the box that contained Seren's heart.

"I'll find your sister," he told me. "I'll send you a telegram the moment I do. You go and bury your dead."

So I'd gone.

I felt easier when I'd arrived in Blodyn Village to find the telegram already waiting for me. I felt easier still when Seren's heart lay quiet in the earth.

And now?

Now I'm ready to take Awela home.

The train stops at a village a ways outside of the city—Breindal's station is in ruins, torn to pieces by the Gwydden's trees. I hire a horse, hardly dipping into my heavy purse of silver, and ride on toward Breindal.

Whatever it was that happened that day, when I lost Seren to the wood, the Gwaed army that appeared so unexpectedly saw me as the boy who stood against the Gwydden, and destroyed her. That isn't the whole truth—it's hardly even a piece of it. But it was enough to make the Gwaed soldiers—or rather, their leader—give me everything I asked for.

Breindal City is destroyed. The Gwydden's Wood marched very far, and corpses lie tumbled about with the stones. There are hardly enough people to clear them, and it will be a long, horrible job. Everywhere are the remnants of Enaid and Elynion's quarrel. The death and ruin they left behind them.

But the world is not gone, I think. *There is a chance yet, at life, at peace.*

My heart is heavy as I pick my way through the rubble of the city gates, then up the hill to the palace.

Gwaed flags fly from the roof, a violet sword on a white field. I'm not surprised, but tension squeezes my throat as I climb from the horse and hand the reins to a scrawny stable boy.

I'm ushered into the same drawing room where I waited so long for the king. This time, I'm barely there a minute before the door opens, and Rheinallt comes in.

He looks different than he did all those weeks training with Baines and me and the rest of the soldiers. His pale hair is tied back at the nape of his neck. A pair of sapphire earrings flash in the light pouring in through the windows. He's dressed simply, in the Gwaed violet and white, but that doesn't disguise the way he holds himself like a king. I wonder I never saw it before.

Rheinallt didn't desert Baines that morning. He'd been sent by his parents to spy on Tarian, to learn if there was any truth to the threat of the wood. He left to meet his army, to lead them into battle and come to Tarian's aid. Turns out it wasn't an inn Rheinallt was set to inherit—it was a kingdom.

"Will Tarian be no more, then?" I ask without preamble.

"Elynion had no heir," Rheinallt answers apologetically. "I will not lie to you about my parents' intent. It makes it easier—"

"That you didn't actually have to assassinate him."

He grimaces.

"Tarian will be absorbed into Gwaed, then?"

Rheinallt nods.

"And the Tarian nobility?"

"I will do what I can for them, if they swear oaths of loyalty to the Gwaed crown."

He doesn't have to spell out what will happen to them if they do not swear.

Rheinallt glances out the window, tension in the set of his shoulders. "I'm sorry you won't stay. I would have you on my council."

"I've only come for my sister, Rheinallt."

He grins. "I know, idiot. Just wanted *you* to know the offer still stands, if you ever change your mind. And know you always have a friend in the crown."

"I've had enough of kings and crowns," I say softly.

He sobers. I know he's thinking of Luned and so many others. Gone forever.

"How's Baines?" I ask.

"Recovering, thank God. I couldn't be deprived of both my friends at once."

"Will he—"

"Walk again?" Rheinallt shrugs. "The doctors don't think so, but he's stubborn enough for anything."

I smile. "He is that."

"Here." Rheinallt hands me a roll of paper. "The deeds to your father's house, as promised. It cannot be ceded to the crown. It belongs to you and your family, as long as it may endure."

"Thank you." My throat tightens. I know there's more.

"Your father's body was found." Rheinallt's eyes flick to mine. He doesn't elaborate; I don't want him to. "We can bury him here, if you wish. Or—"

"He wouldn't want that." I swallow down the acrid taste of bile. "We'll take him home."

Rheinallt nods. "I'll arrange it."

"Thank you," I repeat. The words are heavy on my tongue. I ache for my father. My mother, too. But at least—

"Bring her in!" calls Rheinallt to the door.

Awela barrels into the room, taller and tanner than I remember her. "WEN!" she shouts, and leaps at me, nearly knocking me off balance.

I scoop her into my arms and cradle her against my neck, trying and failing not to weep before my friend who will be king.

"The oddest thing," Rheinallt says. "We found her and her nurse in a little hut just outside the palace walls. The nurse swore a tree had hidden them."

I smile through my tears. Seren helped us, one last time. "Come on, Awela," I tell my baby sister. I kiss her cheek. "Let's go home."

I visit the hill where I buried Seren's heart every day for a year.

Sometimes Awela comes with me, but more often I go alone. I play my mother's cello for her. I play the phonograph—a new one, that I sent for from Saeth. I sing to her. Sometimes, I peer up at the stars and tell her about the constellation that burns in the sky in place of the one her mother put there: Astronomers have named it Gleddyf, Sword, but I know better. I know it's a tree. Her tree.

I always feel at peace when I'm with Seren on the hill, though my grief is never far. There is a void inside of me where she was meant to dwell. I tell her that, too.

I buried my father in a patch of earth beyond the garden, with the pieces of my mother's smashed phonograph. I know they're together now. I know they're at peace. They, too, are gaps in my heart that will never be filled.

On the first anniversary of the night I laid Seren's heart to rest, I find a green shoot pushing its way out of the earth. It grows rapidly, taller every day. It becomes a tender plant. Then a sapling, fierce and strong. It's white and silver, like she used to be. The tree unfolds shining leaves, and a patch of violets grows at its base.

After six months, the birch tree is as tall as me. Now every night I sit beneath it, mesmerized by the dappled moonlight filtering through its leaves.

On the second anniversary of the night I buried Seren's heart, her tree stands strong against the stars, a memorial in white and silver. But it isn't enough. It isn't her. It never will be. I feel somehow as if I've lost her all over again, or if I've realized at the last that she is truly, wholly gone. Grief is an ocean, and I am drowning in it. I weep beneath her tree.

The wind whispers through the leaves, grazing past my cheek. My tears dry. I comfort myself with the memory of her. With the quiet night and the sweet scent of violets.

ΕPILOGUE

I DREAM
    of wind in my leaves,
    of roots drinking deep of the earth,
    of sunlight warm on bark,
    of rain soothing and sweet.
I dream
of a voice
speaking to me in the moonlight,
of a boy
pressed up against my trunk.
Sometimes, there is music.
Sometimes, there is weeping.
I think perhaps the boy was precious to me, once.
I think perhaps I knew his name.
He touches me with soft fingers.
He sleeps beneath my boughs.
Perhaps he dreams.

Perhaps
of
me.
I remember little things
in the darkness of my dreaming:
I remember that the world has color and light.
That it bursts with joy and beauty.
But I remember pain, too.
The slick feel of blood.
The dark rush of dying.
And I remember the sensation
of a heart beating inside me,
measuring out
the
moments
of
my
life.
I have no heart now.
I think I gave it up.
Outside of myself I feel the change of the seasons.
The brisk spice of autumn,
when my leaves fall
from my branches
to carpet the ground.
The sharp cold of winter,
the wet cling of snow,
the bitter glass encasement of ice.
The heady rush of springtime,
new leaves unfurling free from my branches,
flowers pushing up from the earth at my roots.
The suffocating heat of summer,

when I live for the cool wind of evenings
that wash me clean
in the starlight.
There is a longing inside of me.
A sorrow I cannot comprehend.
I want to sleep deeper.
I
no
longer
wish
to
dream.

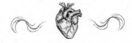

A cool wind whispers past my cheek. It smells of violets.

I am gradually aware of my body pressed into the grass, of a root beneath my arm and twigs scratching at my bare feet.

But it is the weeping that brings me to myself. That makes me realize I am more than what I have been for so long.

I open my eyes.

I stare up into the deep green leaves of a birch tree in high summer, their edges dipped in starlit silver. The smooth gray trunk shines against the hill and the dark line of the woods just beyond.

I touch my body, my face, my hair. I am human, and that surprises me.

I dreamed I was a monster.

I push up onto my elbows—it is only then I remember the weeping.

A boy is curled up a pace away, hugging his arms around his chest, his dark head bent, his body shaking.

Joy sears through me at the sight of him, but I don't understand why.

"Why are you crying?" I whisper, and marvel that I command the gift of speech. Have I spoken before? I am not sure.

He jerks his head up. All of him goes still.

"Why are you crying?" I repeat, tilting my head to one side.

"Seren?" His voice is incredulous, his face wide with shock. He radiates a profound, impossible joy. "Or . . . or is it Bedwyn?"

I blink at him. "I think I am called Seren."

His eyes glint with sudden moisture. "You don't remember?"

"What am I to remember?"

He sucks in a sharp breath, his body sagging. "Do you know who I am?"

I squint at him. He has a handsome face, but I am sure I've never seen it before. I shake my head. "What are you called?"

"Owen," he says heavily. "Owen Merrick."

"Why are you crying, Owen Merrick?"

I watch him consider his answer. I wonder why it is hard to find. "I thought I'd lost you."

"Have I been lost? I have been . . . I have been dreaming for a long time, I think."

"Three years, Seren," he whispers. "It's been three years since I buried your heart." He runs his fingers through his hair, glancing up at the birch tree that almost seems to bend over us, listening. "It took one year until your tree sprouted, another year for it to grow. And yet another year for you to come back to me. Perhaps . . . perhaps it will take one more, for you to remember."

Something pulses within me, and I place one hand on my chest. "My heart," I say in wonder. "It's beating."

His smile is laced with grief. "I gave up my soul, as you gave up your heart. It seems both have been returned to us."

There is something else, too. Filling up the deepest part of me, a place I think was once hollow. It's bright and strong. More than that, it's mine.

I drink in the depth of the summer night, and I am glad I have stopped dreaming. I am glad to be awake. I turn back to the boy. "Will you tell me, Owen Merrick, all the things I cannot remember?" I stretch out my hand to him, and after a moment's hesitation, he takes it. His hand is warm and large overtop of mine.

"I will tell you," he says. "I will tell you how the Gwydden's youngest daughter forsook the monster her mother made her. I will tell you of the boy who lost his heart to her, and how together they kept all the world from crumbling to nothing more than leaves and stars."

I smile into the sky, and scoot closer to him, our backs pressed up against the silver birch tree. I close my eyes, and listen to his story.

ACKNOWLEDGMENTS

BOOKS ARE STRANGE THINGS, AND THE GROWING OF THEM IS BY no means a solitary endeavor.

The concept of this book was seeded in Prescott, Arizona, in a cabin among the pines. I was busy writing *Beyond the Shadowed Earth* when the idea of a tree siren popped into my head. I don't know quite where it came from (where do ideas actually originate? I haven't the foggiest), but I jotted it down in the idea file on my phone to save for later. Another key piece of this book came from a conversation I had with my husband about the concept of a gender-swapped "Beauty and the Beast." We agreed it would take a special kind of boy to fall in love with a monster (*waves at Owen*).

So first of all, thanks to the Prescott woods (am I allowed to thank trees? It seems fitting for this book, anyway), and to my husband for always being willing to talk about interesting things.

A huge thank you to my agent, Sarah Davies, for loving the concept of this book and always championing me and my work.

To my editor, Lauren Knowles, for her brilliant insights and frequent brainstorming calls, and for referring to the ending as "emotionally compromising."

To the entire team at Page Street—I can't believe this is our fourth book together! Thanks for always taking care of my words and making them look so very beautiful.

Thank you to Hannah Whitten and Charlie Holmberg for reading early drafts—other eyeballs than mine are invaluable, and both your sets were greatly appreciated. Thanks to Hannah and Anna Bright for brainstorming with me about the king's silence spell. (I know it's horrifying; you can blame them.) Thanks to Jen Fulmer, stalwart CP extraordinaire, for her insightful notes and all-caps comments. Thank you to my whole wonderful writer pod for our never-ending group chat filled with commiserations, celebrations, and every sort of thing in between: Hannah Whitten, Steph Messa, Anna Bright, Jen Fulmer, and Laura Weymouth.

Thanks to writerly friends far and near for always being willing to chat with me: Amy Trueblood and the entire AZ YA/MG Writers' Group, Addie Thorley, Naomi Hughes, Meredith Tate, and so many others. Thanks to Hanna Howard for being my forever kindred spirit, and for our continual text thread full of all-caps comments, flagrant emoji overuse, and oceans of exclamation points.

Thanks a billion to Ashleigh Hourihan, my dear friend and bookish cheerleader—I'm so glad you won that giveaway of my very first ARC. Thanks to all the Bookstagrammers for their beautiful photos of my book babies—I'll never get tired of ogling them.

Thanks so much to my BFF, Jenny Downer, for a thousand and one cups of tea, and even more conversations.

Thanks to my amazing family for always being proud of me. Love you all.

An enormous thank you to my husband, Aaron (yes, I'm thanking him twice! He deserves it) for bearing with me throughout the creation of yet another book, and for wrangling our bear cub—I mean toddler—so I could write. Aren't you glad you're stuck with me? Love you.

Arthur, you were younger than Awela when I started writing this book, and you'll be nearly twice her age by the time it comes out. I hope you don't mind that I've immortalized part of your toddlerhood in fiction. You exhaust me—I love you to bits.

And to my readers: Every single email, comment, tweet, and message about my books means the absolute world to me. Thank you so much for reading and loving my words. Twelve-year-old me is in awe, and to be honest, present me is, too. Thank you.

ABOUT THE AUTHOR

JOANNA RUTH MEYER IS THE AUTHOR OF THE CRITICALLY ACCLAIMED *Echo North*, as well as the companion novel duology *Beneath the Haunting Sea* and *Beyond the Shadowed Earth*. She writes stories about fierce teens finding their place in the world, fighting to change their fate, save the ones they love, or carve out a path to redemption.

Joanna lives with her dear husband and son, a rascally feline, and an enormous grand piano named Prince Imrahil in Mesa, Arizona. As often as she can, she escapes the desert heat and heads north to the mountains, where the woods are always waiting.